DADDY'S HOME

DADDY'S HOME

A. K. ALEXANDER

THOMAS & MERCER

Published by Thomas & Mercer
P.O. Box 400818
Las Vegas, NV 89140

ISBN-13: 9781611098082
ISBN-10: 1611098084
Library of Congress Control Number: 2012916949

To Aunt Anita who, after

Dad, is my biggest fan.

1

Holly Jennings wanted to get this son of a bitch. She needed to see him stretched out, strapped down on a gurney. She yearned to watch as the hypo hooked up to his vein released the venomous fluid that would flow through his body, causing it to gradually shut down. Better yet, Holly wanted to take her 9 mm Glock, put it to his temple, and pull the trigger.

Blow the monster's brains out.

She slid down the steep incline, brushing off the leaves as she got to her feet, and took a pair of latex gloves from her black bag, smoothing them over her hands. Even after four years of working the Crime Scene Unit for the San Diego PD, Holly still hadn't gotten used to that acrid rubber smell and the puff of powder that flared out as the gloves snapped into place. It was like a wake-up call to her body.

Here we go again, Holly, grit your teeth.

Even her years of experience with death scenes never made the next part easier. No matter how many times she had faced smells so foreign to the average nose—even those not so average, like Holly's—the vile aroma always hit her hard. That first breath ignited images of violence—images completely opposite of anything normal, like a plunge into the depths of hell. Then, too, there was always something about each victim, each situation, that caught a detective, or herself anyway, off guard. Each victim had been a real person with a real life, and within a matter of days, hours—or hopefully for his or her sake, minutes—became a statistic. Sickening. Yet, in spite of the shattered bodies and the putrid odors, Holly had to admit it was a job she mostly relished.

Holly stepped along the perimeter of the taped-off crime scene, walking in a straight line and with trepidation, hands behind her back—not an easy task while also carrying her bag, but a necessary one. Holly played by the rules. *Keep the crime scene intact, and don't fall on your ass. The boys are watching.* She glanced back and saw both her partner, Chad Euwing—whom she could screw up in front of and laugh about it over a shot of tequila—and Robb Carpenter—whom she wouldn't even think about messing up in front of; he'd run straight to the higher-ups, who would love to demote a skirt if given a chance. So much for equality.

Robb was full of stupid one-liners like, "Didn't you miss your nail appointment?" Or maybe, "We're a little hormonal today?" Asshole extraordinaire.

Holly reached the little girl first. She knelt down, and the natural instinct to touch her gave Holly an intense head rush. *Shut down the emotions. Do your job. What kind of freak would do this to an innocent child?* Only two weeks earlier she'd been in this exact position when a child and his mother had been violently slain. Was she dealing with the same killer here?

Focus. Think. Work. Examine. It was again time to examine the UNSUB's heinous work. The unknown subject of an investigation. The killer. The savage. She pulled out a small recorder from her coat pocket and pressed the Record button. "Time of day: ten hundred. Tuesday. Approximately fifty-five to sixty degrees, clear weather, post rain. Victim 1: female child. Approximately age four. Blonde hair. Eyes closed. Wrapped in cellophane. Starburst wound at base of left temple. Entry: UNSUB is left-handed. Looks like someone braided her hair, put ribbons in it—UNSUB?"

She leaned in closely. The smell of decay and death wafted past, nauseating her. It always did—another thing she knew that she'd never get used to. *Hold on. What was this?* She pocketed the recorder and took her magnifier from her bag. Gold links. *He took a necklace from you, didn't he, sweet girl?* She scanned the wrapped body and face closely. There was a smudge of brown next to her lips. Not blood. *What is that?*

"He's a collector," she yelled up to Chad. "Did we find anything missing on the Collins little boy or his mom? You talked to the grandparents about jewelry?"

"Yeah. No one said anything about any jewelry being gone," Chad shouted back. "We know what he took at that scene." The grave tone in Chad's voice didn't go unnoticed.

"This one took something from the kid, too. Got your camera?"

"Right here." Chad held up his 35 mm.

"Then come on down. Let's get some pictures." Holly looked back at the child, whose facial color held a greenish-purple tinge. She'd been out here for at least forty-eight hours. Luckily, it had been cold and rainy, preserving the body far better than if this had been a typical Southern California week.

Looking again through the magnifier, she noted that both maggots and beetles were prevalent. *You certainly took some care here, didn't you?* You wrapped her up nice and tight. The time and obvious care the UNSUB had taken, wrapping up the child in the plastic wrap, had also helped to keep her body intact. *Maybe you're still on her. Your cologne. Your hair. Something you wore. I'll find it, you bastard. If you left something, anything, I will find it.*

The sound of crunching leaves underfoot, as well as Chad's humming of "Sunshiny Day," announced his arrival. She used to hate it when he did that. But humming helped Chad to get through the scene. Every investigator had a tactic. Hers was to get as deeply into the killer's head as possible when confronted with a victim. She had to detach herself in order to solve the crime. Later, she could think about the victims as they once were—living, breathing human beings.

"The gunshot to the head was at close range. At least she didn't suffer." Holly shuddered. "Well, let me rephrase. I don't think she suffered at the moment of death. Who knows what occurred beforehand. Look here." Chad bent down next to her. "Soot around the wound."

"He didn't wipe her clean?" Chad brought the camera up to his eye, focused, and started snapping close-ups.

"No."

"Like the last kid." Chad lowered his camera.

"Exactly like the Collins boy. And I don't think this is about him being in a hurry. There's more to it. He feels responsible somehow. In his sick way, empathetic. The gunshot wound offends him. I'll head over to Psych later and see if we can't get some help with the profile. My initial impression is that he doesn't like killing the kids."

"Then why bother with the kid? Why not find a single female vic? What is it with the kids?"

"Well, assuming that we're dealing with the same UNSUB, I don't know. We could be dealing with someone totally different from the last scene. We'll know soon enough when we check out the mom." Chad gave Holly a knowing look. "Here, get a snap of her neck. See that?" Holly pointed to the few lengths of chain around her tiny neck.

"She wore a necklace?"

"Yep, and he took it. He carried her down here. Then yanked off the necklace. Any footprints?" Holly asked.

"With the rains we've had over the last couple of days? No." Chad shook his head, and started clicking the camera again. "What's that caked on the side of her face?"

"I don't know." But the word "cake" did ring true—chocolate maybe. Mark Collins had had peanut-butter cookies in his stomach contents. "Maybe this bastard gives them goodies first. A real compassionate type, huh?"

"Twisted, Holly. This is one of the more bizarre cases I've seen. 'Here kiddo, let's have cake and ice cream before I murder you and your mom.'"

"We're not dealing with your average psycho here." After Chad was finished snapping away, Holly bagged the bit of chain. "Let's check out Mom."

They walked another five feet down and to the right before reaching the woman's naked body, face down, a blue tarp tattered but still taped to her. "He didn't take any time here," Chad noted. "Looks like he basically dumped her and got the hell out of here."

"I think you're right. My bet is he was extremely angry with her, or whoever she represents to him. He doesn't care about her. He's pissed off, and she's the root of his anger. He didn't bother carrying her down. He tossed her like a bag of trash."

Chad snapped several photos of the body in that position. He then rolled her over with his gloved hands. "It's possible she's a mother figure to him."

"That's one train of thought. Or a wife, girlfriend, even a sister. Someone else besides a mother may have raised him. Could be a grandmother. I don't know. But his hate is deep-seated, and it's directed at the women. This isn't really about the children, by what I've seen so far. That is, if he is the same killer who murdered Patricia and Mark Collins." Holly shook her head. She was frustrated by the dead end that particular murder investigation had led her to. The killer on that case was meticulous and left nothing at the scene. The similarities, however, were alarming.

The Collinses had been taken late at night from their Hillcrest home. No one had seen a damn thing. Patricia Collins was the quiet type, not very social, and a dedicated single mother. The only lead they'd had was that she had belonged to both the local gym and a dating service, neither of which had turned up anything.

Patricia had only had one date through the service, and the man had checked out completely clean. Holly had the police chief breathing down her neck, and these new murders, if they linked up to the Collinses, would have him in even more of a tizzy. Holly didn't like dealing with Tom Greenfield in a tizzy.

Holly nodded at Chad, who pulled back the blue tarp covering the mother. "Oh my God!" Holly gasped, bringing her free hand up to her mouth. She had to look away momentarily. Her heart pounded hard against her ribs.

"Yeah. I guess you could say he was pissed," Chad muttered before firing off shot after shot of film.

The woman looked to be in her early thirties. She had been badly mutilated. Anguish and fright splashed across her face, her eyes frozen wide open. Holly's gut said the killer had done the mutilating before he killed her. The woman had suffered quite a bit, whereas he had killed the child quickly. Oh, God. Had she witnessed the brutality her mother had endured?

"Why would he cut off her breasts?" Chad asked.

The tarp was torn open enough to see the horrid wounds the killer had inflicted upon the woman. Holly shook her head. *Stay in his head. What are you so angry about? Why her?* Holly sighed. "Anger combined with wanting to either strip her of her womanhood or of her motherhood. I don't know. He's one sick fuck."

"So what do you think? Is he the same one who murdered the Collins boy?" Chad asked.

"He didn't mutilate Patricia, except for the finger." Holly stared blankly at the missing ring finger on this victim's hand. "And, uh, yeah. He's saved himself another ring finger. I'd say he's the same killer. It adds up. Both kids shot in the head at close range. The medical examiner and ballistics will give us a better idea. The difference is in the mutilation here. Our other gal cooperated with him; maybe thought she would get out of it alive. He only severed her ring finger, and the ME believes that was done postmortem. I don't think he did this after he killed this one, though. I think he tortured her." Holly bent down next to the woman and picked up the woman's stiff hand. "She fought back, though, before he cut it off. See the blood and skin on the other fingers and nail beds?"

Chad bent down and took Holly's magnifier from her. "We're gonna get DNA off this. Let's hope he has a prior."

Holly knew the chances of DNA were slim. Serial killers were usually very careful. *You fought him, didn't you?* "You did good. We'll get him, I promise you. I'm gonna find him for you," she said in a barely audible whisper. She glanced back over at the body of the child. "Carpenter!" she hollered up to Robb. "Get down here. What the hell are you doing? We might have some fibers. Bring your kit, and let's get some measurements and sketches drawn up. This scene isn't going to stay preserved forever."

"You okay?" Chad asked.

"I can't stand that asshole. And you know he can't stand me, especially if I'm running the scene. He's still bent that he didn't get promoted to my position."

"You earned it. Ignore him. That really gets under his skin." He winked at her.

Holly was fully aware of her title as Ice Princess around the department. She'd even caught a whiff of rumor about bets being placed as to who could get her in the sack.

She looked at her watch. It was almost lunch hour, and she had a forty-minute drive to make it to Chloe's school. Her daughter's second-grade class had plans for their Thanksgiving festivities. *Damn.* She had promised her that she would be there. She had already missed one dance recital and a school play this year. "Can you handle this from here? I promised Chloe I'd make it to her school assembly and Thanksgiving feast. Make sure Carpenter and the boys stay in line. I don't want any mistakes. Our perp is good and careful, but he'll screw up somewhere along the line. When he does, I want him behind bars until they've got him strapped to that gurney. I don't want him out on a technicality because of something we got careless about."

"Count on me."

"Thanks. I know I can. I'd stay and hold the fort, but Chloe…"

"Go, for God's sake. I can handle this."

"Call me if you get anything new. I planned to take the rest of the afternoon off and spend it with her. This morning she sent a big guilty arrow through my heart about how I'm always working. I know I shouldn't take off, and Greenfield would skin me alive if he knew, but that might hurt less than my seven-year-old's therapy payments down the line."

"No problem. Family first. You do what you need to, and I'll plan to meet you at the medical examiner's office in the morning."

Robb Carpenter passed her. "What's the matter, Holly? Your thong up your ass today?"

She kept walking. She heard Chad tell Robb to go fuck himself. *Good friend.* Behind the wheel of her Jeep, she pulled down the mirror and applied her tawny-colored lipstick, hoping to look more like a mother than a cop. She also put on some mascara, bringing her hazel eyes to life, and quickly brushed her short auburn hair back behind her ears. A little better.

Holly quickly got onto the freeway and sped down the I-8, heading west, noticing the whites of her knuckles as she gripped the wheel tightly. She hated admitting that she had wanted to leave the scene. It wasn't something she would typically do, although today she did have a good excuse. *That poor woman, what she must have suffered...Her breasts. My God!* Holly put a hand up to her breasts. *He studies his victims, knows them, or at least of them and their situation. What's his motive? Why is he doing this?*

He wasn't some recluse, killing randomly. He had specific reasons for the women he chose. He carved up women just like her— young, single, and with a child. It was now up to Holly to track him down before he savagely butchered another family.

2

The little girl with dark hair braided into two pigtails and eyes the color of Tiffany blue scanned the faces of the parents in the audience. Holly raised her arm and waved it wildly. She scrunched in between a couple of other parents in the far back of the auditorium, as it was standing room only for the stragglers—most of them dads.

Holly saw a smile spread across Chloe's face as she raised her index finger in front of her chest and wiggled it. Yes, she'd definitely seen her. Holly made the same gesture back—their special wave.

Wow, the kid looked so cute. For once, Holly felt a little like Martha Stewart. She had stayed up into the wee hours putting the finishing touches on the Indian squaw getup that Chloe was wearing, and she looked absolutely adorable in it. It was necessary for her and Chloe to maintain some semblance of normalcy, and sewing a costume for her daughter was one way that Holly could do this. Having a mom who was a crime-scene investigator was far from normal.

She would like to be home more often and envied the mothers who could be. But in reality, Holly knew that staying at home would also stifle her. She was a cop by nature—three generations.

Her folks had four children—all girls. Her dad, Ben, had kept hoping for that one boy to follow in his footsteps. He'd been FBI himself and had helped design the profiling system years ago.

Holly, the youngest, was surely supposed to be that boy. But she knew he was just as proud of her—if not prouder—than if Holly had been a boy, because he appreciated how hard she had worked to get to where she was. Her dad also understood the discrimination she dealt with on a daily basis.

Holly reached into her bag and pulled out her compact video camera. She would have to send a copy of this to her parents, as it looked as though they wouldn't have a chance to be together over the rapidly approaching holiday. Her folks had decided to fly to Hawaii for Thanksgiving to visit her oldest sister Beth. They had begged for her and Chloe to come along, but Holly knew that she couldn't take off the time from work. She also really, really hated to fly. The thought of it made her squeamish.

So this year it would just be her and Chloe. Then, of course, there was Brendan. Holly knew that he would ask Chloe where the two of them were going for the holidays.

Before turning on the camera and raising it to her eye, she took a sly look around to see if she saw Brendan, something she could do quickly and without being noticed. Yep, there he was in the opposite corner, doing exactly what she was—scoping it out—and their eyes caught. *Shit.* His arms were crossed, and he wiggled his index finger in a greeting to her. He had obviously been watching her for the last few minutes, enough time to get the special wave down. She laughed.

The children started singing, catching her attention. There was Chloe, all braids and smiles, dancing around with gusto that would make any Indian tribal council proud—*or at least* this *mother anyway.* That kid did have her dad's enthusiasm for life, as well as his enigmatic smile. The thought of Jack gave her the same feeling in the pit of her stomach it always did, as if she'd been sucker-punched. But she would not think about him, or that fateful day almost eight years ago. She would not think about Jack. Not today. As if that could be remotely possible.

There wasn't a day that went by that she didn't think of Jack.

She would definitely not look back over at Brendan O'Neil. *Damn him.* He had to have not only those sinfully green eyes and tousled blond hair that always looked as if he'd stepped in from a windy day, but also that Irish lilt in his voice. And if Holly didn't watch it, she was pretty sure he could talk her into just about anything. *Nuh-uh, no way.* She had a daughter, and she had cases to solve, and right now there was a serial killer on the loose to catch.

A few more chants and a song about a turkey-gobble-gobble led into a poem written by Chloe. Her beautiful child stood tall, as tall as she could get at seven, and recited her Thanksgiving poem:

"I am an Indian, brave and tall. I shared with the pilgrims, one and all. We danced and sang on that first Thanksgiving as we ate corn and turkey and mashed potatoes, too. It was really good. And the pilgrims were my friends. I am an Indian, brave and tall."

Chloe bowed as applause rang out through the crowd. Filming it, Holly bumped the camera as she lifted her hand to wipe away a tear. That was her kid! Brave and tall. *Yep.* She wanted to run up to the stage and twirl that angel around, but thought better of it and waited the five more minutes until a few more children had read their poems. Chloe's was by far the best.

After the presentation, parents milled around in the classrooms finding their assigned seats for the feast the children had prepared. That was where Brendan found her and Chloe.

"Amazing. That was some poem, Miss Chloe. If I didn't think you were going to grow up to be a beauty queen, I'd say you've got a mighty good chance at being a poet."

Ah, that accent.

"Thank you, Dr. O'Neil," Chloe said, her face turning a faint tinge of pink. Brendan's daughter, Madeline, tapped Chloe on the shoulder and whispered something in her friend's ear. The girls laughed.

"Mommy, I'm going to get you a plate now, okay?"

Holly tried to hold up her hand to stop her, but the girls were heading toward the cafeteria, where the feast was being served. The school was not as organized as it usually was. Chaos filled the air along with the seasonal smells of turkey and cranberry.

"Ah, let them go, Holly. They like doing this. Gives them a chance to take care of us for a change. And we must take advantage of that, now don't you think?"

Holly heard her nervous laughter and stifled the embarrassment she felt. She knew she wasn't exactly in glamour mode at the moment. "I suppose we should."

"Good. It'll give us a chance to chat. It's been a while. I've tried calling, but you haven't called back, and you've all but disappeared from yoga class."

"I know. I'm sorry. I'm on a case, and I'm extremely busy." His woodsy-smelling cologne wafted her way. Interesting, the way a scent like that could remind a woman of just how long it had been since she'd been with a man. Part of her wanted to smack him and run away for being that reminder. The other part, well, it had ideas, too.

"You need to take care of yourself, Holly. At least, if you don't want to call me back you should get in and do that yoga. I know what it's like to raise children alone and hold a job, remember? The yoga keeps you grounded."

Yes, she did remember. They had this talk over pizza with the kids, which was simply a chance thing, and again over lunch one weekend while cutting out construction-paper states that the children in the class would use to do their own personal puzzles of the

United States the following week. Holly had wondered how truly random it was that Brendan also volunteered for the same job. She had to admit they'd laughed quite a bit and had a good time, even agreeing to have a glass of wine together when they were finished, which they did. But Holly left after the wine and an appetizer feeling confused, a little high, and yes, unfaithful, which she knew was absolutely silly. Would she ever get Jack out of her system?

Brendan had two daughters he was raising alone and was a veterinarian with his own practice. He was a hard man not to like.

"Listen, Holly, when we had wine a few weeks ago, did I offend you in some way?"

"No, no, I had a great time."

"Then what is it? I can't understand, because I had a great time, too. I was hoping we could get together again," he said.

A paper plate of food came crashing onto her lap at that very moment, and she looked up and saw her wide-eyed daughter looking desperate. "Oh no, Mommy."

"Ah, jeez," Brendan said grabbing a napkin and beginning to wipe the mess off her legs.

Holly grabbed the napkin from his hands, and rather than cleaning it, she wound up smearing canned cranberries into her slacks, along with marshmallows mixed with sweet potatoes. Chloe burst into tears, and Holly muttered, "Shit." Then glanced around at the eyes of other parents staring at her. "Sorry." She looked back at Brendan who was wearing a smile of amusement, and she couldn't help but start giggling. "Okay, I'll see you at yoga tomorrow night, deal?"

"Deal."

"Now, Chloe, come here. It was an accident, baby." Chloe looked up at her mom. "It could happen to anyone."

"Your mother is right. That it could. I drop things all the time. Ask Maddie here."

"I'll get you another plate, Mommy."

"Oh sugar, don't do…"

Too late. The child was off and running again, always aiming to please her mother. Madeline was in tow. As they disappeared, Holly's cell phone rang, a call coming in from the office. Brendan nodded at her as she gave him that look that said, I've got to take this outside.

She walked around the corner of the school and flipped open the phone. "Jennings here."

"We've got a locale on our vics." It was Chad. "Cleaning lady says that the woman and little girl are always there when she arrives, because the mom invariably has a list of duties for her. But today, she uses her own key to go in, starts to get breakfast for the girl, then realizes they aren't there. We called the mom's work. She's a computer analyst. They said that she hadn't called in yesterday or today. The assumption was she took off early for the Thanksgiving holiday. Apparently she had that kind of lee-way being that she was more of a consultant for their company than anything. But they did say that it was strange for her not to call."

"Where's the company located?"

"Twenty-eight, twenty-nine State Street."

"Not too far from where Patricia and her son lived. Looks like he's got himself an area. Call the local schools and find out where the little girl went. Maybe there's a connection, if the kids went to the same school."

"I'm on it. I had to leave our scene in the east county. Carpenter is wrapping it up. The call on this came in about a half hour after you left. Maureen took it, and she's handled it really well. Better watch out, she might be after your job, too."

"Isn't everyone?" Holly laughed, but she also knew that this was a job like any other, and one could be taken down or moved up a notch depending on the way cases were handled. Maureen was a good friend on the force, but she was also a damn good detective.

"Another thing, Holly."

"What's that?"

"He left us a little something that solidifies the fact that this was the victims' house. I think you'll find it very interesting."

"I'll be there in twenty." She looked down at her pants. The cranberry matched nicely with the brown wool. *Oh, well.*

She walked back into Chloe's classroom. Her daughter was there, new plate in hand and a huge smile on her face. Holly did what she had to and sat back down in the chair made for children and frowned as her butt eased over the sides. She should get back into yoga again, maybe add some kickboxing to the scheme. That weight was creeping up on her. Holly felt about five pounds overweight, but her friends told her that was plain silly. She knew by most standards it was, but by hers it wasn't.

She quickly ate the mishmash of food Chloe had piled together and drank apple cider out of a paper cup. She glanced back over at Brendan who was seated at Madeline's table. He made the *namaste* sign at her, bowing slightly with his hands together in prayer at his forehead.

"Listen, Chloe, you need to go to aftercare today. I'm sorry, but I have to go back to work."

"But you said that you were coming home early, and I could go with you after the feast like all the other kids get to," she whined.

"Not all of the other children get to go home with their parents right now. You know that, and you like aftercare."

"They do too get to go home, and I don't want to go to aftercare. I want to go with you."

"Baby, please. I need to go to work."

"You always need to go to work. I want to play with you. You said we could go to a movie."

"I know, and I'll be home as soon as I can. Maybe we can stay up late and pop popcorn and eat candy, okay?" She hated doing this to her little girl, but there was no choice. Doing this job was what put food on the table.

Chloe frowned. Brendan approached them. "A dilemma?"

"My mom said that she would take me home after the feast, and we could go to a movie. And now she's going to work." She did a good job of making the word "work" sound like the epitome of evil.

"Well," Brendan said as he got down on his knees to Chloe's level. "Sometimes mommies and daddies can't help that their work calls them. Trust me, I know your mother would much rather be with you than go to silly old work, but it's just the way it is. Like you have Mrs. Franz as your teacher, and you can't always go off and play when you want. That is sort of how it is for mums and dads. Their bosses are kind of like their teachers."

"Stupid," Chloe muttered.

"Agreed." Brendan nodded, crossing his arms in front of him in an imitation of Chloe's stance. Then he brought his finger up to his head and tapped it. "Listen, something has just come into my brain, a wonderful idea. Why don't you come to our house today and play with Madeline? We would love the company, and we just got the new Zac Efron movie on DVD. You do like Zac, now, don't you?"

"Yes," Chloe said, a hint of a smile spreading across her face. "Can I, Mommy, please?"

Holly flashed Brendan an "Are you sure?" look and replied, "Of course. What a wonderful idea."

"Good, then we're set." Brendan smiled.

"I'll call you. I don't know what time it'll be."

"No worries. I'll save you some dinner."

"No, you don't have to do that," she replied.

"Then I'll wait until you get there to make it," he said.

She shrugged. "I'm not getting out of it, am I?"

"No way. You make it sound like you have to go to the garbage dump or something. I promise it will be better than that. We'll have a great time."

"That's what I'm afraid of," she muttered as she left her daughter's classroom. She knew that Chloe already liked Brendan and Madeline, and he was definitely using the girls' friendship to his benefit. Who knew? Maybe that was a good thing. Maybe it was time to let go and find someone to come home to and snuggle with. *Maybe it was time.*

But thoughts of Jack came rushing to her, and she had to admit to herself that the time might never be right. Could you love someone again after loving the only man you ever thought you would love? *Vowed* to love? Holly didn't know if that was possible, and she wasn't sure if she wanted to find out. Her life fit her the way it was. No complications. There was work, and her child, and everything ran on a schedule in an organized manner. That was how she liked it.

She did not need the extras life could bring. Or did she? Was Brendan O'Neil an extra? Or could he, in fact, be a necessity?

3

God, they are so fucking beautiful to watch! Young thirty-somethings in khakis and white T-shirts, looking as if they'd just stepped out of a Gap ad. Some of them had the requisite denim jacket, others wore sweats with tight sweaters, one or two needed help badly and definitely did not fit in...*But oh, dear God, the others!*

Young, scrumptious, delicious women, all here with their sweet children, here in La Jolla, where all the beautiful people lived. But much to Gunter's consternation, most of them were attached—and deeply so—with wedding rings that marked dollar signs in the millions. Maybe he'd get lucky, though. Doubtful.

Look at that one go by. Wow! There's a personal trainer on Daddy's payroll, indeed, with that tight ass, and the abs peeking out from under the belly shirt. Her nips nice and pointy from the chill in the air. He licked his lips. *Oh, and what a cute kid, with that golden hair shimmering in the sunlight.* Thank God the rain had let up a couple of hours earlier. Being locked up inside was no place for a man like Gunter Drake. He needed sun, and the laughter of young children, and yes, the sight of their beautiful mothers. He still couldn't understand how the last two turned out so very badly. It had all gone so wrong.

Gunter Drake hated killing children. It's not like they ever deserved it. Their bitch mothers were the ones who really deserved it, and they were always the ones who started the problems—the lying, conniving, and manipulations. And these were the reasons Gunter Drake had to punish them until…well, until they descended into hell. Because that was where they were going. Gunter's children, however, would all be in heaven waiting for him. Because, after all, he was a good daddy. The children told him so, but it was way too hard to raise a kid without a mother, and until Gunter could join them all in heaven and get a little help, he would keep looking until he found the perfect family.

The truly sad part for Gunter was that this last wife and daughter he had taken had seemed so perfect. The little girl with big blue eyes and long, sunny-blonde curls cascading down her back. He knew that if she had given him a chance, those gorgeous eyes would have learned to light up at the sight of him. Gunter Drake had so much to give. He knew he was the best daddy. But then there had been the other one, his wife. She'd made a good first impression— petite, same blue eyes as her daughter, thirty-something, with the body of an avid kickboxer. That hadn't helped her in the long run, though, after she'd turned on him.

It was always the woman, wasn't it? They were really good at making the kids dislike him. What the hell was that about, anyway? *Women*…His eyes brightened as he glanced around the park and watched a brunette beauty pushing a toddler on a swing. He leaned back against the bench and took in the sights.

He would find another pair. That much he was sure of. *No problema, baby*. At six foot two, he was built, with plenty of muscle to squeeze. Longish dark curls framed his high cheekbones, and he had deep, dark-brown eyes that Gunter knew could mesmerize women. He loved to hear people say that he reminded them of

Johnny Depp, but old Johnny had nothing on Gunter. He was a wuss. Gunter was a real man.

He glanced at his watch, noticing a smidge of blood on its face. He wiped it with his leather jacket sleeve.

He reflected on the other night again. The police would not find many leads. Except for what he'd intended them to find. His footprints would be hard to locate because of the rains. But damn, that had made it so slippery, and it had taken all his strength to hold on to the child and make it the twenty feet down to where he'd positioned her gently and kissed her cheek. "Good-bye, darling," he'd said. His gloved hand had grazed her neck. *Ah! A treasure to keep. How foolish! Can't forget a trinket from the sweet child.* He had torn the keepsake from around her neck and taken one last look, brushing the back of his gloved hand along her pale face. Should've covered it, too. He didn't like leaving it exposed after having wrapped her so painstakingly in cellophane, like the true gift she had been. *Idiot!* Gunter reached into his jacket pocket and brought out the necklace, the one with a ruby in the center of a gold heart. He fingered it. It was sweet. Like Sara had been. This was his reminder—Sara's sweet little gold heart.

Gunter hadn't bothered to take such care with the wife. All her damn fault anyway. If she'd been a good girl, done as she'd been told, none of this would have happened. Once he had finished her off, he'd had no choice but to go back into the girl's bedroom and take care of her, too. It was so difficult to raise a kid on your own these days. Gunter didn't want that responsibility. He really hadn't had a choice.

The child had pleaded, "Where's my mommy? Where's my mommy?"

He had hated seeing the tears in her eyes. Her crying for her mother was not at all pleasant. Whining was so nerve-wracking. Gunter hated it. He'd had to do it quickly, because he had already become emotionally attached to the little girl. He had covered her mouth with his beefy hand and remembered the way he'd killed her mother. He couldn't do that to this precious child. She didn't deserve to suffer because of the sins of that bitch she had been forced to call Mother. He'd removed the pistol from his belt. The silencer on, just in case. He'd been through this before, and sadly it had ended the same way. He'd squeezed the cold, metal trigger. She'd gone limp in his arms. He'd held her tight, rocking her. "I'm sorry, baby. Daddy is so very sorry."

He caught himself saying the words out loud.

The hottie who'd been pushing the kid on the swing a few minutes ago was walking by and gave him a funny look. He noticed another one of those damn wedding rings. He had rules about married women.

What to do? What to do? Watch and wait, and hope the perfect woman and the perfect kid walked on by. That was exactly what he was looking for.

4

Holly pulled into the Golden Hill neighborhood—not the best in town, not the worst. The house was an old Craftsman style, probably built somewhere between the '20s and '30s, when McDonnell Douglas was busy building war planes in San Diego, preparing for World War II. It looked pleasant, as if someone was an avid gardener, and the woodwork around the house had obviously been refinished. Roses abounded in the front, including climbing roses surrounding the porch entry.

When she stepped out of her car, the scent of jasmine and roses hit her. Looking at the quaint little house, no one would ever think that atrocious violence might have occurred here.

Taking a look around, she noticed the typical gathering of neighbors that appear when police cars arrive and a scene is roped off with the telltale yellow tape. She flashed her badge at a rookie guarding the entrance and walked up the porch steps. Before entering, she turned around, faced the street, and looked hard into the faces of the curious. *Are you out there? Did you come back here to watch us?* She doubted it. Many times an UNSUB would make his way back to the scene of the crime to relive the experience. But something told her, not this guy. *What were you thinking when you climbed these steps? What the hell did you want?* She knew that was a rhetorical question. What he wanted was obvious and clearly demented. He wanted blood, and he was most definitely a sexual predator. She hoped he had not abused the child. She would not know that until they all met with the medical examiner.

A neighborhood like this was filled with nosy neighbors. That much she was sure of. There were quite a few elderly people, and she knew that at least one of them had to be the neighborhood watchdog. She would have to weed out who that might be. Maybe somebody saw something.

As she passed through the entryway, she noted that the house appeared even more charming than the yard. It looked as though the woman who'd kept this home might have sub-scribed to *Martha Stewart Living*. Apple-cinnamon potpourri filled the air, but there was a staleness to it. It was hard to tell when they were here last. Now officers tromped through it. She scanned the French Country–style living room for Chad. He saw her first and waved her over. As she entered the room, she could see that the bay windows faced a canyon. *Is that how you got in?*

"There is no sign of forced entry," Chad said. "And there is no trace of blood, nothing that indicates violence."

Holly nodded. "He did a good job cleaning up."

"Or else he didn't kill them here," Chad replied.

"Possible. Do you have anyone talking to the neighbors yet?"

"Your favorite man is at work," he said, referring to Robb. "He arrived just after I spoke with you, and he told me that the scene out east is wrapped. There are still a few black-and-whites hanging out. He told them to keep the tape up, not knowing if you might want to come back out and take a look."

"Oh, and I'm sure he referred to me in the kindest way pos-sible," Holly said.

"One can only guess, but yes, he does make it quite clear to anyone who'll listen that you are not his favorite of ladies."

"Asshole."

"You know it."

"Good thinking on getting him out of this house and scrounging up the neighbors for answers. I get tired of the browbeating. I like you more and more each day. So do you think our killer came in through a back door? Do any of the locks look jimmied?"

"Actually, no. We did find a window cracked open in the kitchen. It also faces the canyon. We're dusting for fingerprints right now," Chad said.

Holly followed Chad into the small kitchen that looked cleaner than hers had ever been.

"Our man knows how to cover his tracks really well," she said. "Today was the first time the housekeeper had come back since last week?"

"Yep. She cleans every Tuesday. But from what she says, there's really no need to. The woman was immaculate, and all the housekeeper did was the extras like the oven, the windows, and laundry. She said this gal was a neat freak."

"Uh huh. That's apparent. Who's talking to the housekeeper?" Holly asked.

"Maureen did. But she sent her home. Apparently she was pretty shaken when she found out that the woman and child had been killed."

"I'll have to swing by her place and speak with her. She may be able to give us a better insight into who this family was and the kind of people the mother hung out with. I suppose it's not likely we got any prints, then?" she asked the tech, who was going over the dining area with the fingerprint kit.

"Not a one. He wore gloves. I'm almost positive."

"He left something of himself in this house," she replied. After pulling on her own gloves, she picked up a photograph of the victims. Mother and daughter smiling into the camera, Mickey Mouse standing next to them. They both had the same smile with dimples on either side. They presented a picture of perfect happiness.

You bastard. I will get you.

"What were their names?"

"The mother was Shannon McKay, and the little girl was Sara. We're still checking on the dad. Neighbors confirmed they divorced four years ago and that he moved back East. He's already been contacted and is on a flight out here."

"Okay. Let's get this place squared away. There has to be a trace somewhere, a hair, a fiber, something. Go through it with a fine-tooth comb. I think you might be right. I don't think he killed them here, but he did something here, and I want to know what, and how in the hell he got them out of here. There's got to be a neighbor who witnessed something. Have Carpenter find out. Have you found where Shannon kept her paperwork?"

"There's a secretary desk in her room. I haven't gone through it yet."

"I'll do that. She should have stuff from her daughter's school, her bills, etcetera." All the things that Holly herself would have. "She might even have info about one of those dating services. Our last woman was linked to one. We need to recheck that angle."

"Do you think it's someone she knew?"

"I think anything is possible. I'm not ruling out that she answered the door for him and let him in herself. I think this guy fits into society in some way. He knows how to blend in. His psyche is warped, but he blends all right. It means he's smart and knows exactly what he's doing. He is extremely calculating. He likes the kids, not just their moms." She wrinkled her nose and shook her head. What was she missing? "Maybe I was wrong at our other scene when I said that it isn't about the children. Maybe it's only about the children, and he kills the mother for getting in the way. It would be her natural instinct to protect her child. When she does, he becomes outraged. I don't know." Holly shrugged her shoulders. "I guess it's another theory to suggest to Brooke," she said, referring to the PD, Dr. Brooke Madison. "The other family was what, only three, four miles from here?"

"Three point seven."

"Damn, you're good." She winked at him. "As I said, let's scope the local schools. Hey, you said he left something for us."

Chad smacked himself on the forehead. "Shit. I almost forgot. Where's the letter?" he called out.

"A letter?" Holly's mental wheels started working. This could be a big break for them. Before going into police work, Holly had been a nurse for the criminally insane. She hadn't worked the psychiatric ward, but she had learned enough to play couch shrink. She attributed her reliably good intuition on criminal cases to what she had learned those couple of years working in the prison. It was also one of the reasons she believed that she had moved up the job ladder as rapidly as she had.

Chad nodded his head.

"I've got it tagged and bagged," said Maureen Baldwin.

"Can I see it?" Holly asked.

Maureen, the tall redhead with a knockout figure, walked over carrying a clear bag with a piece of paper inside it. "Get a load of this," she said in a husky voice.

Holly took it and, through the plastic, read what the UNSUB had written.

Dear Sirs,

I'm sorry that things turned out like this. I really did love my family, and I would never hurt them on purpose, especially my daughter Sara. She was so beautiful and sweet, and I know that she really loved me. But Shannon had a mind of her own, and for some reason turned her back on me. So I had to do what I had to do. I think any daddy in my situation would have done the same thing. I am very sorry.

Fondly,

THE VERY BEST DADDY

P.S. I will find love again.

A cold shiver raced down Holly's back. "This fuck is sicker than I thought. Does he actually think he's the husband and father here? If he didn't kill them here, then he either came back here and wrote this after the fact, or the whole thing was planned from the beginning. He left the note, then took them and did the deed. I don't get this at all. Why in the hell did he leave this? We've got to find him fast. He's baiting us."

"We're going to get a handwriting analysis on this," Maureen said.

"Good."

"Jennings, media just showed up," Robb Carpenter yelled as he sauntered through the front door.

"Damn."

"They want you."

She looked at Chad. He shook his head. She hated the media. Usually the chief did these things, but his wife was at the very end of a difficult pregnancy, and he was with her at the hospital.

"Hey, Holly, I'll do it. I know how you feel about those maggots," Maureen said.

Holly sighed. "Thanks. Don't give them much, please." Holly hoped she wouldn't regret this decision. She didn't think that Maureen was really after her job. But when it came to camera crews and inquisitive reporters, Holly got tongue-tied. She always tripped herself up, and Greenfield would be on her ass. Yes, sending Maureen out to the wolves was truly her best bet.

She watched Maureen walk briskly past the smirking Robb Carpenter and step outside. Holly stood at the front door—within earshot but out of sight.

At once, questions were hurled at Maureen by a swarm of reporters. "Where are the bodies, Detective? Is it true he's a serial killer? What are you calling him?"

"The Family Man," one of them shouted.

Oh, God. Now I'm really in trouble. Holly knew it was bad once the media coined a name or phrase to attach to the killer. *Who's the jerk who called in the vultures?* If it was someone on the force and she found out who, she'd burn 'em alive.

Maureen held up both her hands, still in the rubber gloves, and said loudly above the din, "Listen, there is an ongoing investigation. We do not have a lot of answers yet. No, I cannot confirm whether or not this is a serial situation. That is all I have to say for now. I'm certain the department will be arranging for a press conference as soon as possible. Until then, please be conservative with your comments."

Maureen handled the reporters beautifully. However, Holly knew it was highly unlikely the news crews would curtail their reporting. The media was all about sensationalism. Maybe there was a reporter or two out there who would heed her advice. Doubtful. By the time the story hit the papers and TV news that evening, it would be hugely blown up, and the San Diego community would be frightened, outraged, and rightfully paranoid. It would be a community up in arms, one Holly really was not ready to deal with, and she knew that her boss would feel the same way. The chief also shied away from the media as much as he could, but the cameras came with the job, and lately he'd had his share of media exposure with high-profile cases over the last few years. Holly would have no choice but to give the media a press release.

Chief Greenfield had way too much on his plate with his wife's pregnancy.

She turned around and muttered to the uniformed officer on the porch. "See if you can't get them to back off for me. Explain that we really have a job to do here."

"Yes, Ma'am."

"You can call me Holly or Detective."

He nodded, his southern drawl giving him away as he touched his forefinger to his cap in a quick salute. He was far more respectful than most of the cops. They still had a hard time coping with her gender. She and Maureen would go out over beers occasionally and joke about it. They laughingly called it the power of a certain female part.

Maureen came back inside the house. "Good work, Detective," Holly said. "Want to grab a drink when we wrap?"

"Yeah," Chad said. "Brooke and I are heading over to The Tavern around six, if it works out. You guys up for it?"

"Sure," Maureen said. "After today, I'm gonna need a stiff one."

"I'm not touching that at all," Holly said. "I can grab a drink, but just one. I've got to pick up Chloe at a friend's house. He's also expecting me for dinner." Holly realized that she'd slipped when Maureen and Chad exchanged curious glances. "No, no, don't you two get any ideas. He's a friend from Chloe's school. His daughter is in the same class."

"Sure," Maureen said. "Nice cover."

Chad winked at her.

"Let's get back to work, Cupid and his sidekick. I want to get this letter to Psych and see what the good doctor has to say about our UNSUB." She tapped the sealed evidence with her finger, reading it again.

"What do you mean?" Maureen asked.

"I think we need to expect some overtime on this. The media is on it like flies on fresh shit. Once this is all out in the open, it will get ugly out there until we get this sicko. I think I'll walk the scene. See what I get. Has anyone called Shannon McKay's parents?"

"Not yet," Chad replied looking down at the ground.

She knew that was going to fall on her shoulders, and she dreaded it.

"But they have called her several times," Chad said. "Their messages sound worried, and they were planning for her to drive up north for Thanksgiving. I checked their locale. Looks like they're up in the Napa area. You might want to play that last message."

Holly saw the blinking light on an answering machine hooked up to a kitchen phone. She pressed play. There were messages from a few friends. She jotted down their names. One said that she wanted to stop by, but since Shannon had the week off, she assumed she'd taken Sara up to Napa early. The woman on the machine, named Judy, jokingly said that she was a little peeved at Shannon for not letting her know that she was going away, and that she would've gladly looked after Petie. Holly wrote down the names Judy and Petie.

"Any trace of a kitty or dog?"

"There's a dog bowl, but no dog. He must've taken off."

"Any photos of the dog?"

"One over there." Chad pointed to a side table next to the sofa.

Holly walked over and picked it up. A snapshot of Shannon and Sara at Christmastime. A Yorkie terrier with a small Santa hat on its head sat on Sara's lap. "I need to get the vet's number. I better check those records. If she was as organized with her records as she was with this house, we might find something. Maybe our man has the dog. We know he likes to take things."

Holly slowly crept through the house. She drowned out the voices and activity going on around her as best she could. She would probably have to come back once the chaos died down, but maybe she could still find something.

The house was small, a two bedroom with one bath. She came to Sara's room first and swallowed hard at the sight of Barbie's townhouse, the same one Chloe had. This was a little girl like most little girls—like her little girl. An emotional surge rushed through her, and she fought hard to hold it back. Holly wanted to catch this fucker now, more than anything she had ever wanted. She needed to wipe him off the face of the earth, because he killed children. She knew in her gut and mind, down to her soul in fact, that he wouldn't hesitate to kill her own child if given the chance.

Chloe's face flashed through Holly's mind. She had no choice but to go forward and dedicate herself to tracking and killing this monster. This was more than a murder case. Equating Sara McKay with her own daughter made this a personal quest.

Sara liked Barbies, and she liked to draw and paint, which was evident by the various illustrations throughout the house. Some of them were taped on the walls, some in frames. All put up, Holly was certain, by a proud mother. It reminded her of her own home, which, too, had some charm and definite age to it. It was in the Loma Portal area of town where there remained some Spanish-style homes and a few scattered Craftsman houses—very similar to this part of town. Holly was known to decorate with Chloe's artwork, and seeing the pictures that adorned the walls of a dead little girl's house tugged at her hard. The reaction alarmed her. *Distant. Stay distant. You can't get involved like this.* Emotions had to be shut down. She was good at that. But it was hard to do in this situation.

Holly walked into the room. A canopy bed with floral duvet was the first thing she noticed. It looked expensive, handmade, nothing like what you might buy at a department store or an outlet. *I don't think Shannon had a lot of money, but she definitely wanted the best for this child.*

She bent down and glanced inside the Barbie case. Everything was organized to a T. *Like mother, like daughter.* Something was missing—out of place—and it took Holly a few minutes to figure out what that was. There was Doctor Barbie, wearing her white doctor's coat, Mermaid Barbie in her getup, and a few others. But there was a set of Barbie clothes to the side of the case, which was odd, since everything else was clearly in place, and each Barbie was inside her own compartment except for one—Beach Barbie. Holly recognized the sunglasses and pink, high-heeled sandals that Beach Barbie wore. But Beach Barbie was nowhere to be found, and one of the compartments in the doll case was missing its doll. Holly suspected that Sara had had enough Barbies to fill the case. He let her take a doll with her. He took them to his place. But how? *Shannon struggled with him. She did not go out of here without a fight, and he would've had to control both of them.*

The whole thing baffled her. Holly didn't know how he got in or how he got out with the two of them. It was possible that he still had the Barbie to keep as a treasure. *He has to be one strong son of a bitch, because Shannon would have fought like hell.*

Holly then went into the bathroom, located between the two bedrooms. It was also small, but done as nicely as the rest of the house, with a retro pattern of black and turquoise tiles from days gone by. Holly scanned the bathroom. Nothing appeared out of order. She opened the medicine cabinet and found a couple of prescriptions for Sara, including albuterol for a ventilator. *You were asthmatic.* There were a couple of inhalers and even a prescription for prednisone—a strong steroid. The child must have been a pretty bad asthmatic at that. Prednisone was not a drug that physicians gave out lightly. *Did you have an asthma attack when the killer had you?* Stress could bring it on. If she was frightened and gasping for air, and he didn't have her medicine, he could have panicked. *Is that what sent him over the edge?* Holly didn't know. It would mean more questions for the medical examiner.

She jotted her questions in her notepad and then stepped into Shannon's bedroom. Clean, as she expected, just like the rest of the house. The bed hadn't been slept in. He hadn't taken them from their beds. *Did you know this bastard, Shannon?*

Holly breathed in deeply: stale air mixed with the slight smell of rose from a diffuser on the wicker nightstand next to Shannon's bed, a decidedly tropical style with a bamboo headboard and a floral print on the duvet. *A romantic?* There were candles everywhere, but so far no one on the team had determined whether or not there was a lover in her life. If there had been, she'd kept it low-key. Sara was definitely her mother's first priority, and if there was a man in Shannon's life, she more than likely kept him clear of her child, unless they were serious.

In one corner stood the desk that Chad had mentioned. Holly sat at the wicker-backed chair and folded down the front panel, revealing compartments and drawers. She pulled open the first drawer. Stacks of bills and presumably important papers lay before her. She picked up one of the stacks, a rubber band securing it, and began rifling through it. Mainly basic bills—utilities, phone, cable, plus a gym membership. *Have to check that one out.* Another stack. She snapped the rubber band and flipped through. These were all medical bills, primarily for Sara—asthma, allergy specialists, pediatrician, a gastro doc, and an endocrinologist. Most of the docs were located up at Children's Hospital. Sara must have been a sickly child. This troubled Holly even further. *So do you intentionally prey upon the weak?* She knew she'd have to look further into Sara's medical conditions. It probably wasn't really important, but there could be something there.

One more stack. It contained information on school activities and programs that Sara was involved in, including an acting class and piano lessons. There was also a sheet of paper discreetly stuck inside a blank envelope. Holly pulled it out, and as she read it, her heart raced a bit faster. Fetish and Fun? *What do we have here?*

Mom wasn't only a romantic, she was also apparently into the rough stuff. Holly looked over the receipt for black leather wrist studs, a blindfold, whip, and the super-deluxe, large-man dildo.

"Find anything?"

Holly jumped and nearly fell off the chair. "Jesus, you startled me," she said, turning to see Chad.

"Sorry."

She handed him the receipt and looked back into the envelope to retrieve a second piece of paper. Chad let out a low, long whistle. "Mommy liked a little S&M, huh?"

"Yeah, and she wasn't necessarily playing with people she knew. Look at this."

The second piece of paper she handed him had on it a phone number to a dating escort service that boasted confidentiality for players who liked to live life on the edge. "Now, what do you think that means?" she asked Chad.

"I don't know, but I'd say we'd better find out. Say we pay a visit to her friends over at Elegance Dating Service."

"I don't know if we should go busting in as cops. This isn't your average dating service."

"You think someone ought to go in undercover and do some fishing?" Chad asked.

Holly nodded.

"Who?"

Holly pointed at him.

"Oh, no. Besides, don't you think we might find out a little more if we send a woman in?"

Holly slumped back in Shannon's chair and sighed. "I'll send in Maureen."

"You can't do that. She just gave a press conference. Her face will be all over tonight's newscasts. Trust me, people don't forget someone who looks like Maureen."

"Fine. I'll do it."

"No time like the present."

"Now?"

"You want to solve this thing, don't you?"

"You're a real pain in the ass. Grab a crew and let's head out."

"Good idea."

Holly watched as Chad left the bedroom. She bagged the separate sections of mail, let out a long breath, and shook her head. The voice in her head screamed at her that this was about to get very, very interesting. And possibly very, very ugly.

5

Exhaustion settled in as Holly shimmied into the Lycra red dress. Wow, that was attractive. She noticed her breasts were nearly popping out the front as if she'd just appeared in a photo shoot for a Victoria's Secret catalog. Somehow, though, she didn't think her five-four frame would've worked as a sexy model. But she would have to throw caution to the wind and step out in this instance. Somewhere a killer was waiting for his next set of victims, if he hadn't already found them, and Holly knew it was up to her to find the sadistic madman.

Regardless, this really was the last thing she wanted to be doing at almost five o'clock. That drink was calling her name. But it was at least an hour away. She had already put in a call to Brendan letting him know that she might be later than expected. He didn't seem put off by it, and said that he'd get the girls to bed if need be, as it was a school night. That familiar pang of guilt hit her in the center of her gut. Another child's parent shouldn't be putting her child to bed. She knew that it was her duty. Right now, what choice did she have? And she knew the truth of the matter was that if any other parent was going to be putting Chloe to bed, she'd just as soon have it be Brendan O'Neil. The thought made her bite her bottom lip, close her eyes, and pray she could fight the lust welling inside her. The care he gave to his children and her own daughter made Brendan even more appealing.

She walked into the squad room. Robb let out a low, long whistle. "Well you won't make Supermodel of the Year, but I'd do you." Holly looked him square in the eye and said, "Carpenter, you make one more sexist, chauvinistic remark to me today, tomorrow, or ever, for that matter, I'll serve you with a sexual harassment suit so fast your dick won't ever want to do another woman again. You'll hate my kind so much, you'll go homo on all of us."

Robb's face reddened. He looked as if he was about to comment when Chad said, "I wouldn't, pal."

"I'm out of here. You two can handle this the rest of the day. I've got to head back over to the McKays' neighborhood and speak to a few more neighbors," Robb said coolly.

"And we will miss you," Holly shot back. She placed her hands over her heart and batted her eyes.

Robb stormed out of the office. Chad shook his head at her. "You two are terrible."

"Hey, he started it, and if he can't take the heat, it's not my problem. I don't care what he thinks. Let's head out and get this over with. I'm ready for a margarita on the rocks."

"Okay, you're the boss. And a hot one at that." He winked at her.

"You watch it." She shook a finger at him. "You may be getting a letter from my attorney, too."

"You wouldn't."

Holly laughed. "We better move out," Chad said. "I told Brooke to meet us at The Tavern around six fifteen."

"Hopefully this goes as simply as planned."

Maureen spoke up. She'd been laughing under her breath since Holly had ripped into Robb. "It's basic. I made you an appointment at Elegance Dating Service. I explained that I was your assistant, and that as you were a very discreet person, you would like to meet with the owner himself. The woman on the other end said that wasn't a problem, and that he usually is the one who does all of the interviewing anyway. They pride themselves on the 'services' they provide, claiming they truly are unique. And get this, they're very 'hands-on.'"

Holly and Chad both snickered. "I bet," Chad said.

"Okay, so you'll meet this Mr. James, William James, to be exact. He must really think that name is important because his receptionist enunciated every syllable," Maureen said.

"Great, not only do we possibly have a kinky pervert on our hands, he's also a self-important one," Holly added.

"Is there any other kind?" Chad asked.

"I asked Robb if he could run a background check on him," Maureen said. "But seeing that he cut out of here early, my guess is he'll let that go for the night."

They all laughed.

"Before we head out, why don't you ask Craig Anderson to do it. Greenfield gave him a desk job after he came back from rehab last month, and he's working evenings. Poor man is really gonna have to prove himself. Sometimes I think Greenfield is way too hard, but I'm not getting into the politics of that," Holly said.

Office politics was the last thing any of them wanted to get involved in inside the station. Same with office romances, office gossip, office anything-other-than-work. It could mean slicing one's own throat. Greenfield ran a tight, closed-mouth ship. "Put Craig to work," Holly said, "take his mind off his troubles while we're out having a drink. I'm sure he'll be far more eager than Robb to get it done. If he finds something, have him give us a call. Or if it's too late, ask him to leave a report on my desk for the morning."

"Will do. I'll meet you guys out in the van," Maureen asked.

"See you out there then," Chad said.

He and Holly walked out to the surveillance van. Holly would be driving her own car. "Your wire on?" Chad asked.

"Wouldn't leave home without it. But I'm not going to show you where it is."

"I trust you. Get in your car and give me a check."

Holly got in and started singing. Chad got out of the van and said, "You've got a good voice. I always knew you liked 'Sunshiny Day.'"

"I did that for you."

Maureen came out and walked over to the van. "We're set. Craig was just happy someone gave him something to do besides filing reports. I hope Greenfield comes around where Craig is concerned. He's a good man, and before he got really out of hand with the booze, he was a good cop."

"Greenfield is not one to go light on people he considers weak. Craig is lucky he let him keep his job. By the way, does anyone know how Greenfield's wife is doing?" Chad asked.

"No, but I think I'll check in with him in the morning and send over some flowers from all of us," Holly replied, climbing in her car.

"You are such the politician," he said.

"Right on up there with the president," she joked. "Now let's get this over with."

The dating service was only moments away from the station, located downtown on Fourth and B, a decent enough area. Maureen and Chad pulled into an empty parking spot right across the street. The van's disguise showed it to be a cable company vehicle. Chad sat up front dressed in a cableman's uniform.

Maureen was working the communication center in the back of the van. Holly knew the plan was simply to go in, do a little fishing expedition, find out what these people knew about Shannon, and whether or not there was any apparent illegal activity going on. If they or this William James knew something, then Holly's crew might be able to gain some advantage. Holly had the distinct feeling that this guy was going to slip right into her category of filthy slimeballs.

"I cannot believe that I'm doing this. We really should have sent you in, Maureen," Holly whispered into her wire as she started to walk the half block up to the dating service's entry. She noticed a leering homeless man and a couple of construction guys heading into a bar for a couple of after-work beers. They whistled and looked her up and down.

"Nice ass," one said.

"Nice tits," another one replied.

She kept walking. A strong urge arose to pull her Glock from her purse and go Jennifer Garner à la *Alias* on them. She whispered, "Assholes."

"I think you look hot, too, baby," Chad laughed over the wire in her ear.

"Watch it. I know where you live, cable guy."

Maureen cut in, "Leave her alone. You'll be fine, Holly. We've got your back."

"Okay, you ready?" Chad asked, his jovial tone downshifting.

"Ready as I'll ever be," she replied.

She felt like a hooker in the spiky high heels, low-cut, slinky red dress, and more makeup than she had ever worn before. *This is gonna suck.*

She opened the door to Elegance Dating Service. A discreet sign just inside the door read, "We provide a place to meet for those people with the love of pleasure." *Oh, God, this is really gonna suck.*

Holly tried her best to stay balanced on her spiked heels, but it was damn hard. She approached the front desk where a way-too-thin peroxide blonde sat behind a black-lacquer desk—tacky all the way. A red velvet couch sat in the center of the room; in front of the couch, a coffee table held a black vase filled with fake flowers the same color as the gold silk drapes. The room looked like something out of a bad Vegas casino or a Mafia boss's home.

"Can I help you?" the blonde asked.

"I have an appointment," Holly answered.

"Do you mean an interview?"

"I suppose I do." Holly shifted as perspiration made her itch at her pantyhose line.

"Hmmm, name?"

"Katrina Richards."

The blonde looked down at her scheduler. "Yes, Mr. James will be with you in a moment."

"Thank you."

"Would you like some coffee, water, tea? A glass of wine, perhaps? We can even mix you something stronger. It might help relax you during the taping process."

Wonder where they got their liquor license? "No. I'm good, thanks." Holly sat down on the couch, sinking nearly all the way into its plush fabric. She reached for a magazine and crossed her legs and tried to look comfortable. She wondered if the receptionist knew Shannon McKay. She decided to take the gamble and see what she said. "My friend sent me here. She said she'd met some really great people, and that I might like it."

"Really? I'm sure she was right. So, who is your friend?"

"Shannon McKay. Do you know her?"

The young woman looked up at her from the paperwork she'd been shuffling, apparently with the intent of looking busy. Something in her eyes—was it a look of fear, anxiety, anger, the knowledge of something bad? Holly didn't know, but whatever it was, there was definitely something other than mere recognition.

When she replied, her voice was far sharper than it had been only moments before. "You know, we get so many people coming through the door, and it is really hard to keep track of who everyone is. I can't say that I know your friend. But I'm certainly glad that she recommended us. I'm sure you'll find our service as satisfactory as she told you."

"Oh, I'm sure I will."

Shannon would have had to go through the receptionist to get an interview. *Why is this woman lying?* There was something far more sinister going on behind the guise of this dating service. Holly felt it in her bones. And she couldn't help but wonder if it would lead her to Shannon and Sara's murderer.

6

William James, one of his many aliases, sat in his lavishly decorated office, all modern in black and fuchsia, behind the two-way glass that reflected the comings and goings in the waiting room. Yes, he was a voyeur. In this business, that wasn't a bad thing. In fact, as far as he was concerned, it was a prerequisite.

What he saw on the other side of his window today absolutely fascinated him. She was a beauty indeed, and she looked brainy too. Like a hot teacher type with the glasses and all. But once the glasses came off, those women were nothing less than totally doable. This one on the other side of the mirror was far more than just doable. She was gorgeous, and he would love getting a piece of her ass. But then he'd heard her mention Shannon's name over the hidden speaker system, which he used anytime he saw something of interest and wanted to listen in.

Why was she asking about Shannon? Shannon never mentioned a friend, and certainly none as radiant as this one. All Shannon ever talked about—when talking was involved, that is—was that little girl of hers.

William liked little girls.

He stood, smoothed down his black V-neck cashmere sweater over his gray silk slacks. Yes, he was a catch, but not just any woman could have him.

Only the special ones.

He left his office through the back entrance, as was his practice. There was never a need to tip anyone off about the two-sided glass.

He approached the front room, breathing in deeply. Ah, her scent. What was that? Gardenia? Freesia? No, tuberose. It was definitely tuberose. Probably wore "Fracas." Not only was she beautiful, but she also had style, a certain element of sophistication. Maybe she did know Shannon. That could be bad. Or maybe it could be good. This was going to be very interesting.

The young woman stood as he entered. Seeing the tight dress hugging her curves made it difficult to contain his obvious arousal. But for now, he would have to do just that.

"Ms. Richards, is it?"

"Yes." She extended her hand. Nice, soft, but her nails weren't long or polished. Just very plain. It didn't fit the image. They would have to work on that.

"Nice to meet you. Would you like to step into my office?"

"Sure."

For these occasions, William used a different office than the one behind the window. There were only a few special people allowed into that world. Maybe the lovely currently following him into his more appropriate place of business would be one of the lucky few. Time would tell.

They entered the office, which was overflowing with flowers in Art Deco vases. William loved flowers. There wasn't anything else that came close to capturing the essence of a woman. "So, Ms. Richards, what brings you to our service?"

"Actually, a friend of mine suggested it. She said that she had quite a bit of luck with meeting people here." The woman winked at him.

"Ah, yes. And who was your friend?" William wondered if that wink meant that she knew something about him and Shannon. He shifted uneasily, making the leather in his chair creak. It took a lot to make William uneasy, but this woman was immediately getting under his skin. What was it about her? Something different from any other woman he'd met before. She exuded a type of power that he didn't find in many of the clients who came through the door. Oh, sure, there were some who held his interest by their controlling nature. It was fun at times to allow the woman to be in charge. But this Ms. Richards...well, it was a different thing from the dominatrix-type control he enjoyed during a full moon. Yes indeed, she did make him uneasy.

"Shannon McKay."

He'd planned on this moment the minute she'd slipped Shannon's name past her lips inside the reception area.

"Shannon McKay? I'm afraid that I don't recall her." He leaned back in his chair, trying to act relaxed.

"I don't know how you could miss her—blonde, beautiful, blue-eyed. And a whole lot of fun, if you know what I mean."

"Not really." Oh, yes, he did. But the vibe he'd been getting, that feeling that this woman was in total control of the situation, had only grown stronger in the course of a few seconds.

She leaned across his desk. Wow, he could almost see down her dress. She was hot.

"Oh, I think you do know what I mean."

"Nope."

"Well, then, maybe I am in the wrong place." She stood.

William stood up as well. "Wait. I'm certain that we can find you someone very special here."

"Oh, no. I don't think so. If you didn't know Shannon, then I don't believe that you can help me. You see, I know that she met some very nice people here, lots of fun, and she said that she was sure I would have a very good time with those same people."

"Why don't you get names and numbers from her then, if she was—is—so willing to share."

"I would do that. However, I haven't been able to get a hold of her for a few days, and I figure that maybe she's out of town. And you know how we can all get when we're feeling a little...needy." She placed her hands on her hips and smiled coyly.

Yes, he did know that feeling. "I think maybe you're right. Maybe you should try to reach your friend, because for the life of me, I certainly cannot remember a Shannon McKay."

"Fine. Thank you for your time. I may be back."

She stood, and William escorted her out of his office. She brushed against him. What did this lady really want? What had Shannon told her? As fine as she was to look at, and as much as William had wanted her when she'd walked into his building, he couldn't wait to see her go. "I'm sorry we couldn't be of any help."

Ms. Richards waved a hand at him and left the building. Perplexed, he watched her go.

"You okay?" Darla, his receptionist and his on-again, off-again, asked after the woman walked out.

"Yes."

"Do you think she really knew Shannon?"

"I don't know. But I want to know exactly who she is. I don't believe she was here for a date." He left Darla staring at him, knowing that her stupid little mind was spinning. He regretted ever telling her anything about that night with Shannon.

Ah, the things they had done. Shannon better not have talked to anyone about that night. He'd discussed the consequences of talking about their escapades and what they could mean for her charming little daughter. But Darla didn't have anything so sweet to be blackmailed with, and she wasn't nearly as bright as Shannon. He might have to take care of Darla. She could talk if she grew angry enough. And this Katrina Richards...what did she know exactly? He'd have to find out a little more about her. Damn, he'd have to find out a whole helluva lot about her. There could be no loose ends in his kind of business, and Katrina Richards, if that was really her name, could be a loose end.

7

"That perverted bastard knows something," Holly said. "I feel it right down to my soul. I'd like to get a subpoena and search that place."

"On what basis? That you think William James knew Shannon McKay?" Chad asked. "I agree with you. He's a slimeball. I could hear it in his voice while you were in his office. But let's face it, Holly, unless we get something more than the fact that he's creepy, we've got nothing to go on."

"Hopefully Craig will have found some dirty little secret on him by the time we get back to work in the morning," Maureen said.

"If he doesn't, I say we go back in there anyway and bully him a bit. Get him to 'fess what he knows." Holly took a drink from her margarita. The tart mixture of tequila, lime, and splash of Grand Marnier went down smooth. She checked her watch. It was a little after six. Time was running short, and she knew that she'd have to go easy on the booze. Just because she was a cop didn't give her a license to drink and drive, and she should probably finish only three quarters of the strong margarita.

"I'm betting that he has himself an expensive attorney on retainer who is just as sleazy as he is. So if we want to get him yapping, our best bet is the way we went about it. If nothing turns up on him, you're going back in, Holly. It's the only answer," Chad said.

Holly held up her hand, fingers crossed. "I'm hoping and praying that Craig turns up something, because the last thing I want to go and do is play Miss Trampy Tina with that scuz again."

"Seriously," Maureen said. "I'll be shocked if we don't find something on him. At least enough info to bring him in and throw some questions his way. I'm going to grab another drink. Anyone want one?" she asked.

"Not me. I'm good," Holly said. "Besides, looks like there's quite a group at the bar, and by the time you get back here with it, I'll probably have to head out and pick up Chloe."

"Okay, nice job today. There's a friend at the bar I'd like to say hi to." Maureen waved and sidled over to the bar, right on up to one terribly good-looking man who Holly knew was Maureen's trainer at the gym. He was Maureen's once-in-awhile, convenient affair. That was Maureen for you, and Holly sometimes wished she could be more like that herself. But men and relationships were far from convenient for her, and she had a child to think about. Then, of course, there was Jack, and each time she thought about him, it pretty much destroyed any hope for what she might be able to find with another man.

"So where's the good doctor?" Holly asked Chad. She could swear she saw him blush.

He looked at his watch. "She should be here any time."

"Something is up, partner. What is it?"

"Nothing." He took a long sip from his gin and tonic.

"I've got a hunch that it's more than nothing. And my hunch tells me that it starts with a capital B, and ends with an MD." She grinned at him.

"I have no idea what you're talking about," Chad said.

"Sure, sure. Go ahead, play dumb. You know what I think? I think every time anyone mentions Dr. Madison, you start fidgeting, and a little color rises to your cheeks. I've also noticed that she's joined our evening bar sessions in the last month, and I haven't said anything. Come on, since when does the office shrink join a bunch of detectives for drinks after work?" Chad started to protest, but Holly cut him off. "Now, don't get me wrong. I like the good doctor. I think she's a real sweet gal and one helluva psychiatrist. Without her, I don't think we could get into the minds of some of the bastards we hunt down. She's good. Really good. And we want to keep her happy so we don't lose her to the Feds."

"But? 'Cause I know there's a 'but' in there," Chad replied.

"At least you're not denying that the two of you are screwing." Chad gave her the evil eye. "I guess all I'm trying to say is, keep your relationship under wraps." Holly laughed. "Guess that's what you're doing. No, seriously, you know that Greenfield would have a shit fit if he knew that you and the doc were fooling around."

"Believe me, I'm just as versed on Greenfield's policy on fraternization as the rest of the force." He paused. "Holly, I really like her. No one has ever made me feel this way."

"That's great. It really is. But before you go getting yourself in some kind of trouble with the boss, see if this thing lasts past the bump-and-grind stage. If it does, then you may want to let Greenfield know that you and Brooke are serious."

Chad nodded. Holly could see by his expression that he was somewhere in between embarrassment and relief. "Um, Holly?"

"I know what you're gonna say. Don't worry, your secret is safe with me. However, if I were you, and I didn't want anyone else knowing, I might think of taming down the after-work drinks and staying real low-key. If you don't, it won't be long before the cat is out of the bag. Let's face it, you aren't the best at keeping your emotions in check."

They both knew this to be true about Chad. When he was taken with a woman, he had a hard time hiding it. Holly suspected there had been something going on between Brooke and Chad for about two weeks now. Tonight, she had confirmed it.

Not only was she a bit fearful of losing Chad as a partner if Greenfield found out, but Holly had the distinct feeling that once Brooke had him wrapped around her finger, she could easily break Chad's heart. Holly did not want to see that happen. Chad was the brother she never had; growing up with sisters, she'd really wanted a brother at times. All that female energy under one roof had not been easy, to say the least. Holly loved her sisters, but she was glad they were now all grown and living separately. They were actually much closer that way.

"Okay, Inspector Clouseau, now that you have me and my love life figured out, I have a few questions for you," Chad said.

Holly set down her drink and put on her best I-don't-know-what-you-mean face. "What kind of questions?"

"I tried that innocent act on you a few minutes ago and you didn't buy my line. What makes you think I'm buying yours? I've got a feeling about you too, Detective. I think there's more to this man who's the parent of a little girl in Chloe's class. If I'm not mistaken, there's something behind those eyes at the mere mention of this guy. Is there something I should know?"

Holly set down her drink. "There is nothing you should know. It's exactly what I said it was. I have to pick up Chloe at a friend's house."

"Yes, you did. But you also said at the dad's house, which means he's divorced. I am a detective, remember?"

Holly shrugged her shoulders, not sure she wanted to get into this with him.

"Holly?"

"What?" she asked sheepishly.

"Who is he? Am I right? Are you interested in him?"

"Oh, fine. I opened the can of worms by giving you the third degree, so I guess trying to close it now isn't possible. Yes, I am kind of interested in him. I guess. We had pizza with the kids one night, but only because I had to pick up Chloe from him, and it worked out that way. And then we did some volunteer work for the teacher and wound up having some wine afterwards. That's it, nothing more to tell. He encouraged me to take a yoga class with him, so I have been, but with this case and all, I haven't gone for a few sessions. That's it. Nothing more to tell." There, she'd let it all out. Well almost all of it anyway. She'd finally confided in her partner and best friend. What she didn't tell him was how good it had felt to be around Brendan.

"I had no idea that you had a thing going on, Holly. I knew you might have a crush or an interest, but it sounds like you've got a thing." Chad finished off his drink. He was obviously looking around for Maureen to get him another one, but she was far too busy flirting with the personal trainer to take notice.

"Want the rest of mine? I've got to get going," Holly said, shoving her margarita over to his side of the table. "It's not a *thing*. Yoga class and a couple of glasses of wine don't constitute a thing."

"Oh, no, you're not skipping out on me after dropping a bomb like that. But, yeah, I will take the rest of your drink if you don't want it. I didn't mean you telling me about the class and your wine date made it sound like a thing. It's the sound of your voice when you talk about him. And I can see it in your eyes."

"As I said, it's nothing. It certainly isn't a *thing*. He's a nice man I've spent a bit of time with, and we enjoyed each other's company. But I am not ready to get involved."

Chad shook his head. "Really?"

"Yes, really." Holly stood just as Brooke walked into the bar, all long-legged and dressed as if she'd just stepped out of Neiman Marcus. She let out a low whistle. "Someone is dressed to impress."

Chad glanced at the door and turned away.

"Are you blushing?" she teased.

"No."

"So what does this guy do, anyway?"

She rolled her eyes at him and said, "He's a vet. He's a nice man, that's it. End of discussion," she hissed, giving his arm a hard knuckle-rap.

"Hey, you're brutal. I hope this guy can hold his own." He looked back over at the entrance. Brooke was still trying to get through the crowded bar. It was one of those places that was standing room only once five o'clock hit.

"A vet, huh? Cool, cool. You like animals."

"I work with you, don't I?"

"Low blow, Detective."

"You are so lucky I don't tell Brooke that I know the truth. But since you're a relentless ass, I'll tell you this much. He's cute, he's nice, he's funny, he's a good dad. I don't know. He's about as close to perfect as any man could get, I suppose."

"Boy, has he got you snowed. You know that we men are all liars. But since you're the one who used the word perfect, tell me, what's the problem?" Chad asked, eyeing her suspiciously. "Or should I answer that and say that Jack is the problem?"

"I knew I shouldn't have said anything." She grabbed her purse off the booth.

"You know what, I'm glad you did, because every time Jack's name comes up you run or change the topic as fast as you can, and personally, I think you need a shrink to work that out. But since I know you well enough to know you're not about to puke your past traumas and emotional hang-ups while lying down on a therapist's couch, you need to talk to me."

"I suppose it is about Jack." She turned and waved to Brooke who caught her eye and continued pushing her way back to them. Then she stopped at the bar to order what Holly figured was certain to be a cosmopolitan. Or maybe something a bit more demure, like a simple glass of Merlot. Holly didn't have Brooke figured out yet.

"Of course it is. Holly, it's been nearly eight years. Don't you think he would want you to move on?"

Holly shook her head slowly. "I don't know. Yes, he probably would. But I can't get over what happened that day."

"You were not to blame for his death."

"You know what? I can't talk about this anymore. Yes, I like this new man, but I do have issues to resolve."

"You are not going to resolve them by doing nothing about it."

"Chad…" Holly's cell phone rang loudly, and she was relieved it did. "Jennings here."

"Holly, it's me, Brendan. I'm calling to check in and to see what time you might be by."

"Right. Sorry, I'm running a bit late." She was chagrined that the Rolling Stones were playing loudly on the bar's speaker system behind her, and it wouldn't take much for Brendan to figure out that she was no longer at work.

"Not at all. If you want, she can stay the night. But she'll need her school clothes for the morning."

"No. Maybe she can stay over this weekend, but on a school night, she knows the rules. She's a jabber mouth, that kid, and she'll keep poor Maddie up all night."

"Sure, and don't I know how they like to talk." He laughed. Nice deep, gentle laughter. "I only asked because tomorrow is a half day, the day before the Thanksgiving holiday. But I understand. You still up for dinner?" he asked.

She glanced over at Chad who was studying her, an amused smile on his face. Brooke had made her way to their booth and was scooting in next to him. Holly raised her eyebrows. Brooke waved. Holly waved back. She felt her own face grow hot as Chad started to laugh quietly, pointed at her, and mouthed, "Holly's got a crush."

Holly frowned at them, as she replied to Brendan, "That would be nice. Thank you. Say around seven thirty?" She was now locked in for dinner.

"Good deal."

She clicked her phone off, faced Chad, and said, "Not one word. Not a single freaking word out of you."

Chad continued laughing while Brooke looked puzzled, which was a rare occurrence.

"Beware. I know things about you that others don't," Holly remarked.

"You wouldn't."

Brooke's jaw dropped. "What do you mean? What does she mean, Chad?"

Holly looked at her watch. "Oh, look at that, I gotta run. Good seeing you, Doc."

"Holly…" Chad called after her.

"See you later." She looked over her shoulder, saw Brooke still looking puzzled, and had to laugh. Well, Chad deserved some razzing, and she was sure Brooke could give it to him.

"Have fun tonight, you man-eater," he yelled.

"Screw you."

Chad caught up to her before she made her way out. No easy task with the filled bar. "Jokes aside, partner, I think if you like this man that you should think clearly about it. Jack would not have wanted you and Chloe to be alone. I promise you that you can love again. You really can. The Holly Jennings I know can do pretty much anything she sets her mind to."

"Bye, Chad. Be careful with the doc." She made it to the front of the bar and closed the door behind her, drowning out the chaos. She saw Chad watching her through the large-paned windows as she walked toward her car. He waved one more time. She flipped him off, and although she couldn't see him, she knew he was laughing, just as she was.

As she turned the corner and headed across the street to the parking lot, she couldn't help but wonder if there was any truth to what Chad had said. Could she love again? How would Jack have felt about Chloe?

Jack had never even known Chloe.

He'd never even known that his daughter had been born.

8

Holly took in a deep breath and let out a long sigh, actually relieved to be standing in front of Brendan's front door and ringing the bell of his Spanish-style home, very similar to hers, in fact. They only lived a few blocks from each other in the older, historic neighborhood. For a little while at least, she would not have to think about the madman stalking single mothers and their children, how his crazed mind worked, or where he might strike next.

As much as she hadn't thought that she'd want to come here tonight for dinner, she realized that her stressful day had changed her mind. It was nice to actually have a place to go after work other than the cop bar or home. She'd gone home first to change and wipe off some of the makeup she had put on for their little covert operation.

She knew that tomorrow would be another kicker, as they were all working overtime on this case. She didn't know what she would do with Chloe. Her regular babysitter had a new boyfriend and hadn't been available much lately. *Knew that was coming once the girl hit sixteen and got those braces off.* She'd have to find a new sitter, and soon. She considered her only recourse might be to ask Brendan again. God, she hoped she wasn't overstepping the boundaries. She didn't want him to think that she was using him.

She could hear Brendan and the girls laughing loudly, so loudly that between their noises and that of a dog barking in the background, they didn't even hear the doorbell. She cracked open the door and couldn't help but smile at the sight before her. There were Brendan and the girls, dancing like mad in the living room to the latest Britney Spears hit. The barking Labrador looked as though he was cheering them on, his tongue lolling out of a big grin.

Holly yelled, "Hello!"

"Oh, jeez," Brendan said and rushed to turn down the stereo.

"Da-ad," Madeline whined.

"Mommy!" Chloe came running over and wrapped her arms around her.

"Hi, baby."

She glanced up at Brendan, who was standing there red-faced and soaking in sweat, the result of the workout with two seven-year-olds and the embarrassment of Holly catching them.

"Thought you might ring before you got here," he said.

"I'm glad I didn't. I would've missed the show."

His face turned another shade of red. "They're such dorks," a voice from behind Holly said.

She turned around to see Brendan's older daughter, Megan, standing in the hallway entry. Holly had only met her twice before at the school. She was a striking girl, with long dark hair that waved like her father's, but the color she surely got from her mom, as Brendan was so blond. Her eyes definitely came from her father, though—that intoxicating bright green. The kind of eyes that could unnerve a person if that was the desired effect.

"Nuh-uh, you're the dork," Madeline chimed in, making a face at her older sister.

"Girls, girls," Brendan pleaded, trying to catch his breath. "Megan, say hello to Ms. Jennings."

Megan looked Holly over with a scowl on her face, finally uttered a disinterested, "Hello," then turned on her heels and strutted down the hall.

"Wait a minute, Meg. Could you excuse me for a moment?"

Holly nodded and watched as Brendan went after the fifteen-year-old girl.

"She is so busted," Madeline said. "She and Daddy haven't gotten along lately. He says that she needs to be nice to his guests. I think it's because she misses our mommy." The little girl flipped back her long hair, the same blonde as her father's. She was the spitting image of him. Holly couldn't help but wonder what their mother looked like and where she was. Better not to ask. She also couldn't help but wonder about the reference to his other guests. Did he bring home a lot of women? That would change her mind about him. What could be worse than parading all kinds of women in front of his daughters?

"My mommy left us, you know. I don't think she liked us anymore."

Holly looked down at the little girl. What to say to something like that? She racked her brain.

Chloe saved the day. "I bet your mommy loves you very much. Sometimes mommies have a lot to do. Maybe she's at work for a long time."

Holly decided it best to change the subject. "So what's for dinner?"

"My daddy made us chicken nuggets and fries. We already ate. Chloe had ten chicken fingers! He's a good cook."

"Sounds like it."

"But he made you something yucky."

"He did? Hmmm…"

"Yeah, Mommy. He made you chicken something blue. It looks gross."

Holly stifled a laugh. "Oh, yes, it's probably disgusting. Did he call it Chicken Cordon Bleu?"

Madeline and Chloe nodded simultaneously. "Yeah, that's it. My daddy made me try it once and I didn't like it. I like chicken fingers and french fries a whole lot more."

"I bet you do."

"Hey, Chloe, wanna go play Barbies? You can be Beach Barbie."

"I can?"

"Yes, because you're my best friend."

Chloe looked at Holly. "By all means go and play Barbies."

She watched them scamper toward Madeline's room. The thought of the two little girls playing Barbies, and especially that Chloe would be playing Beach Barbie, brought back the memory of Sara McKay's room. It hurt right in the center of her gut and spread into her heart. That monster had destroyed a child as innocent as her own.

She would see him into the grave.

And here she thought tonight would be free of all reminders that evil lurked somewhere outside the door, somewhere inside the city.

She caught Brendan staring strangely at her, holding out a glass of red wine. "You okay?"

She took the wine. "Just a little tired. It's been a long day. How about you? Everything okay with Megan?"

Brendan turned and headed into the kitchen, which opened directly into the family room. He went behind the center island, took out lettuce, tomato, and carrots and chopped away. Holly sat at a barstool opposite him. She ran her fingers across the jade and black marble. Smooth and cool to the touch.

"To answer your question about Meg...I don't know that everything is all right. I don't know what to think anymore. I mean, she's fifteen, and fifteen-year-old girls act ridiculous sometimes, right?" Before Holly could answer, he went on. "She disobeys me, sneaks out to see this misfit boy all the time, spends more time with his family than her own. Hell, I don't know. She says she's not, you know, doing it with him. But I'm not sure. Girls these days and in this country...in Ireland, when I grew up, if a girl or boy disobeyed, a mother and father didn't take any of that. But here I am taking it. My own father would be embarrassed. But I feel so damn guilty." He looked up at her and then took a big swig of his wine. "Ah, jeez, look at me ranting and raving. You don't need to hear all about my problems with my daughter. I am so sorry."

Holly glanced over the rim of her wineglass and replied, "I don't mind, really. What's the guilt for?"

The oven buzzer went off, and Brendan removed a foiled pan, opened it up, releasing a cloud of steam. It smelled heavenly, and it made Holly realize that she hadn't eaten anything since the Thanksgiving feast at noontime.

"You know, I shouldn't have said that. I don't really want to talk about it." He dished out the gourmet dinner made up of the chicken, a side dish of wild rice, and the garden salad that he gave a final tossing.

"This looks divine." She decided that if he didn't want to talk, she wouldn't push it. Maybe she didn't want to know what he was feeling guilty about anyway. Had he driven the girls' mother away for some reason?

"I hope you like it. I already fed the girls. I thought it might be nice to have dinner by ourselves."

He took their plates over to a table with a bench and a couple of chairs around it. Brendan guided Holly to the bench and seated himself in a chair. Their discussion throughout dinner was much lighter, the main topic being their girls, who periodically dashed into the room.

"We were just checking on you," Chloe said.

"Really now? Do we need to be checked up on?" Brendan asked.

Madeline interrupted, "Are you going to be my dad's girlfriend?"

Holly nearly spit her wine across the table and tried hard not to giggle. The wine, after half a margarita, was going to her head.

"Oh, Maddie." Brendan brought his hand up to his forehead.

"What, Daddy?"

"Would you two like to watch a movie?" he asked.

Madeline nodded.

"All of your homework done?" Holly asked.

"Yes," they answered.

Holly looked at her watch; it was almost nine. "Okay, go watch a movie, but only for a few minutes, because we've got to get you in bed."

Chloe and Madeline whined in unison.

"They've got that down pat, hey?" Brendan said.

Holly laughed. "Don't they, though."

"But, Mom, it's a Fun Day tomorrow because it's the day before Thanksgiving. So we won't do anything but have fun," Chloe said.

"She's good, that one. Ever thought about how much it might take for you to put her through law school?"

"Often." She turned to Chloe. "Now, go watch your movie for a few minutes while I help Dr. O'Neil clean up."

"You can call him Brendan," Chloe said. "He lets me."

"Oh. Okay, then."

The girls went into the family room, while Holly helped Brendan clear their plates. As she turned on the water at the sink to rinse, Megan entered the kitchen. "Do we have any ice cream?"

"Why don't you check?" Brendan said.

She opened up the freezer and, while facing it, said, "So, my dad says that you're a cop."

"I am. Actually I do a bit more, I'm a criminalist. I work with a forensics team to help solve violent crimes."

Megan shut the freezer door, a pint of Häagen-Dazs now in hand. "Really?"

Was that interest? Holly wondered. She glanced at Brendan, who shrugged his shoulders. "Really."

"So, you, like, catch killers and stuff?"

"I do. I'm on a murder case right now. It's why your dad had to take Chloe for me. My boss runs me ragged." She laughed and hoped that she'd get a smile out of the teenager.

Megan actually did smile. "That is so cool. I watch *CSI*, like, all the time, and now *CSI Miami*. I love it. I totally want to be an FBI agent. And I've seen every episode of *Alias*. Are you like the chick on that show? I mean, do you dress up and everything, you know, to go undercover?"

Holly thought about the afternoon, but wasn't quite ready to relay the details. "Sometimes, but I don't go all karate style. It's not always as fun and interesting as the TV shows make it seem. But I have been known to kick a little butt in my time."

"Wow!"

"I didn't know you wanted to be an FBI agent, Meg," Brendan said.

"You never asked."

Funny how her voice could change from interested to surly in a second.

"Well, Meg, I'm your dad, I would think maybe sometimes you'd tell me these things, instead of me always having to drag them out of you."

"Whatever. Ms. Jennings?"

"Call me Holly."

"Do you think I could go on a call with you some time?"

Holly finished scraping off her plate. "Sure, Meg. I could probably do that, if it's okay with your dad."

Brendan nodded.

"Cool, thanks." Megan finished scooping out her ice cream, kissed her dad on the cheek, and said, "See you tomorrow. I've got to study for a history test."

"Don't be calling that boy, now."

"Who? Derek? Oh, I broke up with him." She turned and sauntered out of the room.

Brendan sighed and appeared as if a heavy weight had been lifted from him. He looked up. "Oh, Jesus, Mary, St. Peter, and the rest of you, thanks be to you for getting rid of that boy!"

Holly couldn't help but laugh.

"You think that's funny, do you? Just wait until that little lass of yours starts dragging home them scoundrels. You'll be asking for all sorts of help from the heavens."

"I'm sorry. I'm sure it's rough."

"Rough? You have no idea! That child hasn't kissed me on the cheek in months. Made me think I was a leper or something."

"Nah. You're just a dad, and it looks to me like you're doing a good job. She'll come around. Trust me. My dad is one of my best friends. It's all growing pains."

"Indeed. Well, she took a liking to you, which I've got to say is about as close to a miracle as they come." Brendan started loading the dishwasher.

"Ah, so you bring lots of women here?"

"No. You're the first. But Meg doesn't like anyone unless they're a movie star, singer, supermodel, or in her select group at school. The rest of us are useless." He shut the dishwasher door and pressed the start button. The *whoosh* of the system echoed through the kitchen.

"She's a teenager, Brendan. She's normal."

Brendan accidentally brushed up against her. He smelled great, like smoky red wine and the woods. Something electric traveled through her body.

This can't be happening. Whatever *this* was.

Before she even knew what she was saying, Holly slipped and said, "You know, if you'd like me to spend a little time with Megan, get a feel for where she is, give her a woman's perspective, I could do that."

"You would do that? That might be helpful. I'm willing to try anything. I do think it could help. As I said, the child hasn't said good-night, much less *kissed* me good-night, in months. I've got to attribute it to her interest in you."

"Maybe she and I can get together this weekend. I can show her something of what I do. I am working overtime on this case, so I'll probably need to head in for a while. She might be able to tag along. I couldn't give her the details, but she could check out the crime lab, that sort of thing."

"That sounds good. I saw a bit on TV about those murders and in the paper. I'm assuming that's the case you're working. You be careful. He sounds like a real lunatic. I could keep the girls while you and Meg hang out, if it works with what you're doing."

"I'll see. Thanks for the offer."

Holly called out for Chloe, who reluctantly came into the living room, with Megan following close behind.

"I thought I'd say good-bye, Holly," Megan said. "Oh, I know I didn't ask you, Dad, but I was wondering if you and Chloe wanted to come for Thanksgiving dinner?"

Holly felt herself blush. She looked at Brendan whose face was probably the same color as hers. "I think that would be a wonderful idea," Brendan said. "Do you have plans?"

"Actually, it was just going to be me and Chloe. My folks are visiting my sister and her family," she stammered.

"Great, then. We're all set." Meg clapped her hands together and left the room.

The little girls jumped up and down, thrilled to be spending their holiday together. Brendan and Holly both looked a bit stunned. "That's the Irish in her. We like a big holiday."

"So, is there going to be a large group?"

"A few hundred Irishmen, that's all. No, I'm kidding. My folks still live on the Emerald Isle, and since their mum left…well, no, in other words. We were having a quiet Thanksgiving ourselves. Having you and Chloe here definitely fits in more with our idea of a holiday. It'll be splendid."

"I really appreciate it. With these cases and my family away, I didn't make any plans. Normally I would've had something pulled together…And I don't want to intrude…"

"Holly, hush. I'm glad Meg invited you. I would've invited you myself if I hadn't thought you'd have something planned. But I know how work and life can get this time of year. All crazy. In other words, what I'm trying to say here is that we would love to have you."

"What can I bring?" Holly asked.

"How's your apple pie?"

"I make a better cheesecake."

"Beautiful. I like to serve dinner between three and four, but I hope you'll come long before that. In fact, if you'd like to spend the day, well, by all means come along. You can watch a master chef in action."

"I should say," Holly replied. "Your dinner tonight was delicious."

"Indeed. Well, lovely ladies, it seems to be passing our bedtimes, Madeline, yours and mine."

"Good-night, Brendan," Chloe said.

As they said good-night, Holly thought how amazing it was that the day could start on such a rotten note and end so perfectly.

Once in the car, Chloe asked, "Do you think my daddy would want you to be Brendan's girlfriend?"

"Wow, Chloe, I don't know. But don't worry about it. Brendan and I are just friends."

"Will you tell me about my daddy again? Can I see the pictures when we get home?"

"Oh, sweetie, it's late, and we're tired. Let's go home, have a nice cup of peppermint tea, and climb in bed, okay?" Chloe nodded. "Good." Holly reached over and smoothed down Chloe's hair. They drove in silence for the five-minute trip, Holly lost in thought.

Chloe had just reiterated the same questions that Holly was struggling with. With the mere mention of Jack, memories and moments flooded her mind, and the evening she'd spent with Brendan went from perfect into a guilty blur. Ridiculous, she told herself. Jack was gone. She should move on. Once Chloe was asleep, no matter how tired she felt, Holly knew she'd have to type up an e-mail and send it to the one person who might be able to guide her through this situation. The one person who would have insight and advice.

Yes, she would write to her father later tonight or early in the morning with hopes of finding guidance on her issues with Brendan.

And maybe he would be able to guide her with her case, as well.

9

Brendan held the downward dog pose, reflecting on the evening and how so much had transpired in less than two hours. Meg had taken a liking to Holly, and that was unbelievable; that kid disliked all adults since her mother took off three years earlier, only to make an occasional appearance when she felt like it. And here Brendan once thought tradition dictated that it was men who had midlife crises.

The yoga instructor on the home video told him to breathe deeply in difficult situations, and he contorted into positions that he'd never thought he could do before he'd started this practice. What a laugh—an Irish Catholic meditating, breathing, and contorting. Okay, at least he'd been baptized as a baby and gone through the requisite catechism as a child, but Brendan hadn't been inside a Catholic church since Maddie was blessed. What would the priest say now? He took in a deep breath, but no amount of oxygen intake and release could clear his mind the way it should have. He was still very wound up and even confused.

Holly Jennings had that effect on him. She was the entire package—brains, beauty, a gentle being—and well, Brendan was a man. He had noticed, as he was sure that all men had, that Holly

Jennings maintained a great figure. Yes sir, Holly was the real deal. When he'd first laid eyes on her, he believed it was a spiritual thing. Light had shone above her glossy auburn hair, and when those hazel eyes had met his...bam! He knew he'd looked into the eyes of his soul mate. That sounded ridiculous to him, such a damn cliché, but if there were any truth to that saying, then he'd found it in her.

Funny that he now thought like that, because he never would have until recently. That soul-mate stuff was pretty funky as far as he was concerned. Hell, his ex-wife left him for her supposed "soul mate." Brendan had spent a couple of years lifting weights, taking St. John's wort at the pleading of his sister, and reading everything that Dr. Wayne Dyer ever wrote, another thing his sister insisted he do to get him over...Rebecca.

Well, Rebecca had split for her soul mate, leaving behind her three-year-old and twelve-year-old daughters. How could a mother ever leave her children behind? Was he such a poor husband that she'd give it all up? That thought alone made Brendan wonder about penis implants. Silly notion, but he'd met Rebecca's soul mate at the gym, and although Brendan didn't usually look at male counterparts' parts, Rebecca's "soul mate" was hard not to notice. Like a bodybuilder from a porno movie. How could a woman leave her kids and be okay with just every-other-weekend visits? And how many times had she called to cancel those visits? It had been over a month since she'd seen the girls, and Brendan was about to take her back to court and pull out all the stops to take away all her rights. Each time she canceled, he saw the faces of his children melt into sadness (and in Meg's case, anger), and the pain he felt was more horrible than a dagger in his back.

Rebecca had done a number on his family, and if he had his way, he would have her completely out of their lives. He wanted his daughters to be able to move on if their mother really didn't care, and it was becoming very clear to him that this was the case. She was a self-centered bitch. It had taken him the last three years to heal.

He'd even reverted back to his bachelor days for a few months, perhaps in an attempt to prove that his penis was just fine. There was that night the twenty-two-year-old cutie had approached him and a couple of his drinking buddies. She'd actually sidled up to him, and not the jerks he occasionally hung around with and called friends. Him!

But something about those getting-lucky, beer-drinking nights had left him cold and feeling exposed. They were indeed overrated. They hadn't done for him what they supposedly did for other men.

Brendan was a Paul McCartney—a marrying kind of guy. He was as sentimental as his own dad and grandpa, both of them married for most of their lives.

About a month prior to meeting Holly, he'd finally come to terms with his ex's desertion and her need for the whole soul mate thing. He would never have believed that such a thing were possible had he not come face-to-face with Holly.

Swear to the heavens above, a white light had shimmered above her, and he'd been taken with the sense of always having known her. It had been the first day of second grade for both of their daughters at the St. Francis School. Madeline had run up to him, "Daddy, Daddy, I made a friend, a good friend, my very best friend in the whole world."

Maddie was the drama queen in his life, and Brendan cherished that in her. Shiny, wavy, strawberry-blonde curls spread down her back, complementing her sparkling blue eyes. He always wondered about that tinge of red in her hair, until his mother reassured him that it was simply their Irish ancestry showing its bold side. He'd come to believe her as Maddie grew older and took on more of her father's characteristics, including his horribly ugly toes—the two in the middle were much longer than the rest, big toe included. Brendan loved his children. Maddie was the light of his life, and Megan held that place in his heart that only a first daughter could hold. They'd had a tight bond from the time she entered the world, and until a few years ago, he thought nothing could change that. Then her mother left, and Brendan knew that at some deep level Meg blamed him. "Rough going for a bit" was truly an understatement, and Brendan missed the camaraderie he and Megan used to share. But maybe the tide was changing, and if so, he couldn't help but feel that Holly could have something to do with it.

Holly appeared to complement his family like fine wine, and her Chloe fit right into it. Damn, he couldn't believe he was thinking like this. He'd only had a couple of dinners with Holly, a few yoga classes, and some parent-participation time at school. How could he, in his mind, already be walking down the aisle with her?

He knew how he could be thinking it. That day at the St. Francis School, when he first met Holly, was a life-changing day. When Maddie ran up to him all out of breath, flush from the excitement of her first day of school filled with friends and possibilities, he couldn't help but love that little kid even more. With Maddie, the glass was always half full. She'd certainly taught him a lot.

"So you had a good day, huh?" he asked.

"The best, Daddy. My teacher is very nice and funny. Except she kind of has a mustache." She grimaced, and then stuck out her tongue.

Brendan forced himself to stifle a laugh. Maybe he would suggest to the room parent that the teacher's holiday gift should be a gift certificate to a local day spa—with waxing in mind.

"But even better, I met my best friend in the whole wide world. She doesn't have a daddy. He died. I told her my mommy left us, and we only see her sometimes."

Brendan didn't know how to reply, but there was no need to as his bubbly daughter continued talking.

"Daddy, can she come over?"

"Oh, Maddie, I don't know, I've got to get back over to the clinic this afternoon. I need to check on one of my patients, an old pup that's had a hard time today."

"Daddy, please. We can go with you. Come on, can she come over?"

"It's the first day of school, and what's her mum gonna say?"

"Guess you can ask her now." He followed Maddie's eyes as she looked up.

And that was when the bright light came on. Brendan saw the most amazing woman he'd ever seen in his life. Her golden-hazel eyes met his, and Brendan melted. Damn, she was beautiful. He could barely get out any words as she'd stuck out her soft but firm hand, shaking his. "Hi. I'm Holly Jennings. Looks like our girls have become fast friends."

"It does." Brendan didn't know what he was saying; all he could think about at that moment was getting her alone and finding out all about her. "Maddie and I would love to have your daughter over. She could stay for dinner, if you'd like."

"I don't know. We've still got a few school supplies to buy this evening."

Chloe whined, "Oh, please, Mom. We can go tonight after you pick me up."

Brendan watched Holly's face soften. Her daughter obviously had the same effect on her as his did on him.

"I guess. But dinner? I don't think so. We really should get over to the store."

"We'll eat early. Maybe get a pizza or something. You can join us if you'd like," Brendan said. She made a slight face that he didn't quite know how to read. Was it apprehension? Or a "You gotta be kidding me" look? He quickly tried to recover. "It might be easier for you. We could meet you over at Pepe's. It's in the same strip mall as Target where you can buy Chloe's supplies." God, he hoped he wasn't sounding too pushy.

"Yeah, Mommy, that's a great idea," Chloe said.

Holly looked around, as if she'd find an excuse somewhere on the school grounds. Brendan figured she thought he was a loser.

"Fine. Sounds great." Oh, God, she agreed! "I'll meet you guys at Pepe's around six."

"I hate to be a pain about it, but could we make it six thirty? I've got a patient to check in on, and I need to give his family a call. My office is close by. I'm just going to stop in for a minute," Brendan said.

"You're a doctor?"

"My daddy is a vet," Maddie said, showing her perfect smile.

"Really?"

Was there a hint of interest in Holly's voice? "Actually, yes. I've got an older dog that had a cancerous growth and had some surgery this morning. I like to check in on my patients before the long evening stretch."

"Sure. I can understand that."

"So, do you have animals?"

"A cat."

Chloe interrupted, "He's a really fat kitty and not too smart, my mom says. She also says that all he does is eat and sleep. And she says he doesn't even catch mice."

"Okay, well I'm going to head out now, before we get into a discussion about more of the cat's negative traits." She laughed, a hearty yet feminine laugh that Brendan liked.

"We're going to the car, Daddy," Madeline said.

"Be right there," he replied.

"Be good, Chloe," Holly instructed.

"So what do you do?" Brendan assumed by the way that she was dressed (nice khaki slacks and a knit short-sleeved sweater almost the same color as her eyes) that she was a career woman.

"I'm a detective with SDPD. A criminalist, actually. We work with forensics and violent homicides."

"Really?"

She nodded confidently.

"That is very impressive."

"Not really."

"Yes, it is."

Holly started to protest again, but the blaring of his car horn interrupted them. "Girls are getting impatient."

"They seem to be." He looked down at his watch. "Whoops, I'm late to pick up Megan at the high school."

"You have another child, then?"

"Yes, a sophomore, and she's not a happy girl when I'm behind, if you know what I mean. I'm sorry, gotta run. I'll see you at six thirty."

"All right. Bye."

She showed up at the pizza place on time, and their discussion—in between ordering children to use their napkins and not to say words like fart or stupid—was lively and interesting, and Brendan couldn't help feeling further attracted to Holly. He hadn't felt like this in…well, he'd actually never felt like this right off the bat.

He thought about mustering up the courage to ask her out, have dinner alone with her, but the right moment never seemed to present itself. So, on parent night at school, when he noticed that she had already signed up for some volunteer time, he put his name down for the same date and time. That worked out rather nicely. However, he never worked up the courage to ask her out, so instead he encouraged her to come to the yoga class that he'd been taking. She agreed. Inroads made.

Now what?

Something about Holly sort of intimidated him. She still had that glow about her, and he felt as strongly about her now as he did the first time that he had laid eyes on her. Sometimes he got the sense that she felt it, too. But she had a concrete wall for a barrier, and didn't seem as if she was about to let it down.

Even after finishing the yoga video and trying hard to think about nothing, he was unable to shake thoughts of Holly. He'd been through plenty of ups and downs in his life, and he knew right in the center of his heart that Holly Jennings was the one for him. And whether she knew it or not, he would have to take a leap of faith and get out his sledgehammer, because he was determined to bring down that concrete wall around her.

Even if his own heart got smashed in the process.

10

If there was one place where Holly did not like to hang out, it was the medical examiner's office, even though Dr. Peter Lareby was a nice guy. He just worked in such a dismal atmosphere! Holly knew that many could say the same thing about her profession. But as far as she was concerned, she simply found and studied dead bodies, and tied the links together to hunt down the monsters who destroyed human life on a daily basis. What Doc Lareby did to dead bodies on a daily basis made the contents of her stomach do gymnastics. On the days that she knew she would be spending time in the freezing, sterile, small area the doc thrived in, she made certain she kept her food intake to a minimum.

"Hello, Detectives," Dr. Lareby said, as Holly and Chad came in the door. Across the room, little Sara McKay lay stretched out, hard, cold, and blue on top of a gurney. Her face and body almost didn't seem real. More like a figure in a wax museum.

"Hey, Doc," Holly replied. She tucked her hair back behind her ears and started twisting her pearl earring, a habit she fell into when she was anxious. Chad knew it, too. He'd mentioned it to her one day over coffee when Jack's name came up, and she had started fiddling with the damn earring. Since then, she'd consciously tried to avoid doing it. But down here, in this place of death, Holly found herself fighting off a panic attack.

She glanced down at Sara. "What can you tell us?"

Dr. Lareby looked up through his goggles at the two detectives, holding a small saw in his hand. He had kind, warm, gray eyes. No one would have thought eyes like that would see what they did daily. Or maybe everything that he saw was what gave him the aura of sympathy he wore so well. "I can tell you that she was not raped or sexually molested in any way."

"Thank God," Holly said, a sigh escaping her lips.

Chad looked at her with a warning that said, "Don't get too involved here."

"There are no marks on her, no bruises. There are a few scratches on her face that are postmortem. My assumption is that they are from an animal since she was exposed to the elements for almost forty-eight hours. The murderer shot her point blank with a revolver. I honestly don't think that she felt anything. He even closed her eyes afterward. Possibly he told her to before he did it."

"What about asthma? We found prescriptions for an albuterol solution for a nebulizer and some prednisone tabs in Sara's name," Holly said.

"I did find both drugs in her system. I can't say exactly when she took either of them, but I'm fairly certain that they were administered shortly before her death. See here…" He pointed into the lung cavity. "Most of the capillaries are open, but not all of them. Both drugs are fast acting. The albuterol acts faster than the prednisone, because the albuterol through the nebulizer releases directly into the system. Prednisone takes six to eight hours to really kick in, but the effects are longer lasting. Both drugs were in her system, as I said, but the prednisone didn't have time to kick in."

"Which means that he either didn't have them for long, and Mom gave her the meds just before he got a hold of them. Or, she had an asthma attack while he had them and was convinced to give Sara the medicine. Maybe by the mom, or even the little girl herself. It's hard to say without knowing how long he had them for.

"There's another possibility," Chad said. "He could be an asthmatic himself, and if she had an attack while he was with her, he could've administered his own drugs to her."

"You make a good point. But an asthma attack wasn't the cause of death? You know that for sure?" Holly asked.

Dr. Lareby nodded. "As I said, it was the gunshot wound."

"Do you think he's a gun expert?"

"I don't know about expert, the doctor said. "It doesn't take a pro to shoot an unwitting child in the head and kill her. But he might be. More than likely, he does know how to use a gun. Your job is to find out how much he knows." The doc raised his bushy eyebrows in a challenging manner. His brows were the only hair on his face or head. Holly had watched as the doc had gone from a nearly full head of hair only a few years ago to nil. Had to be the job to do that to a man in such a short period of time. "He also fed her a treat as you suggested. Looks like chocolate cake or brownie. And guess what? I found traces of another drug. Flexeril."

"A muscle relaxer?" Chad asked.

Dr. Lareby nodded. "Yeah, and a pretty potent one. I didn't find enough in her system to even come close to killing her, but my guess is that she was asleep a good part of the time while he tortured her mother. He roughed her up quite a bit." The doctor covered Sara with a white sheet and walked over to a gurney parallel to the child's. He ripped back the sheet and exposed a much more gruesome sight.

Shannon McKay barely resembled a human being. Her face was covered in bruises, and once again the shock of seeing her missing breasts made Holly take a step back.

"He definitely raped her. I was able to get a sample, and I've already sent it to the DNA lab. If he has any priors, things will brighten up for you guys."

"If..." Holly replied. She doubted this killer was foolhardy enough to have a prior conviction and then leave a semen deposit. No, she didn't think he had spent any time in jail. But he would. He most certainly would, and when he did, it was going to be on death row.

"Another thing I found curious." The doc rolled the corpse on its side. "They've faded quite a bit, but she has what look to be some kind of whip marks."

Chad and Holly took a step closer and peered down at the marks Dr. Lareby was pointing to. Holly looked at Chad. "From her escapades?"

Chad nodded, a grim look crossing his handsome features.

"Escapades?" the doctor asked.

"Yeah, we found some sex toys in her house, and not the typical fun-once-in-a-while kind of toys, if you catch my drift," Chad replied.

"More than a vibrator, huh? Doesn't surprise me, because these marks were made by some type of whip, and if you look closely, you can even see a mark that may have been caused by some sort of metal stud."

Holly looked down at the ground. It was hard to believe that Betty Crocker-Martha Stewart on the outside was Donna the Dominatrix or Vicki the Victim in the bedroom.

"These marks aren't recent, though. I'd say they're a couple of months old," Dr. Lareby said.

Holly looked at Chad. "Maybe she did meet him through the dating service."

"You didn't find anything like that on our last mother, did you?" Chad asked.

"No. This one fought him off. And either he cleaned up his last set of victims so well because he got scared, or he ran out of time with these two and wasn't as cautious," the doctor replied.

"Which means he could be getting reckless, and if so, eventually he'll really screw up," Holly said.

"Let's hope we can catch him before he has a chance to get reckless," Chad said.

"This is all stuff we need to take up to Dr. Madison," Holly said. Holly could make educated guesses about the killer's background, motives, and where he was headed due to her background as a nurse at the prison, as well as what she'd learned being a cop, but the real expert was Brooke.

"Good idea. Listen, I can't tell you much more other than that the mother died from strangulation. I'd say your killer is extremely strong."

"Once again, the idea of checking out the gyms is a worthy one," Chad said. "We've learned that both women belonged to the same gym. Maybe they put the kids in a day care there."

"I'm not completely finished with the autopsies, but if I find anything new, of course I'll call you both. As I said, I've got samples of all sorts of fibers and the semen on their way to the lab. We should know soon, hopefully on the Friday after Thanksgiving, but I'll be out of town, so you'll have to give the lab a call. Someone should be in."

"Thanks, Doc," Holly said.

"Yep."

Chad and Holly headed out and went up the elevator. "Guess we should go see Dr. Madison sometime today, but first I want to go back to the McKay house. Something is nagging me, like I missed something I shouldn't have."

"You're the boss. Besides, when it comes time to talk to Brooke, why don't you do it? I just, uh…"

"Hard to maintain an office affair, isn't it?" Holly said.

"It's more than that, and I think you know it," he replied.

"Don't get defensive. I know you really like her, and I can respect that, but as I said to you at the bar last night, don't let it interfere with the job. If this little romance you two have going on doesn't work out, you will still have to deal with her. Frankly, she's very good at what she does and so are you, so I'm keeping my fingers crossed that you two can make it. Because if you don't…" She raised her eyebrows and shook her head. "Well, let's leave it at that and hope you pay heed."

Chad stopped and touched Holly's shoulder. She faced him, and he placed a hand on each of her arms, looking her square in the eyes. "I promise you, partner, that my relationship with Brooke will not affect my ability to do my job. I also promise that it won't interfere with our friendship."

Holly swallowed the lump in her throat. "I never thought that it would come between us. Why would you even say something like that? It's not like we're lovers. You're entitled to a personal life with a woman." *What was this all about?* Holly didn't like the sudden sinking feeling in her stomach. *Why would he say such a thing?*

"I know. But sometimes I get the sense that I'm the man in your life."

Holly laughed, the high pitch sounding foreign to her. "Please, bud, don't flatter yourself. I love you. I really do. But as far as being the man in my life, afraid not."

"No, no. I didn't mean it like that. But you know how we are together. I know everything about you and vice versa. I felt responsible for you when Jack died. I guess I still do. I've got a guilty conscience. I suppose it comes from having a Jewish mother."

Holly removed his hands from her arms, holding them as she said, "Listen, you have no need to feel guilty or responsible for me. Live your life, and I'll live mine. Of course nothing will interfere with either our friendship or working relationship."

They stepped out of the elevator, through the front doors of the medical examiner's offices, and headed for the car.

As they drove down the freeway, drops of rain danced from the darkened sky, slowly at first, then quickly turning into a downpour. Holly flipped the windshield wipers to high. "I only love the rain when I'm sitting at home in front of a fire, drinking a nice Merlot, or maybe even a martini."

"Ah, so you're a Sinatra kind of gal," Chad said.

The tension between them subsided a bit. "Maybe a little."

"How was it last night?"

"Was what?" Holly played dumb. It didn't work.

Chad grinned. "You know. The date?"

"It was not a date. And it was nice. Fine. We had a good time." The traffic slowed. "A little rain and people get all freaked out and have to drive like they're from Mars."

"Holly…"

"I'm going to his house for Thanksgiving, okay? There! Yes, I had a good time. I like him, okay? And I'm going to see him again tomorrow, with his family. End of discussion."

Chad opened his mouth to say something.

"Stop. No more."

They pulled in front of Shannon McKay's house.

"What do you think you missed?" he asked.

"If I knew that, we wouldn't be here looking for it, now would we?" Holly pulled on her jacket, slipped the hood over her head, and got out of the car. Chad followed suit.

As they entered the house, they detected a stale odor that hadn't been there before, and the rain had added a smell of mildew to the already musty air. An eerie silence echoed in the space that was now void of a child's laughter, and the drone of raindrops hitting the roof, which had probably seemed so peaceful to Shannon McKay, simply represented a dull sadness now imprinted on this home.

"I may sound stupid, because I've already asked, but can you give me any idea as to what we're looking for?"

"We're looking for anything that might help us dig deeper into that dark side of Shannon."

"So, we're going on a Dungeons & Dragons hunt, triple-X style, huh?"

"Yep. You check around in the front part of the house. I'm heading back to her room," Holly said.

She walked past Sara's room, hesitated, and then kept going. She really didn't have an idea about what she was looking for or might find. She rummaged around the dead woman's desk again. She looked underneath the bed, only to find it as spotless as she'd figured it would be. She searched drawers and found everything neat and orderly. She headed into the closet and flipped through suits, pants, shirts, blouses, some casual things, all of it fairly high-quality stuff. This gal liked to look good.

She bent down and glanced through the woman's shoe collection, all pairs neatly in their original boxes. She had quite an extensive collection—Prada, Charles David, Vincent Longo. Where was she getting the cash for the shop-o-ramas to Nordy's and Saks?

Holly was on her knees and opening one of the last shoeboxes. To her surprise, she found this box didn't contain shoes but photos—very explicit photos of Shannon McKay, and other women and men, involved in a variety of sexual positions. How had her team missed this? She flipped through the first stack, the second, and then came across a whole roll of photos with none other than William James and his receptionist doing very nasty things to Shannon McKay. Some of them involving whips, some chains. Holly bagged the photos and pocketed them. When she stood to go show Chad the goods, she heard an odd noise. It sounded almost like whining. No, a whimper. It was a whimper. It was an animal sound. Holly stopped, listened. The sound was coming from beneath her, but from inside. Shannon and Sara had owned a dog. She opened the French doors off of Shannon's bedroom and stepped out onto the patio. The rain drowned out the whimper.

Holly went outside, rain pounding down around her, and got on her hands and knees to peer into the crawl space. She saw two eyes staring back at her. She laid flat on her belly and scooched under the home. "Here, baby. Here, puppy. I won't hurt you." She was under the house now. The little dog was still whining and shrinking away from her. He was hurt and frightened. Holly reached out her hand. He snapped at it. Then Holly stretched a little farther and grabbed the dog, pulling him out from under the house. She could see the small terrier was caked in dirt and something else. It looked like blood. She tucked him under her jacket, knowing that the dog might have evidence on him, and headed into the house. "Chad! Chad! We gotta go."

"Holly?" he yelled. "What the hell is it? What's wrong?"

They met at the car. Their eyes locked across the pouring rain. "You drive." She pulled the keys from her jacket pocket and tossed them to Chad. He caught them, and they simultaneously opened their doors and slid into the car. She held open her coat jacket for him to see the small Yorkie terrier. The poor dog was shaking, hurt, and in shock.

"Oh, shit. The poor guy looks really hurt," Chad said.

"Not only that. If I'm right, this isn't his blood caked on him."

"Shannon's?"

"Or Sara's."

"Where to?"

She gave him Brendan's office address. He put the flashing light on the roof of the car and sped down Washington, onto the Pacific Coast Highway, and toward Point Loma. Five minutes later, the downpour not letting up, they pulled in front of the vet's office. Holly got out and charged through the door with the pup still under her jacket. There was only one person in the waiting area, with a caged cat that was loudly complaining about his visit to the vet's.

She felt the dog squirm under her jacket. "Shh, shh, it's okay." He obviously wasn't too pleased about being there either. Funny how dogs and kids had that sixth sense about vets and doctors.

"Can I help you?" A young, high-cheekboned, blonde-haired woman looked up from behind the front desk. The door closed behind Holly as Chad came in out of the rain.

"This dog is hurt."

"Is he your dog? Do you know how he was hurt?"

"No, and no. Listen, Dr. O'Neil is a friend of mine. I'm a police officer, and I think the dog might actually be able to help us in a case, and we need to see the vet immediately."

"Oh. You're Holly," she said knowingly. What was Brendan saying to people in his office about her, or to people in general? Well, it didn't matter right now. What mattered was the dog. "Come on back with me. I'll get the doctor."

"Thank you."

Chad and Holly followed the woman who reminded Holly of an Amazon—tanned, beautiful, and at least six feet tall.

They entered an exam room, and Brendan immediately came through the opposite door. He looked at Holly a bit startled. "What have we got here?"

Holly set the terrier down on the table.

"Oh, my. What happened to you, poor boy?" Brendan asked. The dog whimpered as if answering him. "It's gonna be all right, darling. Let me have a look."

"We don't know what happened to him," Chad said. "Actually we're hoping you might be able to tell us."

"And you are?" Brendan looked up from his patient and glanced at Chad.

"I'm sorry," Holly replied. "This is my partner, Detective Chad Euwing."

"Nice to meet you, Detective." Brendan kept one hand lightly on the dog and reached his arm out to shake hands with Chad. "Okay, the pup is definitely in shock and dehydrated. We need to get him on some IV fluids. My guess is he's also got himself a broken shoulder and maybe a rib. By the state of dehydration he's in, I'd say he's been hurt like this for a couple of days at least." Brendan reached up to an overhead cabinet and pulled out a syringe and some medication. He loaded the needle and shot it into the dog's hip. The dog snapped at him. "You are a tough boy, aren't you? You still got some fight in you, even after what's been done to you. I'm impressed."

"What did you give him?" Chad asked.

"A little kicker to take the edge off. In about a minute or two he'll feel like he's shot back some fine whiskey." Brendan smiled at them.

Holly couldn't help but smile back. Brendan's expression warmed her all over, and God, did it feel wonderful, as she was still wet from the rain. Seeing him in his element, she noticed his Irish brogue was a bit stronger than at home. She was very impressed with how gentle he was with the dog, as gentle as he was with his daughters.

Holly was indeed falling for Dr. Brendan O'Neil.

"Okay, here's what we're gonna do with the chap. He needs some X-rays, but I want to get fluids into him immediately. I'm gonna take him into the surgical area, get the pictures I need, and have my assistant Lucy start his IV. She'll also get him nice and cleaned up."

"What do you think happened to him?" Holly asked.

"I'd say somebody took him for a soccer ball. I don't know where the blood came from, though." He pointed to the caked-on patch of blood on the dog's side.

"We have an idea," Holly said. "If he belongs to who we think he does, then his owner was murdered, and that blood could be hers. Do you mind cutting off that piece of fur so that I can send it to our lab for DNA evidence?"

"Not at all." The dog was so sedated he barely fluttered his eyes as Brendan clipped off the piece of fur. Chad reached into his coat pocket for a plastic baggie, and put into it what they hoped would prove to be evidence.

"Thanks," Holly said. "Is he going to be all right?"

"I think so. He's a tough little bugger. Do you know his name?"

"The dog that the ex-husband talked about is in the police report," Chad said. "And I believe he matches the description. But I can't remember the name. Can you?" He looked at Holly.

"I think it's Petie."

"I'll double check and call the station."

"Good, I like to have names for my patients."

Brendan smiled again, and Holly thought she might melt. Cops were not supposed to feel giddy with butterflies in their stomachs! How stupid. She was acting like a lovesick teenager.

Chad left the room, and Brendan took the dog back to his assistant to give her instructions, returning a few moments later. "Poor pup. Whoever did that to him ought to be shot."

"That's what I'm hoping for. He's a sick SOB."

"So you think it's the same man who killed the woman and her daughter who I read about in the papers?"

"Off the record, yes."

"Ah, jeez, Holly, I don't know that I like this."

Now it was her turn to smile. "What do you mean?"

"This doesn't sound like it's safe for you. He's a madman, for goodness' sake. I read what he did to that poor woman and her child, and it about made me ill. To think that you're chasing after him...Well, I don't know that I can take it."

"Brendan, I carry a gun. I've been well trained, and believe me, I know what I'm doing. Besides, what's all the concern? You'd think we've made a commitment or something."

His face turned red. "I...I...I only worry 'cause I care for you. And I care for Chloe. It must be hard having her mom fight the bad guys day after day."

"I suppose it is. There are times when I wish I could stay home, bake cookies, even clean the house. Well, maybe not clean the house, but at least be there when she gets home. But this is my job, Brendan, and I love it. I've worked really hard to get to where I am, and trust me when I say we will get this bastard. Hopefully the dog's hair will provide DNA evidence."

"I pray so."

Chad came back into the room. "You were right, the dog's name is Petie."

"All right then. Me and Petie got some work to do. He needs some fixin' up, so I'll call you later and give you a report."

"Thanks. I appreciate it," Holly said.

"Looking forward to tomorrow, Detective," Brendan added.

"Me too."

As Chad and Holly left and got into the car, Holly held up her hand to once again combat any of Chad's curiosity. "Don't go there. Besides we've got a case to solve."

"Anyone ever tell you that you're difficult?" Chad asked.

"Pretty much every day of my life," she replied, thinking about her dad and wondering if he'd received her e-mail.

11

Holly and Chad went back to the station and headed for Carpenter's office. He was sitting at his desk, eyes closed, feet propped up on an open drawer.

"Hey, sleeping beauty, we hate to disturb you, but—" Holly started.

Carpenter jumped, eyes now wide open. "Shit. I was resting my eyes. I'm allowed that on a break."

"Whatever. What did you and our night man find out about James?" Holly asked.

Carpenter put his feet under his desk and shuffled through some paperwork. "Some interesting info. May want to get Maureen over here, too. Think she went down the hall for some coffee."

Holly nodded and called Maureen from her cell. She quickly joined the powwow with steaming cup of java in hand.

"What you got, Carpenter?"

"William James's aliases include Will James, James Wills, James Williams, William Laine, Laine Williams, and more. But here, you can have the list." He handed it to Holly. "Mr. James spent three years in jail on a sexual assault charge back in 2001. He was also arrested on drug possession with intent to distribute, bad check charges, and fraud, all in the nineties. He used to make poor-quality porn, even starred in a few of his own films, and was really into the threesome and bondage thing. All of this was on the East Coast, back in New Jersey to be exact. He moved to LA in 2005 and down to San Diego just a couple of years ago. I called a few friends up at LAPD and got some info from them."

Holly took note of the way he made a big deal about calling the Los Angeles police department. *Good. Maybe they'd hire him. One could hope.*

"Apparently he pissed off a well-known porn director, and the dude told him to get lost or he'd lose his balls. He was trying to start up his own production company and entice this other guy's girls into his business. So he moved here and, check this out, not only does he own and operate Elegance Dating Service, he also owns and operates Right Connection Dating Service."

"Where Patricia Collins was a member," Holly said.

"Yeah. But he's got a partner at Elegance."

"Who?"

"Darla Monroe."

"She was the gal working the front desk the other day," Holly said.

"And I also got a little more info from one of McKay's neighbors. She said she saw a silver Mercedes out in front of the McKay house earlier in the evening. They may have voluntarily gone with James and his gal pal before or after they played around. Another hot item is that James is an asthmatic."

"Okay. Let's bring them both in. I need to get a warrant," Holly said.

"I've already been by their homes and offices," Carpenter replied. "You know, to sniff around a bit."

Holly raised her eyebrows pointedly and crossed her arms in front of her, "You did?"

"Yes, I did. But don't worry. I didn't do anything against regulations. I knew that you'd want to get a warrant. I just wanted to make sure they were both around. I figured that you two were busy enough at the medical examiner's office."

Holly really could not argue that point. Carpenter had gone on his instincts and done the right thing. When it came down to it, the man was a good cop, but it still didn't change her personal feelings about him—good cop, total asshole. "So they're around, right?"

"Nope. The dating services both have signs up saying they're closed for the Thanksgiving holiday, and when I swung by each of their residences, no one was around. I'm thinking they jetted off for the long weekend. I doubt they know that we're on to them, since you went in undercover."

"What if they put two and two together though, and skipped town?" Holly asked. "We better check airline reservation lists, just in case that's what happened."

"It won't necessarily mean a thing. It is Thanksgiving weekend. Besides, it's the busiest airline travel weekend of the year. By the time we get through checking things out, the weekend will be over, and we can walk right into their place of business, and take them into custody."

"Okay, you do have a good point." Ugh, she hated admitting to Carpenter that he was right, but she was also not above acknowledging the truth here. "Come Monday, I say we take a drive on over to Mr. James's and Darla's houses and see what they have to say. I'll make my calls and get those going."

She looked at Chad, who nodded his head. "Agreed."

"For now, I'd like to talk with Dr. Madison, and see if she can help me get into James's psyche. It should help when we do bring him in for questioning. Chad, you want to come?"

She saw the heat rise in Chad's cheeks. Oh, great, the relationship with Brooke was going to interfere with his police work. If he couldn't even hear the woman's name without getting hot and bothered, well…this could be a problem. "Never mind. Why don't you check out the gyms we talked about, maybe see if James or this Darla might have belonged to one. It could be another link. Then we'll hook up back here afterwards."

"Deal," Chad replied.

"What about me and Maureen?" Carpenter asked.

"Why don't you continue running background on James and see if we can get a complete profile on him, especially what his family life was like, if he's ever been married, and if so, find out if we can talk to the wife, that kind of stuff. If he and his girlfriend are the killers, I don't want to leave any missing pieces lying around. I want to bring them in and seal it up. Case closed. And Maureen, I need you to check out Darla's past, see where she's been and what she's been up to in the past several years. I'm betting she's got a history in porn."

"Okay." Maureen headed back to her desk.

Holly truly felt like they were on the brink of breaking this case. She headed for Brooke's office.

Dr. Brooke Madison sat behind her glass-top desk, peering over her eyeglasses, more than likely a designer brand, looking intently at whatever it was she was reading. She didn't look up as Holly came in. The sight of Brooke, ever the model of elegance and grace, never failed to amaze Holly.

Her modern office reflected her style and subtle taste, managing to look as if a human being worked there even when surrounded by the clutter and mess of the other precinct offices.

Her shiny blonde hair (that Holly knew never went beyond four weeks without a touch-up) was cut into a shoulder-length bob, and her crystal-blue eyes shone brightly, as if she were always on top of the world. Right. Holly knew what (or at least who) she was busy on top of these days.

Holly cleared her throat. Brooke looked up at her. "Must be some interesting reading there."

"Well, hello, Detective. I can only guess what has brought you to see me."

"I suppose you can."

"The Family Man."

Holly cringed at the title, but once the media named the murderer, it had stuck. Even the precinct staff was calling him that. "I'd prefer to call him something else."

"I'm certain you would. I've got some theories about him, and I think I might be able to help you come up with a profile."

"I am here for that exact reason, Doctor. We may actually have a suspect, but up to now, we haven't located him. Once we do, and we confirm he is the murderer, I'd like to know exactly who it is I'm dealing with. What are you thinking?"

"First, don't expect this one to slow down anytime soon. If you don't locate your suspect, or if you arrest the wrong man, he will continue to hunt and kill."

"I was afraid that you might say that."

"And I don't say it necessarily because I think he truly likes to kill and revels in it the way that so many psychotics and psychopaths do. No, there's more to this person than that. He's rather complicated, I'd say. I read your report about the possibility of his considering himself the father in these cases. I also had a good look at his letter. Very interesting. Quite an ego on this one."

"Great. So now tell me what you're thinking about this loser."

"As I said, it's not about the killing. He's got a romantic fascination with family life and what that means to him. My guess is that he was terribly abused as a child." Brooke shifted in her oversized black leather chair.

"It always starts at home, doesn't it?"

"A good share of the time. Here's what I think. He has been searching for the perfect family, and he does a good job finding them, stalking them, and insinuating himself into their lives for however long he needs them to play along with his fantasy, until he determines that it's time to kill. Based on what I've seen in the reports, when the assault happens, the mothers go into a fight-or-flight response. Their main objective is to save their child. I read over Dr. Lareby's reports and noted that he found sedatives in the children. I think that he rapes the mothers while the children are drugged, and all that the mothers can think about is saving their child."

"That would be a normal response."

"Yes. However, it's not working for them."

"No kidding." Holly sighed. "They're dead."

"Once his victim, the mother, starts to fight back, his murderous rage is fueled. This path that he is on probably originates from the abuse that he suffered. My guess here is it's likely to be his father, and—"

Holly interrupted. "Wait. Why do you think his anger is about his father when he's victimizing women? Usually the profile would fit if his mother had beaten him. That would make him want to lash out and kill her."

"Yes, usually. Good question. I'll answer that in a minute. So as I was saying, once the mother fights back, his entire fantasy is destroyed. I mean the perfect daddy, or 'best daddy,' as he refers to himself, would not have a disobedient wife."

"So he thinks he's freaking Ward Cleaver, and she's June."

"That's one way of putting it."

"Once he's been disappointed, he kills them."

"Yep. He goes straight into a rage, maybe not even realizing what he's doing."

"You're not going to tell me that once we get him, he'll be able to plead insanity?"

"It's very possible, and if he gets himself a good attorney, it's likely. And I think he can probably afford a good attorney."

"What makes you say that?"

"My gut says that he's a professional of some sort, and it's very likely that he could afford a skilled attorney."

"Great. So he could be a schoolteacher, a gym trainer, a financial planner, a lawyer, whatever."

"Yes."

"What about a sexual deviant?"

"That's obvious," Brooke replied.

"Specifically, someone who likes the S&M variety of sex?"

"I'm not convinced of that. However, as he so viciously mutilated Shannon McKay, I certainly can't rule it out. I'll have to finish my analysis."

"Anything else that you might be able to tell me?"

"That's about it for now. I'm going to go through the mothers' and children's profiles and cross-reference them. That might tell us the type of women he's looking for and what they have in common. Aside from both being attractive, the victims' physical descriptions are very different from one another."

"He'll probably pick another petite one like our first gal, after the way Shannon McKay tried to fight him off," Holly said. "Let me ask you, do you think he knows his victims, or does he do a random pick?"

"Good question. I'd have to say that he knows them in some way. It might be a very small passing moment, one with either the mother or the child. They might not even remember ever meeting or seeing him."

"Like in passing on a street?"

"Sure. Or more likely the park, the library, places where mothers might take their children on Saturday afternoons."

"Great. Just what I need to be worrying about, every McDonald's and Chuck E. Cheese out there."

"Yes, you probably do until I can get a better profile of him. And no matter where he finds them, he has to blend in and not alarm them in any way. It's not like these mothers took measures to guard themselves. I get the sense that they were not afraid. Not at first anyway."

"So they might have known him better than just a simple smile on the street."

"Possibly."

"Okay. Before I check out of here and let you off the hook for the evening, you said that you had a theory about the rage being against a father figure rather than the mother. That seems odd to me. From everything I know and learned as a prison nurse, I always thought that killers victimize the gender that they hate, usually because of some past connection to a parental figure, so that part I get. But why the father?"

"Here's what I think about that. As I've said, this killer comes from an abusive home where the dad was the be-all and end-all, probably a real angry character. The father took out his rage on our killer, his mother, and any siblings he might have had. Given the way your UNSUB's mind is warped, whatever Daddy was doing to him and his family as a kid was horrendous."

"Are you saying that he's playing the actual role of his father during his escapades?"

"Maybe. I'm not sure yet. He might start out playing as his own father, and then eventually ends up as his own unique father-figure symbol. But I can tell you that his father factors heavily into this."

"Super. So all I have to do is find all of the abusive fathers in this country in over the last what? Thirty-five years?"

Brooke gave a slight, haughty laugh. "If your suspect doesn't pan out, then yes. Not an easy task, my friend. I don't envy you bringing this one to justice. He's smart, but I think if he is angry enough, he might get careless, and you may get a break."

"You think he'll strike again if we don't bring him in soon?"

"Did you have any doubts?" Brooke leaned forward in her chair, rolling her fists up under her chin.

"I was sort of crossing my fingers."

"Unless this guy takes a flying leap off the Coronado Bridge or a set of gangbangers from Logan Heights gets a hold of him, I'd say he's going to strike again very soon. It's too bad you can't locate your suspect. Is it this William James character? Carpenter sent me down a file and had me take a look."

"That would be the one," Holly replied.

"Don't get your hopes up too high, Holly. This James character is a real scary man, and some of it fits. But some of it doesn't. I'm not always right, but keep your eyes on the road and look for all possibilities. I know the lab is processing the bloody fur from the dog, and the semen found on Shannon. Hopefully, we get a DNA match with James off of one or the other, or both."

"You have no idea how much I hope you're wrong," Holly replied. "No offense."

"None taken. But James just doesn't fit into what your UNSUB is looking for. I read that he came from a home where his folks were married for over thirty years until his mom passed away. Doesn't sound like a man with a psychotic need for a close-knit family."

"Maybe not, but no one knows what goes on behind closed doors, and the fact that James is such a pervert and sicko leads me to think that his family didn't compare too well with the Beaver's."

Brooke laughed. "True, true. Our man does indeed have an incessant need for this family that he can't seem to find."

Brooke uncrossed her legs, and stood, gathering her papers together and shoving them in an alligator briefcase.

"Before you go, Detective, can I ask you something?"

Holly didn't like the sound of that. "Sure."

"I know that you're aware of my relationship with Chad, and I hope that you're okay with it. I know how close you are to each other."

Holly had never seen the always put-together doctor so uneasy. It was a bit enjoyable. "I do know, and, yes, he's like a little brother."

"I care a great deal for him."

"That's wonderful. I hope it works out," Holly replied.

Brooke locked her briefcase. "I just wanted you to know that."

Holly nodded. "So you'll call me if you come up with anything else?"

"Sure will."

As Holly left Brooke's office, that distrust she'd felt about Chad earlier in the day resurfaced with Brooke's words. Why was there so much concern for her feelings? What were they hiding? Or was she being paranoid? And if so, why did she feel like that about someone whom she had known and trusted for years?

She rubbed her eyes and thought about how nice it would be to finally climb in bed that evening. However, as tired as she was, could she really sleep? Her partner and his girlfriend were weirding her out, not to mention that she may or may not have found her killer. If it was James, where the hell was he? And, God forbid, would he strike again before she brought him in on Monday?

12

Gunter poured himself a glass of crisp Chardonnay and set it down on the table next to him. He walked back into his kitchen—all stainless steel and white—to take his warm bread out of the oven. This was all a part of his nightly ritual. He was a traditional man, and a romantic one at that. If a wife had been here with him, she would know that. He would rectify that soon enough. The park had not borne fruit yesterday. C'est la vie.

He turned up his oven to 375 degrees and took out the bread, replacing it with a pan of shrimp scampi. His mother had been a good cook and a good teacher, but she had never shown true love and appreciation for his father. As a child, Gunter had felt so very sorry for her and had loved her with all that he had.

He missed her.

Gunter sat down in his recliner and took a sip of his wine, appreciating its complex bouquet, and then reached for the newspaper. He flipped through world events and soon turned to the metro section. There it was on the first page: "The Family Man Strikes Again." The family man. Now that had a nice ring to it. He went on to read the article, which was concerned quite a bit more about Shannon and Sara than himself. That wasn't what he expected.

What a wonderful mother Shannon had been...how devoted to Sara.

Ha! If she'd been so fucking devoted, the kid would still be alive, and they would still be a family.

It hurt his heart, though, to read about Sara and how wonderful she was. He felt his face burn at the thought of what Shannon had made him do to them.

"Bitch," he muttered.

As he continued reading the story, something else caught his eye even more than their off-base psychoanalysis of who he was—because Gunter was as sane as the rest of the men in America. In fact, probably more so. Definitely more so. At least he was trying to be a good daddy—the best daddy. What about all of the deadbeats out there? He was a responsible man. *What about all those men who up and leave their wives and children?* That wasn't his style. Yes, the analysis of him offered by the media and the police was off base, and the woman detective behind the investigation...Who was she, this Detective Holly Jennings? Holly Jennings. The name bothered him. Where did he know her from? Did he know her? *I need a wife to keep me organized. Help me remember all of the things that I forget.*

He reached the bottom of the article, where it said how distraught and devastated Sara's father was. "Well, I suppose you shouldn't have ever left, huh, Dad?"

Gunter folded up the paper, went back into the kitchen with his wine, and finished it while waiting for the timer to go off. Tomorrow was Thanksgiving, and he didn't have to work. He wished he did. It had been slow going this week, and he was a little pissed off about it. He really wanted another family. Desperately. He didn't care to have his turkey day alone. Maybe he would go out and find some of his friends.

He thought about his whore, and how she'd jump at the chance to be with him tomorrow. But she wasn't returning his phone calls, which was so unlike her. *She better be a good girl.* She knew too much, and this scared him somewhat, but he knew deep down she wouldn't talk. She was loyal—completely and totally. Always had been.

Besides, maybe by tomorrow night he'd have the perfect match, and he wouldn't have to spend his holiday alone after all.

13

Holly was edgy because the DNA evidence hadn't come back by the end of the workday on Wednesday, nor was there a trace of the elusive Mr. James and his cohort. The only thing taking the edge off of the day was Chloe dancing around to music from her iPod, while Holly blended cream cheese, sugar, and pumpkin into her one dessert specialty—pumpkin cheesecake. Well, any cheesecake, really. She changed the flavor depending on the occasion, but that's where her dessert skills ended.

They were to head to Brendan's house in a couple of hours for Thanksgiving, and that would be another wonderful distraction to keep her mind off of the case. There was something about that man that was getting to her, and after seeing him with Petie yesterday, it was getting harder to deny her growing attraction.

Holly finished mixing the cheesecake, put it in a Pyrex dish, then into the fridge to chill before baking. Next she checked her e-mail and smiled when she saw that her dad had replied to her message. He went on and on about the amazing sun and ocean, and how he wished that she and Chloe were with them. He wrote a bit about her sister Beth, and Beth's two kids and husband, who was the manager at the Hilton Waikiki. Holly smiled again, wishing that she, too, could be there. Sooner or later, she would have to get over this fear of flying.

Her dad did get serious with her at the end of the letter: *I don't like the sound of this case you're on. Something about it bothers me, and my cop instinct wants you to really watch your back on this one. I'm still searching my brain, but something about this killer reminds me of someone or something from the past, or at least it provokes a déjà vu—type thing in me. I'll figure it out, but in the meantime, stay careful.*

The words sent an icy chill down her spine. What could he possibly be talking about? What did her case remind him of? She'd have to call him later. She was running late leaving for Brendan's. She'd promised him an early arrival when she had called to ask about Petie last night. At least the dog was doing well.

She quickly showered and dressed, taking more care than usual choosing her outfit, selecting a coral V-neck cashmere sweater her mom had given her last Christmas, and adding a nice pair of black slacks that fit a bit more snugly than any she would wear to work. She even went so far as to apply eyeliner and mascara, which she rarely bothered with.

Chloe appeared around the corner. "Wow, Mommy, you look so pretty." She stood there, hands on her hips, wearing her favorite dress and tights, and black patent-leather shoes.

"You look downright beautiful! Look at you! And you picked it out all by yourself."

"I thought it would be a good idea to dress nice on Thanksgiving, because it is a special occasion."

"Yes, it is. What do you say we take off?"

Chloe nodded and began to help her mother gather their things for the visit to Brendan's house, chattering away about how excited she was to see him and Madeline and even Megan.

Holly couldn't deny that she, too, was excited. And more than a bit nervous. She knew that was silly; they were just friends getting together for Thanksgiving. Christ, who was she kidding? She liked Brendan O'Neil because he made her laugh, which got her mind off of more serious issues. He was also smart, interesting, and yeah, so damn handsome that it made her blush just thinking about him.

"You ready?" she asked Chloe, when they reached Brendan's house.

"I'm ready, Mom. Heck, Maddie is my best friend. Are you ready?" A precocious smile spread across her child's face, and Holly had to laugh. Damn, kids were so smart and intuitive.

"Yes, ma'am, I think I am."

They climbed the front porch steps, and before they could even knock, the door opened wide, revealing a very happy Maddie, who said, "I was watching for you. I'm so glad you're here! My daddy is making a mess out of the kitchen, and my sister is laughing at him."

"Guess we arrived on time then," Holly said.

The girls headed straight for Maddie's room, already talking about who was going to have which Barbie today, and where Barbie and her pals might be off and running to on such a special day.

Holly took a deep breath, steadying herself, and headed into the kitchen. Maddie had not been exaggerating when she'd said that her dad had made a mess of things. "Wow!" she said looking around and seeing open boxes of various ingredients, fruit slices on a cutting board, and an open flour bag that looked as if its contents had sprayed out across the counter, some of it adorning Brendan's face.

"I said I was a good cook; I didn't say I was a clean and organized cook," Brendan said while mixing the dressing.

Holly put the cheesecake in the fridge. "What can I do?"

Brendan looked helpless, as if he didn't know what to say.

"Hi, Ms. Jennings." Megan was perched on a corner stool, a book in her hand.

"Hi, Meg, and please call me Holly."

"She isn't really reading that book at all. She's over there peering above it, watching me and giggling under her breath, and for that I'm gonna make her clean this kitchen."

"Oh, Dad!"

"Yep, now get started."

"Jeez!" she protested, but stood up and grabbed a sponge out of the sink. "See what I have to put up with?"

Holly laughed and patted Meg on the shoulders.

"I've got something to show you, Holly," Brendan said. "Follow me."

They walked down the hall and into Brendan's bedroom. Holly felt uneasy being in his room, but knew it was nothing other than jangled nerves. His room was nice, comfortable, and clean. He was a man with a sense of his own style, as everything had a Hawaiian theme to it. "Funny, my folks are in Hawaii right now."

"Oh, God, I love it there. I surf, you know?"

"No, really?"

"Oh, yeah. Used to surf in the frigid waters back home, but once I moved to America and tried the waters here, well, you can imagine my delight. Then I visited Hawaii, the Big Island specifically, and I totally fell in love with it. The girls and I go every summer for two weeks. We have a grand old time."

"Sounds like it. Surfing, huh? You're just full of surprises."

"I suppose I am, yes. It's truly a spiritual thing, though unless you actually do it, it's difficult to understand. It's a good thing that the ocean is so cold in Ireland, or I probably would've never gone to school. Now it's my children who keep me in line, you know?"

"I do. So what's this surprise?"

"It's over here." Brendan walked her across the room to where an animal crate stood against the French doors. "There's a friend of yours in there."

Holly bent down and looked in, seeing two small eyes peer out at her, and a slightly wagging tail on the end of a small body. "Petie! Can I?" She motioned to the latch.

"Of course, but be careful. He's got a broken leg. At first I thought he'd also broken his shoulder and cracked some ribs, but that didn't show up on the X-rays. He's well hydrated, and the shock has worn off, although I'm sure he's got himself a nasty hangover today."

"Oh, come here, little guy." Holly carefully took the dog out of the crate and stroked his silky fur, cradling him in her arms. He licked her face.

"He likes you. But can you blame him?"

"So he's going to be all right?"

"Yep. I'm assuming he needs a home. I'd keep him, but I've got my hands full with the lab and the three cats that come and go as if I'm simply a feed store and good for an occasional scratch behind the ears. Since they've detected Petie's scent, they've been none too happy with me." He pointed to the three fur balls lying on the bed and eyeing them suspiciously. "Oh, please, be nice. None of you have any manners. Disgusting lot, you are!"

"I guess he will need a home. I certainly wouldn't want to leave him here to combat those three. It's a wonder your big dog hasn't been eaten alive."

"He's got good sense. He knows who the bosses are around here. Well, you gonna take him home?"

"Me?"

"You."

"Oh, please, Mom, can we?" They wheeled around to see Maddie and Chloe standing in the doorway.

"I'm feeling as if I've been shanghaied here."

"Mom, pleeeese."

"And you're going to walk him, play with him, feed him, and I say…" she held up her forefinger. "Clean up after him?"

Chloe nodded her head emphatically. "I promise, cross my heart." She made the motion with her fingers.

"Sure, all right. He can come home with us."

Chloe squealed with delight and Maddie giggled. They were a sight. Holly still wasn't completely sold on the idea of having a dog around, even if he was a good dog. She was gone an awful lot, and Chloe had school. She feared that Petie wouldn't get the attention he craved. Oh, well, the dog was theirs now, and maybe he would be a catalyst in helping her make it home on time each evening.

After making the decision to keep Petie, the girls knew better than to play with him because of his injuries, so they went back into Maddie's room. Brendan and Holly headed for the kitchen to find that Meg had done a good job of cleaning up.

"What got into you, girl? I think we'll have to have company far more often," Brendan said.

"It is Thanksgiving. And Holly is pretty cool. She's worth cleaning the kitchen for," Meg said.

"Thanks, Meg." Holly was pleased that the teenager was so warm to her. "Hey, I wanted to ask you if you do any babysitting. I frequently need to work later than expected, and Chloe needs someone I can depend on to take care of her."

"I babysit Maddie all the time. It'd be nice to get paid for it." She gave her dad a dirty look.

"Ah, now that's what family is for."

"Of course, I would pay you. You could also rummage through my police procedural books and some stuff I have on crime-scene investigating."

"Yeah. I'd be down with that," Meg replied.

"Great."

The rest of the afternoon went just as pleasantly and smoothly, except for when Brendan accidentally spilled the gravy on the floor. However, his dog, Whiskey, quickly came to his rescue by lapping it up, which sent the girls into giggles. In fact, the day went so well that Holly hated to see it coming to an end. Stomachs full and dishes loaded to wash, Holly thought it was probably time to exit.

"We should get out of your hair. I need to get Chloe to bed, and I'm sure you're tired."

"Nah, don't go. Have a drink with me," Brendan said.

Holly wanted to, but she knew if she stayed any longer she might not leave at all. *The hell with it.* "What ya drinking?" She heard the flirtation in her voice, and it embarrassed her. *Keep this in check. He's a nice man, a good friend. Our daughters are in the same class. That's it. Sure!*

"A little Grand Marnier sound good?" He raised his brows and flashed that smile again, outlined by his dimples.

"Grand." She giggled at her own pun. "The glasses, are they in the china cabinet?"

"Yep. I'll get the booze."

She took two snifters out of the cabinet. She could hear the little girls playing in Maddie's room and couldn't help but think of Sara McKay and Mark Collins. They should be laughing, too. Playing, hanging out with their families and friends. She tried to shake the thought. The last thing she wanted to think about right now was the case and what she thought William James had done to the victims. The more she thought about that slimeball and his perverted tastes, the more certain she was that he was their killer, regardless of Brooke's analysis. Come Monday morning, William James would be behind bars. That is, if he hadn't already skipped town.

"Holly, you find the glasses?" Brendan asked from the kitchen.

"I did." She came back into the kitchen. One of the cats twined itself through her legs, causing her to lose her balance. The glasses slipped out of her hands, crashing on to the floor, but Brendan caught her before she could do a face plant on to the tile floor. "Oh, damn. I'm sorry." She looked up at Brendan. His gaze met hers.

"I'm not." His face came closer.

He was just about to kiss her when Holly heard, "Hey, Dad? Kate is on the phone and wants to know if I can go to the movies with her older brother and her? Oops, did I interrupt something?" There stood Meg, phone in hand, looking a bit shocked, yet equally amused.

"No, no." Holly scrambled out of Brandon's arms and brushed herself off. "I dropped the glasses." Holly grabbed a paper towel and started gathering the glass together with it.

"The movies? Yeah, yeah. Okay." Meg walked away giggling. "Do I feel like an idiot," Brendan said. "I'll get this. You get a couple of more glasses." He bent down next to her.

"No way. You get the glasses this time."

He brought in two more glasses just as she was finishing cleaning up the mess. He poured himself a shot of the fine liqueur. Instead of sipping it though, he quickly downed it. "I can be a true Irishman. You still want a nip?"

"Better not. I'd love to some other time, though. Gotta drive Maddie home."

"Brendan nodded. Understood. Uh, Holly?"

"Yes?"

"I was wondering...well...are you free Saturday night? I thought it might be nice if we could have a bit of dinner, just the two of us, somewhere nice, no interruptions."

Now what did that book about dating rules say? "That would be nice."

"Good, say, seven? I'll pick you up."

"I've got to get a babysitter," Holly said.

"I'll do it," Meg interrupted. She'd obviously been eavesdropping.

"Maddie, too," Brendan said.

"You gonna pay me?"

"Yes, yes, yes, I'll pay you, girl."

"Deal."

"Damn kid. It's always about the money," Brendan said.

Holly laughed, and they said their good-nights. She and Chloe arrived home well after nine, tired, full of good food, and very happy, both falling asleep in Holly's bed while watching a Thanksgiving special on TV.

It was after two in the morning when Holly found herself awakened by her own screaming and Chloe crying out, "Mommy, Mommy, it's okay. Please stop. Stop crying."

Holly focused on her child, while trying to get a hold of herself. "What is it, Mommy? You had a bad dream. What was it about?"

Holly wrapped her arms around Chloe, "Nothing baby. It was just a stupid dream. I can't even remember it now."

They lay back down, Chloe still cradled in Holly's arms. Holly remembered the dream, so much so that it felt very real to her. But she did not want to tell her daughter about it, not yet, not until she was older. It was the same nightmare she had every few months, the one that kept her from ever truly letting go of Jack.

It was the nightmare of the day he was killed and hearing the words that his body hadn't been found.

That the fire had been so hot.

That there was nothing left. Nothing at all.

14

On Saturday morning, Gunter Drake watched the afternoon soccer game from a spot up on a hill, peering through a high-powered
telescope. At last, he thought he'd found the one. He zeroed in on
that ring finger. Aha! No ring. She was petite, with long dark hair
pulled back into a ponytail. He'd prefer that she wear it down.
They'd have to have a talk about that, if indeed she was the right
one. He still had some research to do on her.

Finding the perfect wife and kids could be a real bitch these
days.

Game over. Gunter strained to see, trying to figure out which
of the boys was hers. He liked boys. Having sons was a good thing.
The girls were kind of a pain in the ass. He could usually get the
boys to warm up to him. He knew how to play it right. Most boys
liked electronics and so did Gunter. Perfect! There he was hugging
his mom. Had to be about seven. They'd won, too. Great! He'd
have to get the boy a surprise for that. He liked finding a pair this
way. It was far more challenging and risky than his usual method.

He watched as they left the field and got into a nearby SUV.
He quickly ran for his Explorer and wound down the road from

the YMCA. Heading to the entrance of the park, he made a U-turn and was able to get in behind her.

Moments later, Mama pulled into a Starbucks parking lot, and she and the boy went in. Gunter followed suit. He stood behind them in line. She smelled great, like roses and vanilla—magnificent. The boy was yapping at her about his game; she seemed distracted. Probably trying to decide if she wanted whipped cream or not. She'd be having some whipped cream with him. That was for sure. The boy would need to be taught some lessons in boundaries. The way he kept tugging on Mama was annoying.

"I want a soda, Mom."

"Sweetie, they don't have sodas, remember? You can have apple juice."

"I don't want apple juice," he continued to whine. "I want a coke."

"No, Jason. They don't have cokes."

"That's so stupid. Why didn't we go to McDonald's? I want McDonald's!"

Why did kids always love those greasy fries and burgers? He'd bring him home a Happy Meal, if that's what it took to shut the sniveling brat up. Gunter bent down to the kid's level. The kid looked at him. "I think it's stupid that they don't have cokes here, too. You know, McDonald's does sound a heck of a lot better, doesn't it?"

The kid nodded. Mama had a bit of an incredulous look on her face. But he knew how to soften that as well. "But you know what?"

"What?"

"Looks to me like you're a pretty good soccer player, right?" The boy nodded. "I just bet you are. Well, did you know that all champion soccer players drink apple juice?"

"Nuh-uh."

"Yes, sir." Yes, he'd done it again. Mama was smiling now. "And something tells me that if you drink all your juice, that maybe your mom will take you to McDonald's tonight, right, Mom?"

"Please, Mom. Will you?"

"Jason, Daddy is coming home tonight. Remember?"

"Oh, you're married?" Gunter blurted out.

Mama again looked at him with amazement, and Gunter took a step back. Smooth move, dipshit. What if she detected something? No. How could she?

"Yes, I'm married. Okay, Jason let's get some juice and head home."

"I'm sorry, I didn't see a ring on your finger and thought..."

"You thought wrong." There was an obvious edge to her voice, and Gunter knew he should back off. She faced the girl at the counter and gave her order, totally ignoring him. She even pulled the kid in a little tighter to her. The boy didn't fight it. He must've sensed his mother's uneasiness. Gunter knew that kids could do that. He knew a lot about kids. Nothing could shut a kid up faster than sensing when their mama seemed a bit jittery.

Gunter was pissed now. He wanted this one. He wanted her bad, and the damn kid needed a better father than the one he had, one who would teach him a few lessons in good behavior. But Gunter had that one rule and one rule only: No married women. No, sir, he was not a wife stealer. Single moms only. That was how Gunter liked it.

He watched Mama and the boy leave. Mama glared at him. She would've been a handful anyway. He took his espresso and sat down.

Then something else caught his attention. A little argument at the table in the corner. Looked like a mother-daughter thing. The girl was about eleven. "But I want to go to Dad's this weekend," she whined.

"I told you no, and I told you why."

"Dad only let me watch one R-rated movie. That was it."

"That was one too many, and until your dad and I get this sorted out, I say no."

"That's so gay."

"Kristy, I'm warning you."

Kristy mocked her mother. Their squabbling carried on for a few more minutes. "You know what, young lady? If you don't cut the crap right now, I'm going to ground you until you're eighteen—no friends, no TV, no phone, no shopping. Nothing!"

Good for her. That kid, too, needed some teaching. Man, oh man, what was it with kids these days? They needed fathers, dads who cared. Gunter could see that these two needed just that, and he was the man to make it happen.

15

Lynne Greene pulled her new Honda into the garage. She loved its new leather smell. She was glad now that she'd worked so hard for her status as an RN two years ago. It had increased her worth and made things much easier on Kristy and herself. God knew Kristy's deadbeat of a dad, with no morals whatsoever, wasn't footing the bill. Why hadn't she seen him for what he really was when she'd fallen so desperately head over heels in love with him at twenty-three?

She didn't bad-mouth Bill, but she sure would have liked to when Kristy pulled that crap about wanting to spend more time at her dad's, like she had yesterday at Starbucks. That kid could be really infuriating. The only reason Kristy really wanted to go to her dad's was because he stocked up on sodas, chips, candy, you name it—pure heaven for an adolescent girl. And she even had her own phone in her bedroom. That was the kicker, along with the TV that included HBO and Showtime. Now Bill was pressuring the kid to come live with him, saying that Lynne worked too late, and he didn't like Kristy being alone for that long.

Lynne didn't like to leave her daughter so late into the evening either, and it was already past seven, but her babysitter had family in town on the Thanksgiving weekend, and Lynne took the day of work for the overtime. She needed it to pay all those delinquent divorce-attorney bills. Besides, Kristy was almost twelve and a pretty responsible kid.

Tonight Lynne would make up for her tardiness as best she could and cook Kristy's favorite, spaghetti and meatballs. She didn't have any Thanksgiving leftovers, since they'd gone to her brother's house up in Del Mar, and with the size of his wife's family, there were never any leftovers. Maybe she should've asked her brother if Kristy could stay the weekend there with her cousins, but there wasn't much room at their house since all the family from Kansas was staying there. At least Kristy was here in her house and not at her dad's.

If only Kristy had some idea of what her father was really like. Who knew? Maybe the kid did have an idea, and simply liked the Disneyland, free-for-all atmosphere her dad provided for her. Lynne was hard on her at times, but someone had to make some rules. There was homework, and chores, and getting up early in the morning to get things done. She only did it because she knew that in the long run, if Kristy had discipline now, she'd succeed later in life. But maybe she should back off a little bit. Try and have some more fun with her daughter. Yes, she liked that idea. She could provide a little bit of Disneyland on her own. And she had the perfect idea.

Before closing the garage and heading in, Lynne called her pal who worked over at the sports arena. "Hey, Thomas, can you help me get a pair of Shania Twain tickets? I want to do something special for my daughter, and I'm sure they're pretty much sold out."

"And what do I get out of the deal?" Thomas asked. They were friends who occasionally spent an evening together keeping each other warm. Okay, he was a booty call. But she needed a little romancing and loving once in awhile.

She thought about her reply for a moment. The truth was she really did like Thomas and would like a more permanent arrangement. Thomas, on the other hand, was a confirmed bachelor, and because of that, Lynne held back. She didn't want to get too close. But knowing that the Shania Twain tickets would make her daughter see her in a new light, coupled with the added bonus of ending her three-month period of celibacy, she immediately replied, "Say next weekend I cook you a nice meal, we rent a movie, and from there…Who knows what might happen?"

"I'll get you front-row seats," he said quickly.

She laughed. "Seriously?"

"Yep. Seriously. Oh, and I love meatloaf. Can you make a good meatloaf?"

"Can I make a good meatloaf? What kind of question is that? Honey, I can make a meatloaf that would put Emeril Lagasse to shame."

"So you're gonna 'Bam!' it up a bit?"

"Don't you know it," laughed Lynne.

"Deal. When do you want to come by and grab those tickets? I've got a little extra time I could spend with you at lunch tomorrow. What do you say?"

"I'll see you tomorrow around noon."

She flipped her phone shut and pulled the rubber band from her shoulder-length dark-blonde hair, feeling kind of like a woman again, more than just a nurse and mother. But right now, being a mom felt pretty darn good. She grabbed her bag, shut the car door, closed the garage, and put the key in the kitchen door lock.

Something made her stop. That music. What in the world? Kristy was listening to Frank Sinatra? What in the hell…? Had Bill exposed her to martini music and told her it was cool? Not that she had anything against Sinatra. She loved him. But she'd just bought Shania Twain tickets, and if Bill had done some weird Daddy spell and made her think Shania sucked or something she'd be pissed. It would be exactly like that bastard to ruin another night for her.

She turned the key and opened the door. Stepping inside, things got even weirder. Lights were off, except for a faint glow of what she presumed to be candlelight coming from the dining room table. Had Kristy gotten out that damn Ouija board her dad had bought her last Christmas? Better throw it away. There was something else though…

She called out, "Kristy? Kristy? Honey, I'm home, and I've got something special to tell you."

No answer. Okay, what is she up to? That smell. God, what was that glorious smell? Onion, garlic, and maybe basil. *What in the hell was going on? This kid didn't even know how to boil water!*

"Kristy!" She raised her voice an octave. An uneasy feeling began in her stomach.

She set her purse down on the clothes dryer, next to the back door. She walked down the hall into the dining room, the candlelight becoming brighter. This had to be a Bill ploy. He'd been begging her to take him back, even putting Kristy in the middle and getting her to join in on sending flowers and cards to Lynne. If Kristy was a part of this…

As she entered the dining room, her mouth fell open. Her glass-topped table was lined with candles and flowers, and elegant dishes sat displayed as if she'd entered a gourmet restaurant. "Kristy! Dammit! Get in here right now!"

Strong arms went around her waist. "Bill! Let me go! This is ridiculous. I am not happy, nor am I persuaded by your sick behavior." She couldn't turn around to see her ex's face. Something didn't feel right. "Bill?" She heard the shakiness in her voice, and blood surged through her nerve endings as she realized that whoever had his arms around her was not her ex. Bill wasn't this tall, or this strong, as she'd discovered when she knocked him out the night he admitted that he had gambled away a good share of their savings. She struggled even harder as the realization came into focus that she did not know who this was.

Kristy. Where was Kristy?

"Darling, I've been waiting all afternoon for you to come home. How was your day?" The man placed his hands on her shoulders and turned her around.

She froze. Who was he? The weird thought that he was handsome crossed her mind. She wiped it away. "Who are you? Who sent you here? Did Bill put you up to this? You know what? I want you out of here. I'm calling the police. Where is my daughter?" Her words were tinged with fear, and each breath caught in her throat. She knew she was speaking out loud, but there was a sensation of not really hearing herself speak. It was like being in a tunnel where the words echoed back. She was reeling from dizziness.

"Now, is that any way to treat your loving husband?"

He locked his large hands around her neck, and stared into her eyes. His eyes were cold, hard, and nearly black.

Screaming with terror inside, Lynne realized this wasn't a joke or a game. His eyes told her a story.

Having been a nurse long enough, she'd seen a number of lunatics come and go, even testified once in a case after a patient had come into the ER with a knife and sliced a large gash across her thigh. This man's eyes told her that he was as crazy as that man had been, and from the surreal scene in her dining room, probably more so.

"Where's my daughter?"

"You know I really don't like it when you refer to her as your daughter. She's mine too. Kristy is being punished. She didn't want to help me make dinner, and so I sent her to her room."

Oh, God, no! What had he done with her child? "You sent her to her room?"

"Yes, of course! What else was I supposed to do? She's at that age where we really need to be setting down a few more rules and making her follow them. I'm certain the next time around she'll be more helpful."

"Can I see her? It's been a long day, and I missed her." Lynne was getting the picture, and knew that the only possibility of getting away from him was to play his game.

"What about me? Didn't you miss me?"

"Oh, um, sure I did. But you know how close Kristy and I are, and I only want to say hello," she said, struggling to get the words out. She had to see her daughter, make sure she was okay, and still... She couldn't bring herself to think that maybe he'd really harmed her. Maybe he was really a mental patient, but harmless. Maybe he just had some deranged family need.

Lynne tried to hold back her tears. A sicko like this could be angered by a show of emotion. *Play it cool, stay calm, focus. Get him to trust you.* All of the things she'd learned working in the emergency room flashed through her mind.

"Wow, this looks like a terrific dinner you've made, honey," she said, trying to speak as calmly as possible.

"It is terrific. You are such a good wife. I thought that you deserved a fantastic dinner." He picked up a glass of red wine, and without ever taking his hardened eyes off her, he handed her the wine.

"Thanks," she muttered. "I really should go change and say hi to Kristy."

"Kristy, Kristy, Kristy," his face reddened. "Are we back to her again?"

Lynne's stomach coiled into a nauseated knot. What if he'd hurt her, molested her? Or worse. The idea of playing along with him was lost in those thoughts as terror took over. She wrenched out of his grasp and ran through the house screaming Kristy's name. His footsteps pounded behind her. He didn't say anything, but she knew she wasn't going to get away from him. She reached Kristy's room and flung open the door. "Oh, my God…" she whispered.

Her child was tied to her bed, blindfolded and her mouth duct-taped shut. Blood from her nose had dried into a trickle. A swollen blue bruise marked her check. Lynne gasped. She could see Kristy's chest rise and fall, and was thrilled to see her begin to squirm at the sound of her mother's voice. Lynne rushed to her and yanked off the blindfold and tape. She started to untie the ropes.

"Mama, no!"

Lynne turned around to see the frightening stranger behind her, his face in a purple rage. His eyes focused into angry slits.

"I told you she was fine," he growled.

"You motherfucker!" she screamed, and her fist shot out. He grabbed it and stopped it before it ever connected, but she brought her knee up and got him in the crotch.

"You bitch! You ungrateful bitch!"

Lynne turned back to Kristy, pulled the ropes from her as hard as she could with a strength that she never knew she had. She grabbed her child's hand, and while the psycho was hunched over, groaning in pain, they ran from the room. Nearing the front door, she screamed, hoping someone would hear her. As she reached out for the handle, she felt a heavy hand grab her from behind. Kristy screamed. He turned toward her, backhanded her, and sent her flying across the room, where she hit her head smack against the brick fireplace.

"Kristy!" Lynne screamed. She knew her baby had probably been knocked unconscious by the blow. That would be the very least. Lynne knew that as surely as she knew right then that her world would never, ever be the same. A fist slammed into her cheekbone and she stumbled backward.

"I cannot understand you women!" he yelled. "I've had it with this shit!"

As Lynne tried to regain her balance and reach her child, he grabbed her and threw her to the ground, pinning her beneath him.

Over the next hour and a half, she lost consciousness several times as she was forced to submit to obscene cruelties she didn't think anyone could ever live through. And she was right. As she took her last breath of air, she prayed to God that when her child's head had connected with the bricks on the fireplace, she'd died instantly. Because worse than what she'd had to suffer physically at the hands of the madman hunched over her was feeling the death of her soul at the thought that he might do the same things to Kristy. That he would torture her precious baby girl.

Let my daughter be dead already. Please let her be dead.

16

Holly fretted about what to wear. She changed three times before deciding on a sleek black dress, something that she had bought a couple of years ago for her dad's retirement party. It was far more expensive than anything she usually bought. The bodice was tight fitting and lined with corset boning, the neck cut in a square line that was low enough to draw interest, but not so low as to appear cheap. She put on a pair of pumps, and after spending extra time on her makeup and hair, she was as ready as she'd ever be. She hadn't had a date in years. The last time she had gone out, at her mother's pleading, had been disastrous when the man she had dinner with made a few lewd suggestions about her handcuffs.

She had later told her mom as politely as possible that her best friend's son was anything but a gentleman.

This was a whole different ball game. She liked Brendan, and her nerves fluttered within as they hadn't since…well, since meeting Jack. Yes, those same butterflies had flown around in her belly when she'd met her husband. Had she known the torment and heartache that marriage was to lead to, she'd have walked the other way. Maybe not. No, she wouldn't have. Their marriage had been wonderful. Together they had created a dream of a child. But now she carried the deep mark in her heart left not only by his death, but also by the brutality of his death.

The doorbell rang, and she shook off her morbid thoughts. Chloe beat her to the door, but knowing the rules, didn't open it. She whispered, "You look so pretty, Mommy."

"Thank you, Chloe." She opened the door to see Brendan standing there with a bouquet of pink roses and lilacs. He had remembered their conversation at Thanksgiving about favorite flowers, when she had told him that she absolutely loved how fragrant lilacs were. "Wow! Thank you."

Brendan handed her the flowers. Maddie bounded past the two of them. Meg followed her. They had agreed that the girls should stay at Holly's for the evening, especially since Meg was Chloe's new babysitter.

They quickly scattered to the back of the house.

After putting the flowers in a vase, Holly turned to look at Brendan. "Thank you again. They're lovely."

"And so are you."

She knew she was blushing, but it felt pretty damn good. "You look wonderful yourself." He did look great, dressed in a black button-down with a nice pair of khaki slacks, topped by a tan suede sport coat.

After Holly explained the ins and out of the house to Meg and wrote down her cell number, they left for dinner.

Over a bottle of Beaujolais and a delicious French appetizer that Holly couldn't pronounce, much less spell, she found herself relaxing. Until Brendan brought up her past.

"I assume you were married?"

Holly nodded and took a long sip of wine. Did he have to go there? "I was."

"Well? I've told you all about my ex."

"Not really. And do we really want to talk about the past?" She didn't want to lay the truth on him yet. Once she did, she knew his smiling eyes would turn sympathetic, and the glittery feelings that were starting to come over her would quickly fade. She didn't want to give up that lovely feeling, not yet. But he insisted on pressuring her to talk. "If you must know, my husband died when I was pregnant with Chloe."

"Oh."

Yep, there they were. The sad eyes.

"I'm sorry. I didn't know."

"Now you do, and now can you see why I don't want to talk about it?"

Brendan looked taken aback, possibly even hurt. "I'm a good listener, you know. I've traveled a rough road myself at times, and it seems to me maybe you should talk about it."

"I've talked and talked about it." That was a huge lie. Thinking to herself and talking to someone else were two totally different things. "Trust me, it's in the past, and there's nothing I can do about it. It's time to move on."

Brendan nodded. "I am not convinced, Detective Jennings, and if you ask me, I think you've been running from this for some time. Why get so defensive if it's truly in the past?"

"Do you like discussing the people you've loved and then seen die?" She shifted uncomfortably in her chair and reached across the table for the bottle of wine. He beat her to it and poured her another glass—this time only half full. Where was the chauvinism coming from? Was he pulling a power trip on her? Because if that were the case, she'd have to say sayonara, bud.

"No, I suppose not, but there is a part of us that has a need to speak of the dead, especially the ones we loved, especially with someone who cares about us."

"Listen, it's our first date. I like you, and I know we've spent some great times together in the last few days, but I'm simply not ready to go there with you. I'm not ready to discuss Jack yet. Maybe sometime in the future."

Brendan smiled. "I like that."

"Like what?"

"That you indicated we might have a future. And I also like that you're willing to say how you feel and tell me when to back off. But I still think you need to talk about your husband. Okay, maybe not now, but if we are going to have a future, then we should have that talk. Because, lady, I haven't felt my heart beat so hard against my chest in ages at the sight of a woman, and I'm not saying that just because I'm feeling this nice vintage here…" He pointed to the bottle of wine. "What I'm saying is, if we're going to plan on spending some quality time together, Holly Jennings, maybe consider a relationship…I want to be certain there are no ghosts sleeping with us."

An image of herself lying in bed next to Brendan crossed her mind, and the tough cop needed to look away, blushing furiously. What did a woman say to that? She was at a loss for words, for Brendan was absolutely right. If she went to bed with him tonight, Jack's ghost would be right there with them. Damn it! How had Brendan so skillfully figured her out, sunk into her skin and bones, reached into her soul?

The truly frightening thing was that not even Jack had made her feel so alive and so like a woman. This man had a charisma, an energy that shouted at her to take a chance for a change. Working over dead, decaying bodies was a cinch, but a man with a heart and soul—and she had an idea he also had a pretty good package between his legs—scared the living shit out of her. Yes, she was gonna have to get out of this and fast, because if she didn't, this was going to lead somewhere. The wine made her giggle out loud at the thought. Because who really gave a shit if it did lead somewhere? What was she so damn scared of? The answer to that was what she and Brendan would eventually have to talk about. But for now, all she wanted to do was drink wine, eat gourmet food, and look at that delicious face.

"What is so funny?" he asked.

"Honestly, I don't know."

They finished the wine and dinner, the rest of the conversation light, warm, easy. Way too comfortable. A long walk on the beach brought them around to the topic of their children once again.

"Are you chilly?" he asked, reaching for her hand.

"Maybe a bit."

He draped his coat over her shoulders and then brought his arm around, squeezing her close. Wow, did that ever feel good.

"So, Chloe really likes Maddie, and the two of them are pretty funny together. Have you ever watched them play Barbie? Very entertaining." Chatter, chatter, chatter. *Keep talking, girl. The night is getting old like you, and he'll have to take you home soon.*

But was that what she truly wanted?

"Hmmm, yes. And did you know that the girls love to watch *Peter Pan?*"

She looked at him, not sure what that meant.

"Yes, they do, and I've watched it with them a few times. And I have a favorite line in that movie."

"Really?" Okay, he had to be drunk.

"I love when Peter says to Wendy, 'Boy, girls talk too much.' And she says, 'Oh, they do?' Peter says, 'Yes they do.' I have to agree with Peter on this occasion. The difference is that if Peter were a smart boy, he would've kissed Wendy to shut her up. Now, I like to think I'm a smart man, or at least have some sense, so right now

I'm going to kiss you. And it's not just to shut you up, but it's also because I want to. Would that be okay with you?"

Holly nodded and said, "Then why don't you shut the hell up and kiss me?"

Brendan did just that. He leaned in and kissed her squarely on the lips. At first it was a sweet, tender kiss. Slow, nice, simple. But as the waves crashed onto the shoreline beside them, the kiss grew heated, intense. Lips separated and passion filled them. Brendan pulled her into him tightly. Delicious warmth came over her and was joined by a chill of excitement, every nerve ending awake and alive. Her stomach twisted into wonderful nervous energy as she felt something hard against her thigh. She knew exactly what that was. She pulled away, and stared into his eyes. A flood of passion and energy passed between them, neither one of them looking away, but taking in everything about each other. It was the ocean that broke the intensity as a large wave crashed on the shore, spraying them with freezing water.

"Oh," Holly exclaimed and jumped back, then began to laugh.

"I'll say," Brendan replied. He took her by the hand and they ran for the car, where he quickly flipped on the heater.

Madonna's voice from the radio sang about dying another day. Changing to a jazz station, Brendan drove as Sade whispered thoughts of perfect love. Ah, so much better.

Brendan came to a stoplight and they both giggled like teenagers when they looked at each other, neither of them with any idea of what to do or say. It was better than being a teenager. Kids were afraid because they didn't know what to do. As adults, Holly knew they both had a very good idea about what to do. The nervousness between them came from pure lust. Or maybe…God, she hated to think it but couldn't help it: maybe something even deeper than lust was causing the wetness between her legs.

The front light was on when they pulled up to the house. Still giggling, Holly managed to unlock the door. The sight before them when they walked through the door touched both their hearts. Meg was asleep on the couch with both her sister and Chloe curled up on either side of her. Holly's chest almost hurt as she sucked in her breath. It was at that moment that she knew. Crazy as it sounded, crazy as it felt, this man, these girls, all of them were meant to be a part of her life with Chloe.

She took a blanket from the hall closet and covered the girls while Brendan mixed them a nightcap. She popped back to her room and saw that her computer was blinking with new e-mail, and the answering machine on her private phone line showed several messages. Screw it. She was having none of it tonight. Tonight was her night with Brendan, and if she wanted to be a normal woman with normal needs instead of a cop for one night, then by God, so be it. Nope, let someone else deal with it tonight.

She walked out of her room wearing a pair of new yoga pants and a J. Crew sweatshirt, ignoring the blinking lights, and headed back to the family room. Brendan was seated in a chair across from the girls, watching them sleep, and Holly wondered if he also felt the connection. That this night could be the beginning of something big for all of them. She hated thoughts like that, but this one filled her mind, and no matter how impractical she told herself the idea was, she couldn't shake it. So for now, with the intoxicating mixture of alcohol and Brendan, she was going to make this last as long as possible.

Taking him by the hand, she escorted him into what she fondly referred to as her library. It was actually little more than a few rows of books stacked in an antique bookcase, a chaise lounge to read and relax upon, and a small TV set inside an armoire, for those nights when she and Chloe disagreed about what to watch.

"So what do you want to do?"

He shrugged and grinned. They sat down together on the lounge and made out like teenagers, learning all the lines and curves and scents of each other's bodies, reveling in their joy with each other. With the children in the next room, they stopped shy of being too indecent, and cuddled in each other's arms. Holly pulled a crocheted blanket up around them. Before long Brendan's rhythmic breathing fell into sync with Holly's, and they were fast asleep.

Sometime shortly after three in the morning, the jarring ring of a telephone woke Holly. At first she grumbled and ignored it, thinking she might be dreaming, or that it was a neighbor's phone ringing. Fat chance.

"Holly, Holly." Brendan's soothing voice woke her, although he sounded alarmed at the ringing.

"It's okay, probably the station. I'm sorry." She left the den and answered the phone on the kitchen table. "Jennings," she muttered.

"Holly, we've tried to reach you for a couple of hours, but got nothing." It was Maureen. "We tried your pager and cell. I know how you hate to have us call the house because of Chloe, but we had no choice."

"Uh-huh." The one night she wanted to run away from it all, turn it off, let someone else run the show…She knew they were about to call her in. It had better be something big.

"What is it?"

"He's struck again."

Holly was now wide awake. "No."

"Not only that, but we've got a survivor."

"Dear God! Can she ID the perp?"

"Nope. She's in a coma. It's pretty bad, Holly. He was especially angry this time around. They must've fought him off as best they could, because he didn't even have time to get them out of the house."

"Hopefully, he left us some trace. Address?"

Maureen gave it to her.

"State Street? State? What was the number again?"

"Seven thirty-five, State."

The number rang a bell, but Holly wasn't sure why. "Do you have the names of the vics?"

"Lynne and Kristy Greene. The mom was Lynne. She's DOA. Kristy has been taken to Children's. A friend of the mom's came by to surprise her late last night, I think hoping for a rendezvous. He said that he had some tickets for a concert for her. He found them. He's real shaken."

Holly almost dropped the phone. She was speechless.

"Holly? Holly? Is something wrong?"

"I'll be right there." Yes, something was very wrong.

Holly knew Lynne and Kristy Greene.

17

Holly changed from the yoga pants into a pair of jeans, leaving the sweatshirt on. There was no time to even consider something more appropriate; her crew needed her, and quickly. Brendan was brewing a cup of coffee for her as she went into the kitchen. The girls were still asleep on the couch, but Meg was starting to stir.

"I'm sorry. I've got to go. Can you...?"

He held up the palm of his hand. "No need to even ask. If you're not home when the girls get up in the morning, I'll take 'em to the Hash House for a bit of breaky, and then we'll go from there. Don't worry about it. I only have to make a quick run into the clinic in the morning to check on the animals. Meg can look out for the girls. If you need to come home and crash, I'm sure we can entertain ourselves. Go do your job."

"Thank you," she whispered, holding back tears that had wanted to fall as soon as she'd heard who had been killed. But now was not the time for tears. She had to put on the poker face that covered the hurt and go to work. "You are a godsend, Brendan O'Neil."

"I beg to differ. You are the one who's been sent to me. Thank you for a lovely evening. I'll see you...?"

"Sometime tomorrow. Although I guess that today is tomorrow. You know what I mean."

He nodded. They kissed again, each now familiar to the other, as though they'd been together for a very long time. Then she was out the door and headed to the crime scene.

She pulled up to the swirling red and blue lights, yellow tape, and the crowd of neighbors who'd been abruptly awakened by the noise. Holly felt the tension rising in her, dreading the sight ahead, and her head started pounding. This was going to get messier with each body if they didn't wrap this up, and soon. Serial killers were not the norm in San Diego. Temperate weather, sandy beaches, and friendly attitudes were the identifying characteristics of America's finest city. She knew that by the time she made it back to work on Monday, after what was to have been a relaxing weekend, the mayor, chief of police, and whoever else had a political career invested in this city would have left a voice mail for her.

She sighed deeply before stepping out of the Jeep. Passing through the gate, she flashed her badge to the requisite rookie at the front entry. He nodded, and she slipped through the door, grateful to have avoided any reporters. At least the media hadn't made it here. Yet. It would not be long.

Quaint, clean, sparse, except for the various pieces of Native American art—from the wall paintings to the many sculptures. Her friend had never lost her love for the native cultures and all they represented to her. A twinge of guilt swirled in her gut. Lynne had talked incessantly about making a pilgrimage to the Incan and Mayan temples. Holly wondered if she ever had. She hoped so.

Holly turned the corner into the dining room, where she heard voices. The splatter of blood smeared across a terracotta wall took her breath away. Terrible and violent things had happened in this house, and the smell of that violence mixed with the chemical agents used for testing evidence brought bile to her throat. A case took on a different look when you knew the victim. It all now blurred into a gray area, but Holly needed it to be black and white; she needed to get back her focus. She took ten seconds to breathe as her yogi had taught her, and settled herself down.

"Hey, Holly. We tried Chad, but he's gone missing too. Any ideas?" Maureen said coming up behind her.

Holly shook her head, but she was quite sure of where her partner was and why he hadn't answered the phone. Damn him. He was busy getting laid and ignoring his phone, when all she wanted was a night of company. Just one night of soothing comfort. Well, maybe more, but she wasn't as irresponsible as Chad. Fine, the truth was, they'd had to track her down, too.

"Body is over there. No one's moved her. Robb is taking photos now. You want a look?"

She was unable to speak, so she just nodded, trying to brace herself for what she was about to see. But there was no preparing for the sight of what was left of her friend. The brutalized remains of Lynne Greene lay unceremoniously—savagely—in a bloody heap on the floor. Holly cried out, "Oh my God!"

"Told you it was bad," Maureen said. "He must be one pissed-off dude. Figure he tied her up to the metal banister of the staircase. There's the ligature marks." She pointed to Lynne's wrists and ankles. "Then he raped her every which way. Untied her when she was too weak to care, raped her again, then slammed her head there against the brick fireplace." Maureen pointed to the fireplace, feet away from Lynne. "Next, he stabbed her repeatedly, then slit her throat. But I can't tell what's postmortem or not. I suppose Dr. Lareby will fill us in on that."

"What is wrong with this fuck?" She said the words loud enough that a group of officers turned and looked. Every fiber in her stung with pain at what lay before her. Totally incomprehensible—totally.

Holly wanted to scream.

She tried to gather herself.

Maureen put an arm around her. "You okay, kid? I've never seen or heard you act like this before during an investigation."

"I'm sorry. I'm a little shaky, that's all. It's three thirty in the morning, and I'm tired."

Maureen nodded, but Holly knew by the look in her colleague's eyes that she wasn't buying it, and who could blame her? Holly was known for her calm exterior, her cool, austere mode of operating, not one to be easily shaken. She had to get it together and work this case. If she let Maureen know that she'd been friends with Lynne and Kristy, it wouldn't be long before she was pulled from the case, and that was the last thing she wanted.

Staring down at the body of her mangled friend, knowing she had suffered hell at the hands of a madman, Holly reaffirmed her will to get the bastard.

"So the child has been taken to Children's?"

Maureen glanced down at her watch. "A couple of hours ago."

"Have you heard anything?"

"Nope. If you want to check in, I sent Fulsom over with her. She's a good cop, good with kids, just in case she wakes up. But I've got to tell you, Holly, I have my doubts the kid will ever wake up, if she even makes it through the night."

The last time Holly had seen Kristy was years ago, when she was only a three-year-old toddler with eyes as bright and happy as sunshine, and a smile to match.

Holly cringed at Maureen's assessment of Kristy's chances. She couldn't help but look back at Lynne, her face so badly beaten it was barely recognizable. Horribly black and blue. A deep purple had set in where the blood had pooled.

Why had she let their friendship die? Jack's face came to mind. She shoved the thought away, angry with him now not only for dying on her, but also for keeping her from a friend over these many years. He had complained constantly that the two women spent too much time together. She'd chosen not to tell him to shove it up his ass, although she definitely should have. A wave of guilt swept over her at the thought. If she had told him, would Lynne still be alive? Would Kristy be at home right now, sleeping in her bed, dreaming about whatever it was girls her age dreamed about these days?

She brought herself back to the present. Holly knew that if she didn't get this vicious killer, he'd continue on his path of slaughtering innocents, forcing too many family members and friends to think in the same terms she now was—in pasts, presents, futures, and what might have been. It was too late now for Holly with Lynne. Way too late.

18

Before heading out to pick up Chloe from Brendan's, Holly continued carefully working the crime scene. It was work that made her sick, but also work that fueled her rage and her conviction to stop the bastard. When she had done all that she could do at the scene, she went straight to the hospital. She had to see for herself how badly Kristy had been hurt.

On her drive over, she had a vivid memory of Kristy as a three-year-old playing with her new Big Wheel. It had been the week between Christmas and New Year's. Things were already on the rocky side in Lynne's marriage, but against Jack's advice, Holly went to visit Lynne and Kristy anyway. The truth was that she'd formed a bond with Lynne and had no intention of breaking it. God! She wished that she'd had more backbone then. She should have told Jack to screw himself and to stay out of it. She remembered it like it was yesterday...

She let herself in to Lynne's house. "Hey? Lynne? Where are you?"

Lynne came in from the family room. "Oh, hi! Come here, you've got to see this." She grabbed Holly's hand and led her to the backyard. Kristy was on the patio making motor noises and riding in circles on the bike. Their old golden retriever watched, appearing annoyed but too mellow by nature and too old to move.

"Hi!" Kristy beamed. "Santa brought me a new bike."

"I see that," Holly replied. "And it's a beautiful bike, too."

The toddler's eyes sparkled; her hair was pulled up into two pigtails that curled into spirals. The beauty of the moment and Kristy's obvious excitement made Holly's stomach flip-flop. A yearning in her womb that had started recently was suddenly screaming at her.

"You can ride it if you want."

Lynne and Holly laughed. "No thank you, sweetie. It's your bike. You ride it." She lowered her voice so that only Lynne could hear what she said next. "And besides, my ass is about ten times too wide," she muttered, sending them into laughter again.

"Want a glass of iced tea?" Lynne asked.

"That would be great."

Lynne brought tall, cold glasses from the kitchen a few minutes later, and they sat at the patio table, sipping iced tea and watching Kristy racing around. They were both silent for quite some time, knowing that Lynne's divorce was causing rifts all over the place.

"I brought you something," Holly said, and handed her a small gift from her purse.

"You didn't have to do that."

Holly batted a hand at her. "Open it."

Lynne opened the gift and inside found a pin with a Celtic cross and an amethyst in the middle—Lynne's birthstone. "Oh, my goodness. You really didn't have to do that."

"I wanted to. I was cruising the antique shops down on Newport in Ocean Beach on my day off, and I saw this and thought of you. I know how much you love Celtic crosses, and I really wanted you to have it."

"It must've cost a fortune."

"No, it didn't, and it doesn't matter what it cost," Holly replied.

Lynne frowned, and reached across the table, taking Holly by the hand. "Look, you mean a great deal to me, and I want to thank you for all of your support with this divorce with Bill, but...God, I don't know how to say this. I know the pressure that Jack's been putting on you about our friendship. Bill came by the other day and we got into it. He said some things about how I'm splitting up you and Jack by expecting you to be my friend and support me through our problems."

"That's stupid! What a jerk! I've never felt you've expected anything of me. You are my friend. It just is."

Lynne smiled, but there was a deep, dark sadness that crept into her blue eyes. "You can say that again. I say it, oh, probably fifty times a day. But the facts are, Holly, I know the 'bros before hoes' thing lasts until they're good and dead. They never really grow up, and I don't see Jack and Bill going their separate ways."

Holly took a long sip from her tea. "So. Let them have their Sunday football games, and you and I can get together. It doesn't all have to change, does it?"

"I don't know. But it might. I hope not, but it might. And if it does, promise me you won't feel bad about it. No matter what happens in this situation, I know how you really feel about me, but I also understand that your marriage comes first, and I certainly wouldn't want our friendship to get in the way of that."

Holly didn't know how to respond, and thankfully she didn't have to as Kristy toppled over on the Big Wheel and started bawling. Her mother ran over, scooped her up, cradling her and rocking her in her arms, all forty pounds of her.

Once she settled down, Kristy said, "I want Auntie Holly to kiss my boo-boo."

"You do?" Holly asked.

"Uh-huh." Kristy held her scraped knee up for Holly to kiss.

"Okay, ready now? À la peanut butter sandwiches!" She kissed Kristy's hurt knee. "Magically cured."

"You stole what the count says on *Sesame Street.*"

"No, I didn't. I borrowed it. See, I'm a good friend of the count's, and he said that I could borrow all the magical things he says."

Kristy giggled, reassured, and they whiled away the afternoon, with Holly telling Kristy stories and having quiet conversations with Lynne that varied from the lighthearted to serious, but all of it with an undertone of sadness.

Lynne had spoken the truth about the friendship changing, and now, as Holly drove up Interstate 5 toward Children's Hospital, the sensation of something insidious and evil sat in the center of her gut, and she couldn't help but hate herself for having failed Lynne and Kristy.

She pulled into the emergency parking at the hospital and placed the police placard on her car. She walked directly to the ER desk and asked for Kristy's room number.

The woman behind the desk rifled through several stacks of paperwork and said, "She's just out of recovery and in the ICU. I can have someone take you up. But I can't guarantee that the doctors will grant you entrance. They're pretty protective of their patients up there. Dr. Lukeman, her doctor, is still on that floor, and he may allow you to see her."

Moments later, after an elevator ride and moving quickly down several long corridors, Holly met up with the doctor. He shook her hand. "Dr. Lukeman."

"Detective Jennings."

"The other detective who was here left about an hour ago. I told her everything we know to this point, and that I would keep the police updated. Nothing has changed. We simply have to wait and see, Detective."

"I understand. But I'd really like to see her."

"I'm afraid I can't let you do that. Besides it wouldn't be at all helpful. As I explained to the other detective, she's in a coma. To update you, she came out of surgery about three hours ago. When she was brought in, she had extensive internal bleeding and a serious head injury. I was able to get the bleeding under control, but we won't know much of anything about her head injury for some time. The neurologist on call took a look, but it's hard to say, with her being in a coma. Another specialist will examine her in a couple of days. Right now, her body needs recovery time."

"So you have no idea how badly she's been injured?" Holly asked, with fear in her voice.

"She had a bad gash to the head, and it's obvious there is some swelling there that we'll have to watch. If it swells too much, we'll have to consider removing a portion of the skull, draining it and then waiting until the swelling goes down to put the skull back on."

The intense tightening in Holly's stomach grew worse. "Look, I know you say it won't do me any good to see her, but I'd really like to."

"Detective, she's not going to wake up anytime soon, and if she does, we don't know how much of her will be there. We don't know if this child will ever be able to put a sentence together again, much less tell you what happened to her."

His crassness angered her, and she couldn't keep herself in check any longer. She was shaking all over, surprised at how strong her emotions were. "I know this child! I've known her since she was a baby. Her mother was a friend of mine. Now, damn it, I'd like to see her," Holly blurted out before thinking.

"I'm very sorry, Detective. I didn't realize. I would never have been so…"

Holly held up her hand. "I understand. I should have told you that I know her. That I love her. I'm sorry. Will you please let me see her?"

The doctor seemed to be evaluating her as he peered through his glasses. He looked awfully young to be a surgeon, but she knew that people thought the same about her in her profession. She had not intended to antagonize him, but right now he was the gate-keeper, and she needed to get past him.

"All right. Now that I know your situation is different from most non-family members, I'll go ahead and let you in. But only for ten minutes."

"Great. Thank you."

He led her to Kristy's room, where a uniformed policeman was posted outside the door. He briefly touched the edge of his cap in recognition as Holly passed into the room. She hoped he hadn't heard her conversation with the doctor.

Holly was not prepared for what was behind the door. Kristy lay still and quiet in the hospital bed that dwarfed her small frame. Tubes were connected everywhere, and monitors guarded her vital signs, their annoying beeps jangling Holly's already edgy nerves. Kristy had been intubated with a breathing tube, and the sound of air pumping into her lungs was ominous and painful to hear. Holly had to close her eyes momentarily as a wave of dizziness caught her off guard.

She pulled up a chair next to the bed and sat with Kristy. "Hey kid," she whispered. "I'm so sorry about this." She bit back the tears that stung her eyes. She gently rubbed Kristy's hand and arm, care-fully avoiding the IV tubes. "I promise I'll get him. I will." She heard the determination in her voice. She was going to kill this fucker, if it was the last thing she ever did.

She sat there with Kristy, images of her as a baby, of when she first walked and how excited Lynne had been…all of the memories came flooding back.

Shortly before Holly and Jack knew that there were problems in Lynne and Bill's marriage, they'd all gotten together for a barbecue.

Kristy must've been about ten months old, and Holly had spent most of the night cooing at her and playing with her. She'd been disappointed when the baby had fallen asleep and Lynne had put her in her crib. She and Jack had left a few minutes later.

In the car, Jack had reached over and grabbed Holly's hand across the seat. "You are so good with that baby, honey. I mean, you're a natural."

"She's a pretty sweet baby. It's easy when they're good." Holly laughed.

"Nah, I think it's more than that. I think you've got it in you to be a great mom."

Holly had laughed even louder. "I'm a cop, Jack. What kind of mother would I make? I fight bad guys and put them in jail. I don't cook, and we both know my cleaning skills aren't exactly the greatest."

"Phooey! You could still be a cop and a mom. I know you could. Yeah, sure, you're as tough as the boys, but I know, even if they don't, that there's a real softy inside you. You've got a heart as big as all outdoors."

"Oh, please, Jack Jennings. You're so full of crap."

Jack had pulled off to the side of the road.

"What are you doing?"

"This." He had parked the car and reached across, placing his hands on the sides of her face. He kissed her long and hard.

"What was that for?"

"I want to have a baby with you, Holly. I want a child."

Holly hadn't known what to say at first. Oddly enough, they'd never really discussed it before they had hurriedly and lustfully run to the justice of the peace after knowing each other only two months. She had always just assumed that they were both focused on their careers as cops. But she secretly had to admit that the thought of a child had crossed her mind a few times in the past months. Every time she saw Kristy, her heart ached for a while after the little girl left.

She'd smiled at him. "You do? Really?"

"I want nothing more."

"You want to go home and get started?"

He put the car in drive and sped the whole way home.

Holly wanted to get pregnant right away, but it took a fertility expert and years to make it happen. Three years and six weeks later came the day she'd gone to the doctor and found out the good news.

It was also the same day that Jack was killed.

"Detective," the doctor said, peeking his head into the room and jolting Holly back to the present. "I let you stay an extra ten minutes, but I'm going to have to ask you to go now."

She nodded, and bent over Kristy, whispering, "You're going to be fine. You were always such a good, sweet, strong girl. Please hold onto that." She delicately kissed Kristy's cheek, and with thoughts of the past still on her mind, left the hospital. Holly was acutely aware that she had quite a load on her plate to take care of.

19

Lost the cool. Lost the cool. Damn! How had that happened? Gunter paced back and forth, the hardwood floors squeaking beneath his feet. What had just happened wasn't supposed to happen. Lynne was supposed to come home, see all that he'd done for her, and be happy, pleased that he took such good care of her. But all she was concerned about was the kid. And there was another mistake—that kid. Gunter thought she'd be a good kid—great kid—but she hadn't been. She'd been a real pain in the ass. Gunter should've seen it all going downhill from the beginning, when the kid put up a fight, refusing to eat any of the goodies he'd just cooked for her. Things had not gone well at all.

"Fuck you!" she had said, spitting out the brownies that he had tried to feed her. He'd had a hell of a time getting her tied up, but he'd finally bound her hands and feet, the little hellion.

He'd slapped her hard across the face. "Now that is no way to talk to your father. I am your daddy, and you will treat me with respect!"

"You're not my father, you demented freak! You're some whacked out screwball and my father is going to kill you. In fact, he ought to be home any minute!"

"No, he won't." Gunter had shaken his head and taken out his duct tape from his tote bag. "Now, for the last time, I'm your daddy!" He tore off a piece of tape and secured it across her back-talking mouth. She had squirmed and thrashed and turned her head from side to side. "Listen, you ungrateful little shit! Knock it off, or I'll make you pay real hard for being such a bad girl."

Well, that was the last time he'd choose a mother with a kid over seven. The older kids apparently didn't get it. Once that little bitch started fighting him, he should've left, because he had known then and there that this was not going to be the perfect family. But one could still hope that the mother would come in and explain the realities of life to the kid, and then they could've all settled down and been extremely happy together—once that kid learned some discipline. But no! Impossible! Mommy came home, threw a fit, and Gunter really lost his cool.

And now he was pants-shitting scared because he'd been so careless.

What if the cops caught on? His own daddy had told him that night, twenty years ago, that you had to get your story straight, memorize it, just in case the cops came sniffing around. Everyone knew the rules in his family; that is, everyone except for their mother. If she'd only played right, his daddy wouldn't have had to…but, no his mother was a very bad lady. Very bad. But Gunter had loved her, really loved her, just like Daddy had. Thinking about her made him think about the other women in his life. There were two others—his sisters. He knew where one of them was, most of the time. The other one, the ingrate…if he ever got his hands on that one, he'd control her, too.

His daddy knew how to control things, and no one had been any the wiser back on that night in 1985—small town, small-town mentality…And then they'd had to move. A couple of cops were suspicious, but Daddy was smarter, way smarter, and after some time had passed, the cops went away. But then, so did Daddy, and Gunter and his sisters were sent away to separate foster homes.

Gunter wondered where his daddy was now. Probably holed up in some old folks home, or maybe he was dead. Well, it didn't matter, because where his dad had failed him, Gunter knew he wasn't going to fail his family. If he could only find the right one.

He couldn't take hanging out here any longer. It was driving him crazy, wondering if the cops were onto him. If they'd found the bodies...And where the fuck was what's-her-name, anyway? Every daddy had a girlfriend on the side, but his hadn't been around in days, and he was starting to get really pissed at the broad. He needed some tension release. He called her number and let it ring several times. No answer, no machine, nothing. He threw the phone against the wall. "Fuck!"

He looked at the time, midafternoon. He'd head out and see if he could find the stupid bitch; then, he'd have to come home and get ready for work. He didn't have time right now to find another family. He was hoping she would do that for him, if he could only find her. She truly understood his needs and supported him. But she would not make a good wife and mother. No way, no how. A woman like that was way too dirty to be a good wife and mother. The nice thing about her was that she really understood her place in life.

Everybody had a place in life. Most people didn't get that, but she did, and he did. His place in life was to be a daddy.

20

Monday morning, Holly picked up the phone in anticipation of who might be calling, hoping to receive some good news for a change. "Jennings here."

The voice on the other end of the phone was just who she had hoped it would be. "I've got that info you asked for, Detective." It was Howard Wheat from the DNA lab.

"Go ahead, Howard. What do you have?"

"The blood that was found on the dog matches your suspect."

"Yes!" Holly balled up her fist in victory. All day yesterday after coming home from the crime scene, she'd waited hopefully for this news. No one on the team had been able to locate William James. The search warrant was signed and ready to go. Holly wanted to get the DNA evidence, just to be certain this was her man. Hopefully by going into his home and businesses, they'd be able to gather enough info about where he'd gone and find him.

She'd already read through recent lists from his dating services to see if Lynne was on any of them. She hadn't found her on one yet and wasn't surprised. Lynne hadn't needed much help in relationships with men, and after her divorce, if Holly remembered right, she'd done a pretty good job of swearing off of them, except for the occasional date. But that had been years ago, and since she'd lost touch with her, Holly had no idea what her recent dating activities might have been. What she did know was that the killer had some type of connection to all of his victims, and now she was getting the evidence she needed to start tying William James to them.

Holly hoped against all odds that James and his girlfriend weren't already halfway to Cabo by now. But they'd be hard-pressed to get that far. The *federales* had already been notified to keep a lookout for them. Holly's team had given them a description of James's car and had faxed an artist's sketches of the two suspects to them. But whether they would be willing to help was an unknown. Holly prayed that wherever James was, he was hiding in a cave nearby, where they might find him soon and get the ball rolling to have him locked away forever, along with his bimbo girlfriend. She had to be involved in some way or another. Holly was pretty sure of that.

"Check this. James's semen was also found on your vic's bra, and his DNA was under her fingernails. However, there was also other DNA under the fingernails on her right hand that doesn't match him. If James did her, then you might want to consider an accomplice."

"I'm already considering it." The noose was tightening around Darla Monroe as well. *But could there be a third perp? Was there some kind of sick sex cult involved in all of this?* "Can you fax me those results? Looks like there's a couple of people we need to locate and have another talk with."

"I'd say. I'll get those to you right now."

She headed to Chad's cube and updated him on the latest. Although she was still distraught over Lynne and Kristy, the idea that they might have figured this thing out, and that they had pretty solid evidence against the suspect, put a bounce in her step.

Chad raised his eyebrows. "Really? Matching DNA?"

"Yes."

"Can I come along for good measure?" Maureen asked. "You might need some backup if he's holed up in his offices."

"Sure, let's go."

They headed out, Robb Carpenter watching as they left. Holly knew he was feeling out of the loop, but she didn't give a rat's ass.

Moments later they pulled up in front of the Elegance Dating Service and, to no one's surprise, found the doors locked and the "closed" sign out front, exactly as it had been Wednesday and through the Thanksgiving weekend. "I knew we should've been keeping tabs on him," Holly said. "Probably skipped town."

"No, I don't think so," Chad said. "He's got way too much cash tied up in these services. He didn't plan on the police finding the dog. Not a very smart criminal, since there's a DNA deposit back in LA taken at the time of his sexual assault charge there."

"I agree that he hoped we wouldn't find the dog. Maybe he thought that when he kicked it, it was history. But there's only one way the man's semen got on Shannon's bra. He had to know that would come up," Holly said.

"There's no law against having sex or having sex with multiple partners. But finding his blood on the dog is different; that's a bit more substantial."

"May I say something?" Maureen had been sitting in the back seat, scanning a fax the lab had sent over.

"Sure," Holly replied.

"Who else do you think could have been involved? Do you think there were three perps in the house that night?" Maureen asked.

"There could have been. Now we have to see which one gives up the others first, after we find them and bring them in for questioning," Holly said. "I'm thinking they had some sort of Manson thing happening, maybe. With weird kinky shit going on. Sort of cultish."

"Here's another thought. What if our UNSUB came in after the sex romp and did his deed then? We know that our second set of victims, Shannon and the kid, weren't killed at home."

"Yes, but we also know there wasn't any sign of forced entry. I'm telling you, I think we got 'em. This guy fits the profile, at least somewhat. He's definitely a sexual predator. Maybe this interests in kids is just now surfacing, and when he tries to mess with the children, the mom goes ballistic," Holly said. "Or maybe..." She bit her tongue, not wanting to think that Lynne was an entirely different person than the one she'd known, because for her to think what she was about to say would mean that Lynne had been someone she would've never wanted to know. "Maybe they include the kids, make them watch. Maybe they're preparing them for the games as well, and none of them have been able to escalate into it quite that far yet."

The car grew silent, each of them considering the monstrous idea. Moments later, they pulled up in front of James's house, all with the same thought: that he lived within miles of the murders.

"Looks like the dating biz is a profitable one," Chad remarked, noting the Victorian-style home in the swanky Mission Hills neighborhood.

"Okay, I'll cover the front door. Cross your fingers that they're really here," Holly said. "Chad, you go around back, and Maureen, you cover that side lawn area. Sometimes these old homes have outside doors in weird places."

Each headed for their stations. Holly walked up the front stairs and rapped on the door. There was no answer. She rang the bell. Still no answer. She walked over to the garage and, finding it unlocked, pulled up the door. A new silver Mercedes sat still and cold. She found Chad and motioned for him to go through the back. She and Maureen crept back around to the front.

She knocked again. "San Diego PD. We have a search warrant." No answer. Signaling Maureen, she said, "Okay, on my count. Ready?"

Maureen nodded.

"One, two, three." Holly and Maureen kicked the heavy door in together. "Police!" Holly shouted. "San Diego PD."

The house was silent, except for the hum of the furnace heating the old hardwood floors. "Looks like he and Shannon shopped at the same design center," Maureen commented.

"Yeah, or else she did his decorating for him."

It was almost spooky to be inside a house where a purportedly single man, assumed not to be gay, had such good taste in decorating that it would put most women's homes to shame. Even more bizarre was the stark contrast between the house and the offices James owned and worked in, which were so Las Vegas tacky. There had to be a woman, or maybe more than one, who'd whipped this house into shape.

Chad came down the hallway. They walked through the house in a coordinated search. James was nowhere to be found. Coming to the third and last door down the hall, Chad found it closed and locked. Stepping back, he raised his foot and kicked it in, revealing an office filled with books, the desk facing a windowsill that looked out over the San Diego harbor and Lindbergh Field. Sitting at the desk was William James, with a bullet hole in his head. The computer's screen before him was filled with pornographic pictures of very young women. His blood was splattered across the screen and the desk.

"I guess we weren't the only ones looking for Mr. James," Chad said.

"Guess not," Maureen replied.

"Shit," Holly said, flipping open her cell phone to call the station. They had another murder scene to investigate.

21

Holly had been so sure that James was their killer, that the tax-payers would be saved a pretty penny. She'd have placed bets on it. Now there was still a killer out there, maybe two, and she'd also put money on it that the other killer had been involved in the McKay and Collins murders. So her city was still not entirely safe. It was possible, of course, that James was the killer, and his partner had taken him out. James's residence had been dusted and searched. His body was now at the ME's office, and an APB had gone out for Darla. Chances were that Darla was in a remote place by this time.

Carpenter called Holly on her cell phone. "She's got five other aliases and a bank account under the name of Jennifer Drake that has been wiped clean of a hundred grand. We're running background to see what we can come up with on all the aliases. Maybe we'll get a hit on one, and we'll be able to see exactly who is behind door number three."

"Okay, Robb. Keep me posted." Her jaw clenched as she flipped the phone shut. It was pretty obvious who had killed William James. The reasons why were not totally clear since there could be a litany of them. It was such a muddle that Holly didn't want to think about it. In fact, she almost didn't want to find James's killer, knowing that it was probably Darla, and that the woman might have had damn good reason. She had a nagging feeling, however, that Darla was just as involved in the horrible murders as James. She wasn't certain how, but if that were true, there was a chance that Darla would kill again. Was it possible that Darla herself was the killer? Holly didn't know, but she wasn't ready to rule out anything.

She headed back from the crime scene and over to the tech lab, where one of the computer techs was dissecting James's computer, bit by bit.

Martin Landon stood up behind his desk as she walked into his office, ran a hand through his stringy, straw-colored hair, and peered at her through a pair of Coke-bottle glasses. Martin fit the computer nerd image to a T, even down to the high-water corduroys and striped button-down. But you could count on Martin to be the one who never forgot anyone's birthday in the office. Oddball, maybe, but a nice guy. "This pervert was into some really sick stuff, Holly."

"I figured."

"He's got all sorts of downloads from kiddie-porn sites and knows all the chat rooms. If you can think it, he's got it, and I'm sure you can't even remotely think of half the stuff. Hell, I can't, and I'm a guy. I can appreciate good porn, but this goes way beyond the bounds. This goes beyond even bad taste."

"Did you contact Sex Crimes and the Internet guys? We might be able to see a nice little spiral from this and catch a few more of the bad guys," Holly remarked, crossing her fingers.

"I contacted them, and they are all very interested in seeing where this case goes. We've already got some of our boys hooked up in chat rooms with these sick jerks. In fact, word from the chat room is one of these losers thinks he's got a thirteen-year-old girl who's gonna meet him at the mall tomorrow night. If our guys can string him along, maybe we can pop him. Who knows? Maybe he'll know something about this James character."

"Good. So can you tell me anything else about our sicko?" Holly asked.

"Actually, I was printing out his e-mails, because I think you'll find some of them pretty interesting." Martin pulled a couple of pages from the printer. "It looks like he's deleted most of them. But on the day he was iced, he'd deleted the e-mails but failed to empty his trash. That's how I found this."

Holly started reading the e-mails, and as she did, she realized that this case was only getting more complicated. She was not nearly as close to solving it with James's death as she'd hoped.

The first e-mail was from William James himself.

I know exactly what you and your crazy boyfriend are trying to do to me. Do you think I'm so stupid that I haven't figured this out? The only reason I haven't gone to the police is because I want to keep my own life private. But I'm telling you right now, if you don't back off and forget your screwy game, then someone is going to get very, very hurt.

WJ

The reply was from someone named Lady Godiva.

You're right about your private life and all its secrets that I'm sure the police would be terribly interested in. But your fixation on the idea that I have devised some bizarre scheme against you is just that. My "boyfriend," as you termed him, is far from a boyfriend. In fact, you know that it's you I love and always have, but you refuse to commit and stop your own freaky games. If I need some company once in a while because you're out satisfying your needs, then so be it. But I assure you that going to the police would be a huge mistake. I do not have any scheme planned. I haven't sold you out, nor do I plan to. So let it go. Can we have dinner and talk about this? I miss you.

Lady Godiva

"No kidding! Have you got a trace on this Lady Godiva's computer yet?"

"Working on it as we speak. But it will take some time. She's sharp and was smart enough to switch her address around and get offline real fast, and with Internet privacy laws..."

"You need a search warrant," Holly finished his sentence. "More bureaucratic bullshit to trash out my day. Don't worry about it. I'll make a few phone calls and see what I can do. It might take some time, too. I think I know who was sending the e-mails anyway. Thanks for the help. I'll let you know when we get the warrant. And keep me posted on the chats going on with the Internet guys."

"You got it."

Holly headed back to the station room, found Chad, and handed him the e-mails. "Get a load of these."

Chad read over them. "What are you thinking?"

"I don't know what to think, but I do know this case is far from being solved. I think Darla is our Lady Godiva, and she holds the answers to this puzzle."

"You think there's another killer out there?"

"Besides her? Maybe. Or when she talks about his sick needs, she was referring to his need to kill."

"Or maybe she was writing about his kiddie-porn cravings," Chad interjected.

"That's possible. But I'm not sure that would bother her so much. Seems that she and William James were two of a kind, and maybe she got into it as much as he did. But I think they're all tied in together, and if there's a third party, we better figure out who it is. Because God forbid that third party is the real killer," Holly said.

"Where do we go from here?"

"We try and track Lady Godiva, and hope she makes a mistake somewhere. If Martin from tech can get a trace on her, then maybe we've got a chance of getting her. Hopefully he will, and if so, maybe she'll screw up and e-mail her other friend. Or better yet, if we can confiscate her computer, which I need to make a call about to a judge right now, then we'll find some more answers."

"Have you checked on Kristy yet today?" Chad asked.

Holly shook her head and grimaced. "I talked to the doctor this morning. He says that her brain is swelling, and they'll most likely have to resort to surgery."

"That's awful. What about her dad, have you spoken with him?"

"Briefly. He's way too upset and stunned. It was pretty awkward since we hadn't seen each other since Jack's funeral. But no, he's not doing very well. For the first time ever I feel sorry for Bill. I never liked him much, you know, when…" She caught herself and realized that she'd just opened the door to getting thrown off the case. What was she thinking? She looked at Chad to see if he'd caught her reference to her friendship with the family.

"I had a hunch, Holly. You've been way too involved in this, and I had a feeling there was a stronger connection than you were letting on. You knew them? Obviously you knew them," Chad said.

"It was a long time ago, partner. You can't say anything to anyone, please. I really want to catch this son of a bitch, and if you tell anyone, you know as well as I do that I'll be pulled off of it."

"You should be. You know the rules, Holly," Chad said, lowering his voice. "You should not be working on this case. I know you've worked on it until you're dragging, but you need to step aside, Holly. It's not good for you."

"Please Chad, don't say anything. I can handle this. I've got to."

"Why? So you can get your revenge on the killer who murdered your friend and nearly killed her daughter? You know that's not how to do this. It'll get clouded, and someone will get hurt. Most likely you," Chad implored, looking at her with concern.

"Listen. Yes, you're right, I want to catch whoever is behind this, and I want to avenge Lynne's killer. But that is not the only reason I'm keeping myself on this case. I've been working it since day one. I know what this bastard or group of freaks, if that's what we're dealing with, is capable of, and I can smell the blood, Chad. I can. I'm begging you to keep this quiet. If it gets out of hand, I'll know. I'll walk away then. I promise," Holly pleaded.

Chad took a step back, crossed his arms over his chest. "I shouldn't do this. I ought to blow the whistle on you. Your staying with this is a bad idea, and I don't think it will benefit you, this case, or anyone involved."

"We all have secrets, don't we?" She was beginning to get angry. "I don't exactly agree with some of your methods or secrets, partner, but I'm discreet because I know it's important to you."

"I don't like the sound of that," Chad replied. He stood back and they looked at each other for a silent moment. "Fine, you've made your point and pleaded your case. I'll shut up for now, but if I see that you're becoming a detriment to yourself or this case, I will go above your head. I'll have to for your own good."

Holly snatched the e-mails from Chad's hands and stormed back to her own cube, where she collected herself and picked up the phone to call the district attorney to get another search warrant, this one for Darla Monroe's house. She knew Chad was still watching her. She could feel his eyes on her. She was angered to no end—at herself for screwing up and saying something, and at him for being such a bastard about it.

But none of it mattered, because no one was getting in her way on this, not even her partner.

After leaving her office, Holly rashly went to see Brooke with the intention of passing on a warning through her to Chad to keep his mouth shut. But when she reached the good doctor's office and stood outside her door about to knock, she changed her mind. This would be a stupid move.

As she turned to walk away, Brooke opened the door. "Holly?"

Holly turned back around. "Oh. Hi."

"Were you coming to see me for something?"

"No not really. Just passing by and was going to say hello, but then realized you were probably busy." Lord, that sounded lame.

"Never too busy for a colleague or a friend."

Holly wasn't sure where, but she supposed that Brooke was indicating that she fit in there somewhere between the two. She smiled, not knowing what to say and feeling very uneasy.

"So this case is keeping you all working around the clock?"

The words "you all" still carried a faint Texas twang that she was pretty sure Dr. Brooke Madison had worked hard, and failed, to get rid of completely. For some reason, that thought helped put Holly at ease. Maybe it was just that even the doctor had her own hidden insecurities. "Yes, it certainly is. It's a tough one."

"You want to come in, tell me about it? Maybe I can give you some insight. I know what I told you the last time we talked, but it appears from the reports I've received that the playing field has changed some, and you're dealing with more than one killer. Funny, I didn't get that in the beginning, but as I said, I'm not always right."

Holly shifted from one foot to the other. Okay, maybe she would have some insight that Holly didn't. It was Brooke's job to crawl into the minds of these monsters and to try to figure out motives and histories. "Sure, why not."

Holly followed the leggy doc into her office and sat down across the desk from her.

"So talk to me some more about this case. Maureen brought the new info to me yesterday about the latest victims. I've been going through it myself, to see what kind of read I can get, but I have to admit this is a strange case. From all that I've read of the reports sent to me, it does seem as though there is more than one suspect involved."

"It does seem that way." Holly handed her the file containing the e-mails she'd brought with her. She hoped Brooke would assume they'd been the inspiration for the visit.

Brooke read over the e-mails. "From these messages, I'd say that we are dealing with more than one psychopath, for that is essentially who these people are. Psychopaths. I told you before what I thought about the killer. Now we have to expand our thinking and consider other alternatives. Most psychopaths are loners; they don't hang out in groups, unless it's a Manson-type phenomenon, as I see you jotted down in the file. Good theory. Maybe this James fellow or this third person is the leader, and the others involved simply don't have enough self-esteem or grit to think on their own. But, honestly, Holly, I don't think that's what it is, either."

Brooke set the e-mails down on her desk and shook her head. She spread her manicured hands across the papers, a ring on her left hand. No diamond, but a ring nonetheless. A blue sapphire in the middle, with small diamonds edged all the way around it—done in platinum—expensive, very expensive. Too expensive for a cop. God, Holly hoped Chad knew what the hell he was doing—assuming he was the one who'd given the doc the ring, of course.

"I don't know what we have, and I'm banging my head against the wall along with everyone else on the team," Holly said. "If there's more than one out there, and our guy was not James, then we still have a killer on the loose, and that scares the hell out of me. After seeing the last crime scene, I know enough about escalation to know that this person is not going to stop any time soon."

"I agree." Brooke stood. She came around her desk and sat down in the chair next to Holly, and in a near whisper said, "Do you believe in intuition?"

"Of course I do. I'm a cop. We follow our gut instincts all the time." Okay, this was getting weird.

"Take it a little further. Say…premonitions?"

Holly pulled back and tilted her head to one side. "What are you asking me?" Really weird.

"What would you say if I told you that I have a friend outside the force who has quietly helped us before, or at least me, in these types of cases?" Brooke crossed her legs.

"Like a psychic? Are you saying that you use a psychic to help you?" An interesting side to Brooke.

"Sometimes. When you all come to me and have questions about a case that I simply can't get answers to, then yes, I have a friend I call who has helped me find answers. The only reason I haven't ever brought this to anyone's attention is that I know what some of the supervisors in this office would think about using a medium, and it could mean my job."

"Uh-huh," Holly replied.

"It's only a suggestion, Holly. What can it hurt? Do you want to give it a try? It's lunchtime. We can go and talk to her now, if you'd like. No one will be the wiser, and it might help you. And if it doesn't, what do you have to lose? Simple folly."

And time on an important case. "I don't know, Brooke. It is a bit out of the norm. And I'm feeling pretty pressed for time on this thing. I hadn't planned on a lunch break today."

"That's fine. Just thought I'd run it past you."

Holly leaned back in the chair for a minute and thought about it. Brooke was right. What did she have to lose? And she couldn't help but be a bit curious about this medium. "Let's go."

"Really?"

"Yeah. Now, before I change my mind. We'll grab a sandwich on the way. I don't think too clearly on an empty stomach."

They left the office, Holly thinking that Chad's Dr. Brooke was full of all kinds of surprises.

22

Anne Nickels was nothing like Holly expected, nor did she live as Holly expected. Anne the psychic was a petite woman with black hair, cut in a pageboy. Her pale green eyes were remarkable, almost the color of celery. She wore Levi's and an Old Navy T-shirt. The house was a two-story Tudor, in Birdrock, north of Pacific Beach and just South of La Jolla—an expensive area. Holly immediately liked Anne, and with the offer of some chamomile tea, she and Brooke settled onto a sofa covered in cream-colored chenille.

"I take it from your phone call that this is pretty important, Brooke." Anne sat down across from them in a winged-back, distressed leather chair, very shabby chic. Brooke had called from her cell phone during the car ride up, counting on Anne's availability.

"Yes. Detective Jennings…"

"Holly, please," Holly interrupted, correcting Brooke.

Brooke continued, "Holly is working a case, and I've been studying the files. There are some complications surrounding the case."

"Okay. Can you tell me, are these the cases that involve the mothers and their children? The Family Man cases?"

Holly nodded. It wasn't like that was too tough to figure out. The cases had been broadcast all over the place.

"Yes, I've been following the media reports, and I see your dilemma. I agree that there are three players involved here. But oddly enough, one player doesn't know about the others. It's a man. Well, he knows, but not in the sense that they actually work together. Do you understand?"

"No," Holly replied. "Is this the man who thinks he was being set up?" Holly asked referring to James.

"No. This is the killer himself. He has no real need for the others. But one of them, a female, plays very strongly in this. She has a real attachment to him." Anne closed her eyes for a minute. "However, he would've done this anyway, without the help."

"So they helped him?" Holly asked, not knowing what to believe and not knowing what Brooke might have told her.

"The woman did. She helped him once, and has offered to help again. He doesn't completely trust her, but part of him enjoys having her around. He likes to keep an eye on her, if that means something to you."

"Can you tell me what she looks like?"

Amazingly enough, Anne described Darla almost perfectly. "Listen, she has a connection to this killer, and I don't know specifically what it is, but I also feel like she's gone."

"Dead? Do you think he's killed her as well? And did this man kill James, too?"

"Wait, hold on. Slow down, please. This is too important to rush, okay?"

Holly sat back in the chair. She glanced over at Brooke who was as captivated as Holly had to admit she was.

Anne closed her eyes again and for several minutes didn't say a word. When she opened her eyes, she spoke. "I don't think the woman is dead. But the man is looking for her, and I think his name is Hunter. But that doesn't feel exactly right, so don't count on it. However, he is looking for her, and he does seem pretty angry with her right now. She wants to contact him, but she's afraid. She's afraid of both him and the police. But her bond to this man is very strong, and although I do think she will eventually make contact, I just don't know when. And to answer your question about Mr. James, this Hunter man did not kill him. The woman did, and I think she's hiding somewhere. That's why I feel she's not close. She is not in San Diego anymore, I can tell you that much."

"Mexico?" Holly frowned. She was buying this. How could she not? The woman knew way too much.

"If I had to put money on it, that would be my first guess. But I can't tell you exactly where."

"Okay. So this man, Hunter, our killer…What about him? Where is he?"

"He's still here in town, very much so. And I feel that he is closer than you think. It's almost like you know him. Or you'll meet him."

Bet I will, sister. When I shoot his fucking brains out.

Anne looked her square in the eye. Oh, God, did she just read my thoughts?

"I don't know how he knows you, but I feel very strongly that he does. He's definitely seen you."

Holly shook her head and sighed. She had quickly gone from almost believing her to not buying a word she was saying.

"Holly?" Anne asked, still staring at her.

"Yes?"

"Did they ever find your husband's body?"

"What?" Holly couldn't have heard her correctly.

"Did they ever find his body?"

Holly looked back and forth between Brooke and Anne. She stood. "We've taken enough of your time. Thank you."

As she opened the front door, Anne spoke again. "Holly, if they never found his body, I don't know if he's really dead."

Enough! What was this medium, or whatever she called herself, trying to tell her anyway? For God's sake! What nonsense. She faced her. "My husband died in that fire. That's it, end of story." She walked briskly to the car. She heard Brooke apologizing and calling good-bye over her shoulder as she followed Holly.

They were silent for a few moments, until Holly got onto the freeway and accelerated, driving at a high speed. This hadn't gone the way she'd thought. She figured maybe she'd get some kind of answer, but what she'd gotten was pure bullshit. And the kind that stirred emotions in her that didn't need stirring. She longed to call Brendan.

"Holly, I am so sorry." Brooke broke the silence. "I don't know what that was about."

"You don't? You and Chad been sharing bedtime stories? What are you up to, Brooke? Are you trying to play me for some strange reason? You and Chad in cahoots to get me off this case? You afraid I'm going to go tell Greenfield that you two are getting it on? So you conjure up this weird psychic scenario, to what...? Get me thrown off the case? Make it look like I'm losing my mind?"

"Holly, I have no idea what you're talking about."

"Whatever. Let's forget this whole thing happened. I've got to get back to work. I've got a case to solve, without you and Madame See-the-Future, much less your boyfriend."

"Holly, I am sorry, really."

Holly gripped the steering wheel. "Save it, Brooke. Just save it. I still have no clue as to what you're up to, and frankly I don't really care. But let me say this," Holly began. "Don't get in the way of me and this case. I'm not going to spill your secret. In fact, I could give less than a rat's ass about who you screw. Screw the entire department for all I care. But leave me out of it."

Moments later they pulled into the station parking lot. Brooke quietly got out and walked away.

Holly checked her watch. Chloe would be in aftercare by now. She decided to go and check on Kristy, then pick Chloe up early. She wanted to get as far away from this place as possible right now. Maybe she could clear her head and try to figure out what in hell was going on. Truthfully, she wanted to go to see Brendan, have him put his strong arms around her, have him hold her tight, protecting her from everything and everyone around her.

23

Gunter couldn't find the stupid bitch anywhere. She wasn't answering his pages, and he couldn't go by the place where she lived for fear the cops might be watching for him to do just that. He knew she had other friends. That was just the way she was. No use fighting it. He didn't want to marry her anyway. Couldn't marry her.

It was still early, so he decided to grab a cup of coffee and sit down and read the newspaper, see if there was anything new about him and his families.

He ordered his usual espresso and sat down outside the Starbucks store, glancing up occasionally to see if any new prospects were headed his way. He was always on the lookout—he never knew what or who might turn up, or when and where. But there was a sour note about a pickup in a Starbucks after the past weekend's fiasco. He needed to be really careful in choosing the next one.

Damned if he could find anything new about his case inside the local paper. There was a small article about the ongoing investigation, but that was it. The lead investigator, Holly Jennings, was mentioned several times. Ah, dear Holly. She had her work cut out for her, now didn't she? Gunter would have to meet her one day.

Finishing the story about the lead cop, his eye caught another article—in the corner of the page. What was this? Local dating service owner shot to death in his Mission Hills Home. Gunter read and reread the article. My God, this was unbelievable. But now at least he knew what had happened to the broad, and he was so pissed off he couldn't see straight.

"Don't worry," she'd said. "It will all be all right. I know what you did. I won't tell anyone. I love you, Gunter, blah, blah, blah… I'll even help you, baby. I know how important it is for you to have a family, and I want that for you. I'll help you find the perfect ones. I'll make it all better for you. That's all I've ever wanted."

Yeah, that had turned out just great, hadn't it? But she had found him Shannon and her kid, and he had liked them really well, until everything went downhill. He wished he had never confided in her about what it was he needed. He wished she had never found out. Well, she'd obviously axed the pervert. Gunter hated that guy. It wasn't as if they'd ever met, but she'd told him all about the freak who liked naked little children. He deserved to die. But after the first family turned sour, and the bitch put two and two together, she said that she'd help him, and that it would all work out. Ha!

"We'll set him up. He'll go down for life with all that kiddie porn he's got lying around. No one will believe that he didn't do it. I'll make sure of it, baby. And by the time they do, you'll have found yourself the perfect family. And me? Well, let's just say that I'll get what I want, too."

What the hell did she want? To have the pervert locked away? Why hadn't Gunter asked her straight out if that was all she wanted out of this? Had she played him for an idiot? He was pretty sure she had.

Now with James dead, it would probably be next week before he could get any idea of what the cops were looking into, or even who they were looking at for the murders. He had to get next to that detective. Holly Jennings. He'd have to figure out a way to get to Holly Jennings and find out what she knew.

He swallowed his coffee and headed over to the Internet café, where he had another espresso and started researching where this detective lived. It took all of thirty-five minutes before he had it narrowed down.

He still had a couple of minutes before he had to get going to work, so he hopped in his car and drove past the address. He could not believe his eyes! The detective whose pictures were in the newspaper was just getting out of a car parked in the driveway, and hopping out of the passenger side door was a little girl. Not older than eight! Oh, boy, oh boy! Maybe he'd have to get to know Detective Jennings in more than one way! He hadn't seen a man's name on the title to the house when he'd located her address on the Internet. So no husband.

This was too damn good to be true.

Gunter Drake smiled.

The perfect family was right under his nose.

24

Karen Whitley looked disgustedly at the plate of greasy food she'd set in front of one of her regulars. She hated her job, hated her looks, and pretty much didn't care for anyone she knew. However, she didn't really know all that many people, and Karen wasn't her real name. She would never, ever utter her real name out loud. Occasionally she thought about that other woman. The one who'd been forty pounds thinner, the one who'd purposely gained all that weight, chopped off all her hair, colored it a mousy brown, and kept her television on all night long. She wanted no one and nothing in her life. At least that was the lie she told herself.

She had to believe that, because she knew that if she didn't, she'd wind up dead.

Stay alone, don't let anyone in or know the truth, because the truth is so evil and frightening that if anyone ever knew it they'd run. She was a part of something sinister and demented, and she'd left all of that behind when she was a kid, but it never really left her mind. That kind of evil, the kind she knew ran through generations of bloodlines, how could she not be tainted with it?

"So Karen, how you doing?"

"Same old same," she said glancing at the large balding man on the other side of the counter.

She'd worked at this diner in the middle of Brooklyn for four years now. The food sucked, the people were sad sacks, all depressed and dragging, and she barely made enough money to pay her rent. But she felt safe here. She'd done it. She'd won. She had been able to escape death and disappear to another coast, into a city of millions, where no one cared what her real name was or where she came from.

She'd even left behind people who had cared for her, and she'd done that to protect them, because Karen knew that at some point in her life the evil would track her down, find her, and swallow her up. It was only a matter of time. She'd been expecting it for a while now. But who knew? Maybe it wasn't coming for her after all. Maybe she had truly escaped it.

"You know, Karen, you really are a pretty lady."

"Gee, thanks, Hank. Yeah right, with my folds hanging over the sides of my apron," she laughed. She knew he wasn't coming on to her. Hank was one of those people who was always trying to make others feel better about themselves. She really kind of liked him. He was as close to being a friend as anyone she knew, except for her cat, Livvie, who was really more of a pain than a friend.

"Nah, you look fine. And I know you're a smart lady. I see the way you handle folks coming in here. Why do you stay? Don't you want something more for yourself? You're a young gal."

"And what would that something more be?" She picked up the carafe of coffee. This kind of talk made her nervous, but Hank was harmless.

"I don't know, maybe a family or a career?"

She stared outside for a brief moment, watching people pass by. Probably on their way home from work or going to work the night shift. She liked the night shift. It meant not having to sleep, not having to dream. She didn't dream when she slept during the day, but the nights…the nights were filled with dreams. If they could be even called dreams. "I'm pretty happy where I am, Hank."

Hank shrugged his shoulders and went back to scarfing down his food. "You could do better, Karen. You really could," he said in between chewing mouthfuls.

"Sure, like maybe the French Riviera or something." She laughed again at her own silliness. Her on the Riviera! What a hoot!

"Why not? You don't have a husband. You don't have kids. Who's to stop you from going to France or Italy or wherever you want to? Me?" He spread his arms out wide. "I'd love to live in one of those exotic places, but I've got a wife and four kids, with two leaving for college in a couple of years and one heading out in a year. I'm tied down. You're not."

"I can't even hardly pay my rent."

"If there's a will, there's a way." He smiled.

"Right." She filled his coffee cup. "Maybe someday."

"So the wife and I are getting a vacation in a week, taking our oldest out to check out schools on the West Coast, if you can call touring our seventeen-year-old around and listening to her complain about what dorks and idiots we are a vacation." He laughed. "If we can ditch the kid for a while, maybe we'll have some fun. Teenage girls can be a real pain in the old buttocks, you know. Love the kid, but I am sort of happy to see her moving out and moving on. It's just gonna cost me an arm and a leg! So we're gonna start in Santa Barbara and head on down to San Diego. The kid's got a brain. If I could go anywhere, it'd be where the sun always shines. I'm hoping she chooses San Diego, 'cause I got a sister out there. We're gonna take some time to visit her. That should be nice, although she's kind of a pain in the old buttocks too, though. Reminds me of my daughter with that stubborn streak of hers. I suppose that's from my grandpa."

Karen drowned him out some. That was Hank—long-winded and filled with all sorts of stories and such.

"Tell you what, though, they better solve their serial-killing thing out there in sunny San Diego before I let her go."

Karen spun on her heels and faced him. "What are you talking about?" The word killing always got her attention.

"Don't you watch the news?"

"I hate the news. I don't want to hear any of that negative crap. I keep it on Comedy Central or the Discovery Channel. I like jokes and animals."

"They got them a mess out there. Some bastard is kidnapping single moms and their kids. They're calling him the Family Man, or something like that. Theory is he wants to live out his perfect family life with them. Sick stuff."

"I guess." A prickly, cold sensation slid across the back of her neck and down her arms.

"The disgusting thing is, this guy cuts the ring finger off of the mom after he's killed them. Makes for a real crime book, huh?"

Karen didn't know what to say. Her body went completely cold, and she nearly dropped the coffee pot. Her hands shook.

"Karen, what is it? You're as pale as a sheet, hon. What's wrong?"

"Nothing," she stammered as she set the pot back on the counter. "Nothing at all." She rubbed her ring finger. She closed her eyes and steadied herself against the counter, her back to Hank. She didn't want him any more alarmed at her behavior than he already was.

What if it was him? What if he was out there? Could it be? Could he be the one killing women and children in San Diego, as Hank said? Oh please, no! Please don't let it be him.

As these disturbing thoughts raced around in her head, she suddenly thought about what Hank had said to her before he'd relayed the happenings on the West Coast. Maybe she should think about another place, even farther away, another place across the ocean. Another new name, new job, new life. Maybe if she did that, she could revive old dreams. France would be nice. But what about those women? Could she go halfway around the world knowing that maybe he was out there torturing and killing them? Or should she get the hell out of here and pretend none of it had ever happened, that she never worked in this diner, never knew Hank or anything about the story he'd told her? She might be able to forget those things, but could she forget what had happened to her? The things that she'd lived through? No, she didn't think anyone could ever forget.

The evil she thought she had escaped had found her again.

25

Holly invited Brendan and the girls to an early dinner with her and Chloe. She was relieved to have the company and to have someone help take the edge off of her truly startling day. She was still waiting for news from Robb Carpenter regarding what he'd discovered about one Miss Darla Monroe and all of her other aliases.

"You're distracted," Brendan said. He tossed the salad, while she poured them each a glass of red wine.

"I am. I'm sorry. It's this case. Please don't take it personally."

"We can go, if you'd like."

"God, no. That's the last thing I want. Actually, you know what I really want, and I haven't been able to stop thinking about it since I left the office this afternoon…?" Wow, she was going out on a limb here.

"I don't know, my dear, but I must say I kind of like the sound of whatever it is you're hinting at."

She socked him lightly on the shoulder. He grabbed her around the waist and squeezed. "No, silly, I wasn't thinking what I'm sure you're probably thinking. Besides, we do have little girls in the next room."

"Okay, guess I got my hopes up."

"Don't give up on that hope, though. I think maybe, eventually, if you play your cards right, you might get lucky. In time that is." Was this stuff really coming out of her mouth? This did not sound like the Holly she knew, or at least the Holly she wanted people to see. But maybe this was the long-lost Holly after all this time. This was the woman she'd been missing. The one who loved to play, flirt, and be a woman—not just a coldhearted cop. That was the woman she'd grown used to, and now to hear this side of her personality coming to life again felt strange, but in a wonderful way.

"So what is it? What have you been thinking about this afternoon?" Brendan asked.

"This. Simply this. Spending time with you and hearing about your day, having you and Maddie here. I wish Meg could've joined us, too."

"I know. But you know teenagers. She has her own agenda. Something about a three-way phone conversation that I believe has to do with the godforsaken word boys."

Holly laughed. "Yes, yes, that bad word. But boys grow into men, and you know there's nothing wrong with a good man."

"You know one, do you?"

"I think I do."

He put his arms around her and gave her a gentle kiss on the lips. They were both guarded, afraid that Maddie and Chloe might pop in at any moment. But it was a sweet kiss, and though not a passionate one, it still sent feelings into territories that hadn't been visited in a long time. Brendan pulled away from her and said, "Well, if you know a chap like that, I certainly hope he doesn't get in my way."

The glow continued over the next couple of hours, and as the girls joined them, chatter and laughter filled the house. Family laughter, familiar, full of fun and intimacy. The more Holly watched Brendan play with the girls, telling jokes and revealing more of himself as he did, the more she knew that she was falling in love with him. However, her mind wandered at one point, allowing in thoughts of what the screwy psychic had told her.

That Jack might still be alive.

She quickly shut out this idea and went back to enjoying the evening. She would not allow anything to spoil this moment, not even the unsettling possibility that Jack…What nonsense!

As the evening wound down, Brendan and Holly knew they each had responsibilities to their children, and giving in to their growing desire and falling into bed together would not be responsible behavior. It was just too soon in their relationship; besides, the girls needed to be tucked into their own beds.

Saying their good-nights at the door, they gave each other a simple hug. Brendan turned back around as he walked down her front path and smiled at her. "Maybe we'll see you tomorrow?"

"That would be nice. I'll call you."

"Good-night."

"Mommy." Chloe was pulling on Holly's oversized sweater.

"What baby?"

"I don't feel so good."

Holly bent down. "What is it?"

"I don't know. My tummy kind of hurts."

"I say we get you off to bed. Okay?"

Holly tucked Chloe in bed and stroked her hair until she fell asleep. Exhaustion overcame her shortly after Chloe fell asleep, and she headed off to her own room. She picked up a book and tried to read, but sleep and mixed dreams took over, dreams of butterflies, Brendan, and then nightmares of fires, Jack, and a faceless killer.

Asleep for quite a few hours, Holly woke hearing cries from the other room. What was it? She rubbed her eyes and looked at the digital clock on her nightstand. It read 2:30 a.m. She heard the crying again, moaning really. Chloe. It's Chloe. Holly whipped back the covers and jumped out of bed. "Chloe! Chloe, honey what is it?" She heard the desperation in her voice. Chloe didn't answer.

Holly turned the corner in the hall and flung open Chloe's door. She ran to her side. "Baby?"

"Mommy?" she cried. "I don't feel so good."

Holly felt her forehead. "You're burning up," she whispered more to herself than to her daughter. Holly had been a mother long enough to know that this wasn't a low-grade fever. She wrapped Chloe up in her blanket. "We need to go see the doctor, okay?"

"No, Mom. I don't want to," she whined.

Holly paid no attention to her protests. She took the thermometer out of the bathroom medicine cabinet. "Here put this under your tongue."

Chloe obeyed and opened wide. Holly laid her back down on her bed. "Hang on. Don't let it out from under your tongue." Chloe nodded. Holly kissed her flaming forehead. She went back into the bathroom and fumbled around for the children's Tylenol, found it and took it back to Chloe. She checked the thermometer. It read 105. *Jesus Christ.* "Oh yes, we have to go see the doctor. Here, take these, honey." Holly gave her two of the chewable tablets. Chloe lethargically chewed them. Holly picked her up again and, slipping her feet into her Keds, grabbed a Gatorade from the fridge, hoping Chloe could get some down. She then searched for Chloe's favorite stuffed animal—a dolphin she'd bought at SeaWorld the year before.

Moments later they were speeding out Interstate 8 East, and then up 163 North. There was little traffic, and Holly made it to Children's Hospital in a record time of seven minutes.

She grabbed Chloe, dashed through the doors, and made her way to the man sitting behind the reception desk. Looking up, he asked, "May I help you?"

"Yes, she's running a temperature of 105."

"Follow me." He led them to the emergency area, where a nurse quickly appeared and pulled the cubicle curtains closed as she stepped inside with them. The man smiled at her and left.

Within minutes, blood had been drawn from Chloe, who was screaming in fear and probably pain.

The ER doc arrived and, after a brief examination, said, "Listen, without any symptoms other than the fever and upset tummy, my guess is that she has a UTI."

"A urinary tract infection?" Holly said.

"That's my suspicion." The doctor, who was younger than Holly (she hated admitting that she didn't quite feel comfortable with that), sat at the edge of Chloe's ER gurney. Her lip jutted out. She was definitely not a happy little girl, but after forty minutes of testing and a question-and-answer session, along with the Tylenol she'd taken at home, her fever had dipped slightly. However, the doctor seemed concerned that it had not gone down enough and that Chloe wasn't showing any other symptoms.

As he returned from checking on the lab reports, he smiled at her, said, "Hi, I'm back." Taking a bright pink marker from his coat pocket, he drew a smiley face on her hand.

"No more needles," Chloe said.

The doctor didn't answer her right away. "Are you having a hard time going to the bathroom?"

Chloe looked at her mom. Holly said, "Honey, tell us if you are. It's important."

"Yes," she said shyly. "I can't go pee pee and it hurts."

"Why didn't you tell me?" Holly asked.

"I don't know."

"Okay, here's what we need to do. We have to run one more test and see if there is anything wrong in what's called your bladder," the doctor said.

"Will it hurt?"

The doctor sighed. "You know what, kiddo, I'm not going to lie. It is going to feel a little uncomfortable. But you're a very big girl, and you were great earlier with the needle."

Chloe started to whimper. Holly put her arm around her. By the time the nurse came back into the room, Chloe had herself pretty worked up. It took the doctor and two nurses to hold her down in order for the doctor to insert the catheter. Holly ached to scream, cry, yell, yank them away from her little girl.

Instead she stood at her baby girl's head and stroked her hair while tears streamed down Chloe's face. "It hurts, Mama. It hurts," she repeated over and over again in a wail.

It felt like it took forever, although it was over rather quickly. Once the medical team left the room to test the sample for bacteria, Holly sat down and held Chloe in her arms, rocking her and cooing. "It's all right, sweet girl. You're going to be okay. Mommy is here. Mommy loves you."

Chloe was just falling asleep when the doctor came in to tell Holly that, yes, indeed, they had found that her child had a bladder infection.

"We'll give her a shot of antibiotics and some to take in liquid form over the next ten days. It's vital that she take it all and on time. This infection is pretty bad, and if she skips any, it could get worse and possibly affect her kidneys. Also, no bubble baths. I'm assuming she may have gotten it from a bubble bath?" The doctor raised his eyebrows, looking directly at Holly. "Um, there's no, hmm, how do I put this. I guess what I'm asking you is, is it possible there's a need to be concerned about abuse here?"

"What?" Holly was aghast. "Doctor, I'm a detective. My daughter and I live alone."

"Just a precaution." He stepped away. "A bladder infection can be brought on by sexual intercourse or…ah, some type of molestation. But I don't see anything here that might indicate that."

"Is that the real reason you cathed her? Were you concerned she'd been sexually abused?" Holly lowered her voice, as Chloe started to stir awake.

The doctor didn't answer for a moment, but kept jotting down notes. He looked up from his clipboard and with a firm stare said, "You wouldn't believe what I see working in here. I take all precautions to make sure the children who come through this ER on my shift haven't been harmed in any way. I needed to cath your daughter to get a decent and accurate specimen. I'm sorry if I've offended you. I'm sure if you speak to your pediatrician tomorrow, which I recommend that you do, you'll find that I've done everything by the book. Now please, as I've said in my instructions, it is vital she take all of the antibiotics. You should see her fever coming down within the hour. I'll fill out your release papers and have the nurse take Chloe's temp one more time after her shot, then you can take her home."

Holly watched him disappear around the corner. She was still in a state of shock. The implication that someone actually could have abused her child was insane. The only man she'd been around lately was Brendan, and she knew that he wouldn't harm Chloe. She felt disgusted and dirty. Wait a minute, damn it. She hadn't done anything wrong. She felt sick at the mere thought that some crazed person might have done that to her baby. She was more determined than ever to make sure Chloe was protected at all costs and at all times. She hated seeing her in so much pain and distress.

An hour later, after more tears and pretty bad bedside manners from the doc and his crew, Holly walked out the door of the emergency room carrying Chloe and feeling every ache and pain possible to mankind in her muscles. As she did, she heard someone walk up beside her. It was the man from the front desk. She jumped even though the area was well lit. She'd been lost in thought and hadn't heard his approach.

"I'm sorry. I didn't mean to frighten you. I was on my break and saw you leaving." He held up a Coke can.

Holly nodded and hit the alarm button on her car, unlocking the door. She slid Chloe into the back seat and buckled her into her seat belt, shutting the door. Turning around, she found the man still standing there. She wasn't in the mood for this. Her conversation with the doctor had been irritation enough. She'd had all she could handle of feeling harassed for one night.

"Can I help you?" she asked.

"Nah. I wanted to make sure she was okay."

"She's fine. Thanks." Holly got into the driver's side and started the engine. She didn't feel like being congenial, even though she was sure the man was simply being nice. The doc had rubbed her the wrong way so much that at this late hour, on so little sleep, she was feeling pretty bitchy. She should've been kinder.

Fuck it. All she wanted was to get underneath the covers with her little girl and get some sleep. As she pulled around the U-shaped drive, she could see out of her side mirror that the receptionist was still standing outside. He seemed to be watching her. *There's something about him—weird. Oh, face it, I'm tired and overworked on this case, and I'm stressed to the max when I start thinking that a Children's Hospital attendant has some strange motive for asking me how my sick child is feeling.* She switched the radio on to the classical music station and drove home, not giving another thought to the man she'd left standing in front of Children's Hospital.

26

Darla Monroe rolled over in the squeaky cot inside the shack where she was holed up in some fishing village, somewhere in Mexico. She was somewhere between Puerto Vallarta and Manzanillo, not sure exactly where and not exactly caring. She was pretty deep into Mexico, but there were still a few "whities" around this place, and if they saw her, and if luck wasn't on her side, they might talk when they got home. Someone smart enough might put two and two together and come to hunt her down.

What she really wanted was to have Gunter with her. It was all she ever wanted, and she would do anything to make him happy, keep him happy, and help him get whatever he wanted. She understood why she couldn't be his wife—sure she did. It was a matter of politics and blood really, right?

Whatever. She reached for the bottle of tequila on a cardboard box next to the uncomfortable bed. She noticed the black strands of hair that fell across her shoulders and remembered coloring it last night down in the river, only yards away from her hut. She took a huge slug of the tequila. Ooh, that had quite a bite. At least it was expensive tequila—agave, the real stuff. But she could pay for it, she had the money. She'd put a bullet right through that perverted, motherfuckin' James, right in the head, and took all the cash. Some of it, anyway. Enough to live really good down here in what was kind of a paradise, depending on how you looked at it. And right now it was looking pretty damn close to nirvana. It was just that Gunter wasn't here with her. She knew he would not, or could not, ever be happy with her. But Darla still ached for him, wanting to ease his pain, knowing exactly what it felt like—enmeshed in him. That's what they were with one another, enmeshed. He just didn't see it that way and only referred to her as his whore, his broad, his slut, his sister. Sometimes she was one woman, and then she was the other when it suited him.

Boy, did Darla Monroe have a story to tell. She had been seven when Gunter had been eleven. Her name was Jennifer back then. She still used that name occasionally. All her life, at least ever since she could remember, no one had ever been nice to her, except her brother Gunter. He loved her. Maybe her sister sort of did, too. But their sister was only four at the time, and what did she know? Darla rarely thought about where little Kimmy might be now. They'd all been spread out when they were sent into foster homes. Darla only could hope for the best for Kimmy.

It was fate that had brought her and her brother, Gunter—her lover—back together. How she loved him. She remembered his caresses and the way he took care of her when she was a little girl. At first it felt really, really wrong. But as they grew older, she knew that Gunter Drake was the only man she wanted. And then they were ripped apart when she was eleven. She really missed him.

"I love you, sissy. I do. I always take care of you, don't I? I'll be a good daddy, just like our daddy," he said to her one night after sneaking into her room.

Their father had beaten their mother almost to a pulp that evening. Darla knew her mommy didn't deserve the beating. So what if she'd overcooked the carrots? She was sorry; she really was.

Darla knew it. But Gunter convinced her that it was Mommy's fault. Maybe it was.

"Daddy loves us, sissy. He does. He told me that he's only trying to make Mom a better person. You'll see. It will all be okay." He slid his hand down inside her panties. She tingled between her legs. Her daddy had done the same thing to her. It was hard to know the difference now. She kind of knew it wasn't right, but her daddy made her lie still and let him do it. Now she let Gunter do it to her, too.

"Daddy says that we all have a place in life, sissy, and you're lucky because you've found yours."

She'd been only nine at the time. He was thirteen. "I have?"

"Yes. Your place is to be my whore."

"I don't know what that means." What she did know was that whore was a very, very ugly word. She'd heard her father call her mother that lots of times, and it always happened when he was being really mean to her.

"Don't you worry, I'll show you."

And he had. Jennifer, now Darla, had become her brother's whore, and she knew nothing else. Even though she wanted Gunter, she knew deep down that he did not want her the same way. Not with the same intensity.

So she'd looked elsewhere for a while and joined up with William after meeting him at the porno awards out in Las Vegas. He was handsome, cool, and seemed to be respected in the industry. She'd made a few films for him and was feeling her way through it all. He asked her out. She gave him a blow job underneath a table inside a bar, and they started spending time together.

Who would've thought that William James would fall for her? Well, he had. Juggling him and her brother hadn't been easy, and when William found out about Gunter, he was not too happy.

"You cheating, lying bitch. Who is this bastard you're fucking?" he'd bellowed.

"Listen, baby, you never said we were exclusive. I know you got your kiddie thing on the side. I also know you do some of the chicks coming through the dating service. I am not stupid. Blonde, but not stupid."

"What are you talking about?" He walked over to the mirror-backed bar in his Mission Hills home and made himself a gin and tonic and sucked it back. He lit a cigar, put it in the ashtray, and made himself another drink.

She was used to this ritual and waited until he was finished. He needed to be nice and relaxed for this conversation. "You like kids. The jig is up, babe. But, hey, we've all got our fetishes, and I'm not gonna blab your secret. However, if I want to have some fun when you're not around, then I will."

William paced back and forth. Darla watched. She knew he didn't like this, but she also knew that he couldn't give her up. She was as much of an addiction for him as his other addictions. She would make this work to her advantage, because Darla had ideas about how William could be of use to her and how he could be of use to Gunter, too.

Darla knew of Gunter's need for the perfect family, and she wanted that for him. She even wanted it for herself. But her real hope was that he would never find one, and that he would come to see that they were meant to be together.

She swallowed another large shot of tequila. She had to get a hold of Gunter, make him realize how crazy this was and that their futures ought to be spent together. But how? Her cell phone wasn't working here in Bumfuck, Nowhere.

She pulled herself out of bed, dressed quickly, and went down to the tiny shack that served coffee and eggs. In her broken Spanish, she asked where she might find a computer with Internet service.

The weathered old woman pouring the coffee looked at her without a clue to what she was talking about.

Darla stretched out her fingers and pretended she was typing. *"Computador. Yo necesito una computador."*

The old woman shook her head. She turned to leave but spotted a surfer who looked like he was from the States coming in for a cup of coffee. He glanced Darla's way. She doubted that this dude was much into the news anyway, in case the cops were looking for her. The hell with it. "Hey, hon?"

"Yo."

"Do you have any idea where I might find a computer down here? I need to write some e-mails."

"Well, chica, you've got about a three-hour drive, but if you head up north toward Puerto Vallarta, you should find something. Most of the larger towns have Internet cafés set up. They might be slow, and it could take some time to get your stuff on through. But that's your best bet."

Not what she wanted to hear. She needed to avoid the larger cities. "Thanks."

Darla headed back to the shack that she'd paid five bucks for, shoved what little she had into her backpack, and readied herself for the three-hour road trip. She knew it was risky, but she had to reach Gunter. She needed to make him see, before it was too late for both of them.

27

Karen Whitley stared at the photograph—the last remnant of an old life. She'd never understood why she hadn't thrown it away, but maybe fate had intervened, maybe there was a reason she'd kept the photo for so long.

Maybe somewhere inside, Karen had known that it would be useful one day, and now she crossed her fingers, hoping that it would be. She prayed it would get into the right hands and stop the evil going on. She wasn't sure that the horrible crimes in San Diego were indeed from the same source of evil that she'd experienced for so long, but there was a sameness to them that couldn't be denied. For that reason, all she would do was mail the picture. Nothing more. That was all. If it worked, then fate will have played a part in it, and maybe (*please, God!*) she could have a normal life, one in which she wouldn't have to look over her shoulder every minute of the day or keep her television on all night to drown out the night terrors so that she could finally sleep.

She closed her suitcase and overnight bags and put her kitty in her carrier. She would make four stops.

The first stop was at the diner where she'd worked for the past five years, handing over the cat to her longtime friend and unwitting confidant, Hank.

"Thanks for taking her. She's a really good cat. I hope she won't be a bother to you or interfere with your trip out West," Karen said.

"No problem, Karen," Hank replied. "My wife loves cats, and hers died last April, so I think this will be a nice gift. She'll have something skinny to cuddle with in the evenings." Hank laughed. "And my mother is coming to take care of the rest of the crew while we're out in California with the oldest. She's a big animal lover. She'll be just fine."

"Thank you. And thanks for everything." She gave Hank a kiss on the cheek. He blushed. She hadn't kissed another human being in years. It felt odd, but pretty good in a way. Maybe she wasn't tainted by the evil. Doubtful, but maybe.

"Send me a postcard."

She smiled. They both knew she probably wouldn't.

Next Karen stopped at the bank and withdrew all her cash—$12,534.17. Not bad. It would do for a bit. Get her started. She'd been frugal and was grateful for that. This was money that she never touched, saving it for a rainy day, putting in a little here and there over the years, making things tight for her, but the knowledge in the back of her head told her to keep doing it. She was sure glad that she had.

Her third stop was at the post office, where she pulled out the photograph she had wrapped in a piece of paper and addressed the priority-mail envelope to Detective Holly Jennings. On the outside, in neat printing, she wrote, "PERSONAL AND CONFIDENTIAL." She didn't want anyone but Holly Jennings to open this envelope.

Karen's fourth and final stop was JFK, where she ordered a glass of wine in the airport bar and ate a hot dog, waiting for her flight aboard Air France to be announced. Karen Whitley was taking a very big chance and leaving all of it behind—all very far behind.

28

Awakening to blue skies and finding that Chloe was feeling much better in the morning helped loosen Holly's tight muscles. The problem was that Chloe was not entirely better, and Holly had a lot of work to do. What a load of guilt! In all good conscience, how could she leave her daughter with a sitter for the day while she went to work on what should have been her day off? On the other hand, how could she in good conscience leave the day to a killer who could strike at any moment at any place?

She poured herself a second cup of strong coffee and quietly crept out onto her back patio, not wanting to disturb Chloe, who'd fallen asleep again. She was putting off leaving for as long as she could, knowing that Chad would be calling soon and asking for her ETA. But sitting out here, taking in the long grass that needed mowing, looking at it creeping onto her brick patio, she didn't want to move. She desperately wanted to forget the killer who'd so insidiously made his way into her life and the lives of the Collinses, the McKays, and the Greenes.

"Mommy?" a little voice behind her said.

"Chloe, hi. You feeling better?" She turned around to see her daughter, hair disheveled, wearing her favorite purple pajamas, and holding her stuffed dolphin.

"A little."

"Good. You've got to drink lots of water today and take all of your medicine like the doctor said."

"I know. I will." Chloe came around to the front of the wicker chair that her mom was sitting in and climbed up into her lap—a sure sign that she wasn't feeling totally better. Suddenly the decision about work was easier.

"You know what, baby? I've got to call Chad, okay?"

"You're not going to work are you?" she pleaded.

"No, not today."

"Good." Chloe smiled and her face brightened a bit.

"Nope. Today is a day for lounging and watching good movies."

"Yea!"

"But first I have to let Chad know. There is one thing I will have to do later on today, but maybe Megan can watch you for an hour while I take care of it. When I come home, if you've been really good, I'll bring you a treat."

Chloe smiled and nodded her head. She jumped off her mom's lap and asked, "Can I watch *Peter Pan*?"

"*Peter Pan*, hmm? Yes, sweet girl, of course you can."

Holly followed Chloe into the house, put in the DVD for her, then went to the phone and placed her call to Chad.

"Long night?" he asked. "You sound a little tired."

"You could say that," Holly replied. "Wound up in the ER with Chloe. Poor baby has a bladder infection. I can't leave her like this today. She's still not totally better. But I do want to head back to the hospital and check on Kristy."

"Oh no. That's not good. Little pumpkin. Poor you. I think you should stay with her today."

"I know, but I need to get by the hospital."

"Okay." She heard the edginess in his voice and knew he didn't totally agree with her going to see Kristy. "If you want, I can come by and watch Chloe then."

"Could you? That would be great. I was going to call a babysitter, but if you could do it…"

"You got it. Say around three? I'll bring you a latte before you head out, jump start your juices."

"You're the best." The sore feelings she'd had toward him from the day before had nearly diminished. Brooke was another story.

"Yeah, well, I also want to hear some more about Mr. Wonderful."

"Nothing to tell."

"I don't believe you."

"You should."

"Okay, partner, I'll see you around three," Chad said. "In the meantime, we're still working on Darla Monroe's background. Hopefully I'll have a full report for you, and we can work at figuring out where she might have run to."

"Sounds like a plan."

Chad showed up on time, coffee in hand. "Thanks for coming over. She's asleep in the TV room."

"No problem. Glad I could help. I've got some interesting info on Darla Monroe."

"Good. Can we go over it when I get back?"

"Sure. What do you think, an hour or so?"

"About that."

Twenty minutes later Holly was walking down the corridor on the fifth floor of Children's Hospital. Something was nagging at her as she walked, but she couldn't put a finger on it. She started to check in at the nurses' station, when over the loudspeaker, the words "Code blue, room five twelve" came through.

"No," Holly said. That was Kristy's room. As she ran toward the child's room, medical personnel swept past her. A nurse with a crash cart ran quickly into Kristy's room. Holly held her breath. Reaching the open door, she watched as doctors and nurses frantically went to work on the eleven-year-old, trying to save her life. As Holly watched in horror, she was frozen in place by the scene in front of her. What seemed like mere seconds was in reality almost forty minutes. No one wanted to give up on the little girl. But it was futile. She was gone. The doctor glanced up at the clock on the wall and called Kristy's time of death.

Holly closed her eyes and fought back the tears.

"Detective?" It was Dr. Lukeman. He laid a hand on her shoulder. Holly opened her eyes. "I'm sorry. We did everything we could." Holly nodded, turned, and slowly walked away. With the hurt crushing her heart, she was unable to say a word.

She made it home and fell into Chad's arms as she told him what had happened. "She didn't make it, Chad. He killed her, too." Chad quietly held her and let her cry. She lifted her head from his shoulder. "We have to get him, Chad. We have to find this monster and nail him to the wall."

"We will, partner. We will."

29

Chad twirled Brooke's golden hair around his fingers.

"I like this music," Brooke said as she put her glass of Pinot Noir on the nightstand. They lay tangled in the bedsheets that had become twisted and scattered during the past hour of heated passion and fulfillment. Candlelight bounced off the peach-colored walls.

They'd fallen into a pattern of spending their evenings at Brooke's house, and to keep Chad's dog happy, she'd had to give a little and allow him to bring the German shepherd-Lab mix named Pedro. They both were finding great comfort in falling asleep in each other's arms. So now, on an almost nightly basis, Chad and Pedro left their unkempt bachelor pad and crossed the Coronado Bridge to get to Brooke's house on the peninsula.

"Yes, it's nice."

"What's wrong, hon?" Brooke said. "I can tell something is bothering you." She sat up, the sheet falling loosely around her waist. It was hard for Chad not to become aroused again at the sight of her bare breasts. Damn they were pretty, and she was so beautiful.

"It's Holly. Kristy died earlier today. Holly was there, and she didn't take it well. I'm pretty worried about her."

Brooke sighed. "I don't think she's at all well. This case is taking a heavy toll on her."

"I think this case is a little rough on her. More than most."

"It's more than the case. She has some unresolved issues about her husband."

Chad shifted under the sheets and sat up straighter. He wasn't sure that he liked his lover analyzing his partner. It felt like a betrayal.

"I think that's changing. Before this latest murder, she'd told me about a new fella she was interested in, and trust me, Holly doesn't show interest in many men. So maybe this is the real thing for her."

"Yes. Hopefully he can help her through this difficult time. She needs some support."

"I think so, too. But Holly is very private. She might not even tell him. And who knows how far their relationship has gone, or if they even have one. It might be wishful thinking on my part."

"You really care about her," Brooke said.

"Of course I do. She's my partner. She's like a sister to me. Hell, Jack was one of my closest friends. I was even a part of their wedding party. I want her to be happy, and I know that's what Jack would want for her."

"Why do you think she's so afraid to get involved?"

Chad had thought about this quite a bit over the years and had a theory, although it sounded nuts, but he believed it was true. He'd never voiced it to anyone. "Jack's body was never recovered. You see, we were working a big drug case, and we discovered the warehouse where the suspects were storing their supply of cocaine. Or rather, Holly discovered it while out on patrol. Even when she was on the beat, she was always getting herself involved in the big cases, sort of through Jack. He was the lead investigator on this case, and Holly was privy to a lot of the information he'd gathered. She put two and two together before the rest of us did and drove out to the warehouse on her own one afternoon. She radioed Jack and told him what she'd thought she'd found.

"He and his partner cruised over to the place where Holly was waiting for them. His partner, Warren Emerald, covered the outside. They insisted Holly stay out of it, which she wasn't happy about, as you can imagine. But she followed orders. They told her to call in for backup. As she headed for the car to make that call, the warehouse exploded into a big ball of flames."

"What went wrong?"

"Not only were these bastards storing their merchandise in there, but they had a nice little meth lab set up inside."

"And the chemicals…"

"Right. You've heard the story before. We assumed Jack was killed instantly. No one could have survived that blast. Warren was badly burned and tossed pretty far, but because he was outside the building, he had a fighting chance, at least a week's worth before the third-degree burns became irreversibly infected and he died. Holly was parked out of sight a good hundred feet away, hidden behind her cruiser so no one would spot her. But she was thrown by the blast anyway and suffered a broken arm. After the whole ordeal was over, she was reprimanded pretty hard for not following policy and for getting mixed up in the case at all."

"That was pretty harsh considering that she'd lost her husband."

"I think that accounts for some of the animosity she feels toward the chief, but he knows that she's a damned good investigator. She went back to work after a really short break, just as she did after Chloe's birth. Back at work before you could turn around. I think it's what keeps her going. Work and Chloe, that's her life." Chad picked up his wineglass and took a sip.

"So what's your take on her lack of intimate relationships?"

"I don't know for sure, but the body was never found. And I think for the first few years, at least, that she held out some kind of bizarre hope that he was alive. Obviously she knew, we all knew, that he wasn't, but she freaked out at first, insisted he could have survived the blast, that it had caused him to have amnesia, and maybe he was walking the streets. Maybe he hadn't gone into the building after all. Crazy, but that's all I can think of."

"People will say and feel some pretty strange things while under that kind of stress and after that kind of trauma. I think you could be right, especially after what happened with Holly and me. I felt terrible about it then, but now I just feel guilty."

"What in the hell are you talking about, Brooke?"

Brooke told Chad all about the visit to the psychic, what she'd revealed to them about the killer, and the possible connection between him and Holly. She also told him what Anne had said about Jack: that he might still be alive.

Chad nearly spilled his glass of wine. "Are you serious? Are you nuts? Of all people to take someone to a psychic. You're a psychiatrist, someone who studies science."

"I study soft sciences, Chad. Granted, psychics are not always useful. But I knew the team was having some difficulty in this case, so I made the suggestion to Holly, and she agreed to it. There is proven validity to the use of psychics in some investigations. I thought Anne might help."

"You thought wrong." Chad flung back the covers and slipped into his sweats.

"Where are you going?"

"To call Holly."

"Don't do that. I promised her that I wouldn't tell you about this."

"Great! Now my partner and my girlfriend are keeping secrets from me."

"It's not like that, Chad. Okay, look, it wasn't the best idea, especially after seeing Holly's reaction and now learning what you've told me, but I truly wanted to help."

Chad walked over to her side of the bed and softly touched her cheek. "I know you did."

"I'm beginning to wonder if she shouldn't be removed from this case. She is too personally involved."

"Policy-wise, she should be removed. If the chief knew that she was friends with the victims, he'd automatically pull her. But just as you promised her you wouldn't say anything about the psychic visit, I promised that I wouldn't tell the chief as long as she could stay focused and remain objective."

"I don't see how she could stay objective. Especially after today," Brooke said. She stood and grabbed her sweater and jeans off the back of her chaise.

"What are you suggesting?"

"I'm saying she should be off this case for her own sanity. I think Holly needs a break. I think you and the rest of the team ought to work this thing. She should get out of town." Brooke headed down the hall and into the kitchen. Chad followed her.

"I couldn't backstab her like that, Brooke. I can't tell the chief or the team what I know."

"I'm a shrink, and I'm telling you that she's too close to this situation, and her involvement is going to hinder this case rather than help it. You wouldn't be backstabbing her at all. In fact, you'd more than likely be saving her peace of mind."

Chad took a couple of steaks from the refrigerator that he had brought for their dinner. Shaking his head, he said, "I don't know what to do."

"Do what's best for Holly. The woman needs a break, and if forcing her into it is the only way she will take one, then that's the way it has to go down."

"Maybe you're right."

Brooke handed him the salt and pepper, and he went out on the patio to light the grill. Maybe she was right, maybe Holly did need him to interfere. She was going to hate him for it, but if he didn't do something drastic, he was afraid that Holly might crack under the strain.

30

Holly dragged herself to work. She was beaten-to-death tired. She'd canceled dinner with Brendan and the girls the night before, explaining Chloe's illness and her need to be with her. Today Chloe was able to go back to school, but she was still on her meds. Holly hadn't even looked over the paperwork that Chad dropped off about Darla Monroe, and she'd forgotten it at home. Screw it. They all had copies.

Her mind went back to the day before, seeing over and over again the doctors trying to save a precious child, one who's life had been so cruelly ripped away from her along with her mother's. There was a dull pain in the center of Holly's heart, but she knew that she had to suck it up and put on her game face. *Go forward, catch this bastard, and kill him.* No way was she going to let him live when she found him. No way in hell was she going to let him get off that easy. She was sure now, as all the evidence was pointing that way, that this had either been a three-member group of killers, or that William James, Darla Monroe, and Mr. X at least knew each other. It was up to Holly to tie it all together and find the missing links.

Walking into the office, she noticed that none of the team was around. She began to feel uneasy and started twisting her earring around. Something was up, and it didn't take long for her to figure it out when she spotted familiar faces sitting in the conference room as she passed by on the way to the locker room. Through the window she saw Maureen, Chad, Brooke, and Robb. And Chief Greenfield was in there as well. What the fuck was going on? He was supposed to be with his wife.

Greenfield saw her pass by and motioned for her to come in. "Hello, Detective," he said. The strain from his wife's difficult pregnancy was showing in the form of dark bags under his brown eyes, and a new crease of lines had cropped up on his forehead, below his receding hairline.

"Hi." She tried to sound upbeat, but knew she'd failed miserably. "What's going on?" she asked, looking around at the mournful faces of her colleagues. Chad would not meet her eyes.

"It's come to my attention that there is a problem with you working on this case."

Holly crossed her arms in front of her, shifting in her chair. "Really, and what is that?" She looked over at Chad, then at Brooke. Brooke looked back. Chad did not. His head was sagging like the sorry sack he was. He'd betrayed her.

"It seems that you had a personal friendship with Lynne Greene and her daughter, Kristy."

Holly nodded her head. "That's true. But it was several years ago."

Greenfield raised his voice. "That doesn't matter, Detective, and you know it. Your relationship with these victims has clouded your ability to make decisions and solve this case."

"Bullshit!" She slammed her hands down on the table, standing as she did. "That's just not true. In fact, we're getting closer each day to figuring this thing out, and I'm an integral part of this investigation. My abilities have not been clouded. I'm clearer than ever."

"I'm afraid I have to pull you from the case, and because of the expressed concern of your colleagues, I'm asking you to take a paid leave of absence until this thing is solved," Greenfield said, spittle escaping his mouth.

"You're kidding me, right? You have no idea what you're saying. I'm the best damn detective you have, and I've worked this from day one, and now you're pulling me. In fact, you're not only pulling me, you're asking me to leave, maybe indefinitely."

"This isn't open to debate. Gather your things and hand over all files you have on the case to Detective Euwing. He's now the lead investigator."

Holly glared at Chad, who still wouldn't look her way. She shook her head in dismay and disbelief and left the conference room. She had never felt so betrayed and angry in her entire life. Chad was not only her partner but was the one person in life she thought she could trust. Like a brother, that's what Chad was. No! That was what Chad *had* been, until he had to be like every other man and get his dick all mixed up in his head. Holly knew that Brooke had instigated most of what had just happened, if not all of it. Maybe this was the source of her distrust about Chad recently, knowing that he'd fall prey to and be influenced by the power of what lay between the uptight doctor's legs.

Yes, Dr. Madison had gotten all worked up and worried that Holly was losing it after the incident with the psychic and her familiarity with the latest victims. Victims? She couldn't even come to terms with the thought that someone she had once been close to had been ripped from this world by such evil. And now she was off this case? Oh, no, she wasn't going down easy. Screw Greenfield, screw Chad, screw Brooke—well Chad was obviously doing that and doing it so well it rendered him insane! *Screw all of them!* She was going to find the bastard who had done this to her friend Lynne and to little Kristy.

Like hell she was turning over her files to Chad. Let him come begging for them. She would solve this case on her own if need be.

Back in her office, she tossed awards, pictures, and miscellaneous notes into a box she pulled from a closet. It was just plain wrong to pull a CSI agent off the case of her life, one that she was literally in charge of, and then expect her to take it lying down. Greenfield was a son of a bitch, she'd always known that. She'd felt sorry for his wife for having such a difficult pregnancy. Hell, now she felt even sorrier that the poor woman was married to him.

But Holly knew that she couldn't point her finger only at Greenfield. Chad and Brooke, and maybe even Maureen, had a part in this. And she sure as hell wasn't looking forward to seeing Robb gloat.

She wanted to sit down behind her desk and just put her head down. She could feel a major headache coming on from all the thoughts flying around. But she was not going to give in. She wouldn't let them see her give in. Was that it? Did they really think she just could not handle it?

"I think you're overreacting," Chad said.

She wheeled around on her heels, nearly jumping in surprise. She'd been so lost in her anger that she hadn't heard him step into her cubicle. "Really? And what you think counts because you've got some special insight into people now that you're sleeping with a shrink?" She'd lowered her voice so much that to her it even sounded like a growl. She saw the surprised expression on his face. She now whispered back, "Sorry, that's right, no one is supposed to know that you're shacking up with the doc. But then I don't betray other people's trust or give away personal information to my superiors." She picked up a small box with dolphins painted on it—a gift Chad had given her on her last birthday. Dolphins were her favorite animals. She added it to the other things in the box.

"Listen, Holly, this isn't about my personal life."

"No, it's about mine." She crossed her arms.

"You knew those people. You were friends with them, even took care of the little girl. Holly, I know that you've been to the hospital and stayed by that girl's side. I saw how her death yesterday affected you."

"Yeah, I was hoping she'd wake up and help us find the person who did this to her and her mother."

"That's not the only reason, and you know it. You are far too involved emotionally. Everyone on the team sees it. This was not my decision."

"Maybe not, but you got the ball rolling. You're the one who alerted Greenfield and you certainly are the one person that the team is going to look to for an opinion about me, about whether or not I can handle this case. You obviously didn't try to dissuade them." She picked up the box and looked pointedly at him. "I trusted you."

"You can still trust me. You know that. Believe me, this is the best thing for you. I know you're angry right now, but I agree with Greenfield and Brooke. Take a break. Go somewhere with Chloe, have fun, and just relax. Once you do, I'm sure that you'll be able to step back and see that we're right about this."

She set the box back down on her desk. "Angry? Angry? I'm furious! I didn't get to where I am in this job by allowing my emotions to control me. I think I know when I could be harmful to a case. I don't need Greenfield, Brooke, or you for that matter, to tell me what I can or cannot handle."

Brooke came around the corner. "I think you do, Holly. At least for now."

"Great. This is just great. While you're at it, how about prescribing some Valium for me so I don't fall apart before your eyes. If anything is driving me crazy around here, it's you guys and your idiotic notions about me and my fitness as a cop."

"No one is saying that you're not a good cop. Everyone needs time off once in a while. It's a stressful job, and you can't do it under these conditions," Brooke replied.

"Right." She picked the box up again and said, "Good-bye, partner." The sarcasm wasn't lost on anyone. "Don't worry, your secret is safe with me." She winked at Brooke and nodded at Chad, who looked away. She could've sworn that he was close to crying.

As Holly marched out the doors, she could feel the energy of their stares weighing her down heavily, and it was almost as though she had to drag herself out. She waited until she got inside her car, and about a mile away, before she crumbled. She sank down in the front seat. Tears didn't come. If anything, she felt a void, completely numb, as if none of it mattered anymore. The whole goddamn situation, the case, her child's constant need for her—none of it mattered right now, she was so exhausted. But she knew it would; when the numbness wore off, it would all matter very much. She couldn't kid herself for long.

She drove a little farther, then reached in her purse and took out her cell phone. Before letting herself think too much about it, she dialed the phone number.

"Point Loma Veterinary Hospital."

"Is Dr. O'Neil available?"

"May I ask who's calling?"

"Holly Jennings."

"Let me check."

The next voice she heard was Brendan's. "Everything all right?"

"I need to see you." Her voice was shaking.

"Sure. Right now?"

"Is that possible?"

"Can you give me an hour? I've got a surgery 'bout under way here, and I need to tend to the poor beast—been run over. Owner wants me to pull out all stops. But it doesn't look good. It may be a little longer than an hour. You want me to come to your office? I can take you for a lunch."

"No. Would you come by my house?"

"Sure, love. Hey, what's wrong? I can hear it in your voice. There's no fooling an Irishman. Well, maybe there is, but I'm no fool when it comes to you."

"I'll talk to you when I see you. Thanks." She flipped off the phone, wanting him at her house as soon as possible. Before she changed her mind.

Right now, all Holly wanted was to feel close to another human being. To Brendan. She needed him.

31

"I don't know what to say," Brendan commented after Holly had told him her story. "I can see how bad this hurts. You know, I don't want to step on any toes or overstep my bounds, but maybe you should take a little trip, get away from here now that you're off the case."

Holly sat up. They were seated on the couch together. "Are you on their side?" she asked, incredulous at the thought.

"What? No, of course not. I think it's a damn shame to see them do this to you. I know how much your job means, and I think I'm accurate when I say I know that you're great at what you do. But Holly, I am a realist, and the truth is that your boss has pulled you off the case and that's that. There isn't much you can do about it."

She leaned back into his arms, seeking their comfort. "I know. I guess you're right. I am a bit sensitive right now. I don't mean to take it out on you."

He pulled her closer, squeezing his arms around her. "It's all right. Just don't let it happen again."

They laughed together. He turned her face toward him, his gaze intense, and the troubles of the day were momentarily forgotten as Brendan kissed her softly, first on the forehead, then trailing his lips over her eyelashes, making her giggle and squirm as a ticklish sensation ran all over her body. Goose bumps rose up along her arms. He rubbed them away, warming her. She ran the tips of her fingers over his bristly cheek. She liked that he hadn't shaved that morning. It gave him a rugged edge.

Holding his face in her hands he leaned in, his lips grazing hers—soft, loving, sweet-tasting lips that sent such a rush through every nerve ending. Holly felt like there were no other two people alive in the world. Their kisses were growing more and more passionate each time they saw each other, and this kiss was turning into the most passionate one yet. They both knew where this was going. The phone rang. "Don't answer it," Brendan mumbled out of the corner of his mouth.

"I have to." She secretly hoped it was her boss calling to apologize and invite her back. But to her dismay, it was not. She knew it wouldn't be, but it was okay to hope.

"Hello? Hello?" No one there. "Hello?" She heard the faint click of someone hanging up the receiver.

"Who was that?" Brendan asked.

She shrugged her shoulders. "Wrong number, I guess." It was odd, but she'd received more than one hang-up call in the last twenty-four hours. Probably some solicitor, but it was odd. And in her state of mind, it added to her uneasiness.

"You sure? You look funny," he said.

"Positive. And I, like any other human being, do not like to be disturbed while I'm making out with a gorgeous man."

"You certainly do know how to flatter." He puffed out his chest. "If I didn't know better, I'd say you're trying to get me into bed."

She laughed. "If I didn't know better, I'd think the same thing myself. However..." She glanced down at her watch. "It's not going to happen today, or at least not right now." She tapped the watch.

"Time to get the girls," he stated.

"You said it."

"Why don't you let me pick them up? You've had a rough day. I'll take them Christmas shopping with me. There's someone I'd like to get a special gift for."

"Really, now?"

"Really, and that's all I'm saying. And maybe if you're nice to me, I'll give you a massage later and rub out all of those knots I know you've formed."

"That sounds heavenly. I am up for that." Even though she still felt pretty horrible about the day, the thought of Brendan buying a gift for her and rubbing her back later helped to lighten the load. "In return, I'll cook dinner for you and the girls, do something I haven't done in awhile."

"Excellent. We'll be back around seven, then."

"Oh, wait." She went to the medicine cabinet in the bathroom and brought back Chloe's antibiotics. "Here, she needs to take one of these, but make sure she has something in her stomach first, and get her to drink a full glass of water."

"No problem."

"She'll try and talk you out of it, you know."

"Please, Holly, I have been a parent for fifteen years. I know all of their sneaky little ploys. I've got my ways." He let out a Dracula laugh and fluttered his fingers up toward the sky.

As he walked to the front door, he turned and said, "Give some thought to my idea of going away. Okay? I think clearing your mind of the case and getting away would do you a world of good. I've got a cabin up in Mammoth, you know."

"No, I didn't know."

"Yes. You could go on up with Chloe and spend a few days there, and the girls and I would come up on the weekend."

Holly thought it over for a minute. It did sound sort of invit-ing. She'd always loved the snow and mountains.

"Better yet, I could send Meg on ahead with you two and let her have some freedom from me. I've been promising a snowboard-ing trip because her grades are so good."

"What about school?"

"Ah, what about it? As I said, Meg's grades are almost perfect, so if she misses a few days, it won't hurt her at all."

"Wow, you are a really cool parent."

"Tell it to my girls. I'm so lax because I'm an old surfer, remem-ber? I missed countless days of school to hit the waves."

"Okay. I'll think about it."

"It would be good, I'm telling you. I also want to get Meggie away from this boy she's been hanging around."

"Another boy?"

"Can't keep 'em away, I tell you. She's too damn pretty for her own good, and she has flirting down pat. Not to mention this boy's hair is too long for my liking."

"And those words from the mouth of a surfer! Bet you never thought you'd say that."

"No comment, other than I was a surfer, and every surfer knows there's only one other thing that comes close to that perfect wave. Since you rarely catch it, you might as well shoot for that other thing, if you take my meaning. And I don't want him looking Meg's way for any of that."

"The truth comes out. Daddy, the almighty protector. I hope Meg knows how lucky she is."

"Please. To her I'm a curse."

"Somehow I doubt it. I think Meg knows exactly how wonder-ful you are."

"I'll see you at seven, love."

"Seven." She heard him drive away, and the mixture of bliss and loss were so intermingled it was hard to know how she felt.

Her mind turned to Chad; she didn't know if she'd ever be able to forgive him. She glanced over at the files on the case lying on her dining-room table. She wasn't ready to go through them yet. Maybe she would go to Mammoth, take them with her, get some fresh ideas. She was still determined to solve this case, on or off it.

She checked her e-mails and saw one from an address that she didn't recognize. Probably spam. She opened it. It was from Daddyman. A cold shiver slid down her spine and the hair on the back of her neck stood up. Was this who she thought it might be, or was this a joke? The brief message read, "You would make a perfect wife." What the hell? No, not possible. It had to be a joke. So many people knew she was working on this case; it was broadcast all over the media.

She thought about picking up the phone to call the tech guys at work for a trace, but then thought better of it. If word got out, it would simply be fodder for gossip, and everyone would wonder if Holly wasn't up to something after being pulled from the case. Worse, they might completely discount the e-mail as a prank, something she thought was quite possible. However, instinct told her to save it, just in case. Maybe if she went away for a few days, she could do her own investigating about where the e-mail originated. She knew a bit about computers. But for now it seemed prudent to discount it as a prank and get on with her day. Besides, she had a dinner to cook for five.

She went to her bookcase in the den and pulled down a couple of cookbooks that she hadn't used in years. Something fun and different seemed like a good idea. Maybe it would feel good to be completely domestic for a change. Aha, there it was: Coconut Shrimp, a vegetable medley, and risotto mixed in a lemongrass broth. Thank

God for her sister in Hawaii and her gift from three years ago—a cookbook of island favorites. Yep, sounded good.

Holly grabbed her purse off of the dining room table and headed out the door to drive down the street to Point Loma Seafoods. As she closed the door behind her, the phone rang again. She heard it as she turned the key in the lock, hesitated for a minute, and then kept on moving. The important people were out shopping, and if it was her mystery caller, then she really didn't want to be hung up on again.

32

Gunter did not want to go to work tonight. He was having too much fun watching Detective Holly Jennings and her comings and goings throughout the day. What he couldn't figure out was why she hadn't been at work all day. That was weird. Didn't she have a case to solve? Was he no longer important? It bugged him. What bugged him even more was when her boyfriend showed up. Creep. Loser. What was she doing with him anyway? That wouldn't go on much longer.

Holly Jennings would soon find herself in the arms of a real man. Real soon.

Gunter checked his watch. Damn, almost seven. Maybe he would make one more phone call to his new obsession. He liked hearing the tension in her voice. There was some fear there, or maybe just aggravation. It would make her realize the need for strong arms around her. One can never tell who's hiding in the shadows of the night. Cop or not, she still needed a man, and he knew that he was the man. He had accumulated quite a bit of information on her and knew everything available about her husband's death. He knew about their daughter, and he even knew where the child went to school.

The face-to-face contact that he'd had with Holly and her daughter—soon to be his daughter—only a couple of nights before had been even more incredible. Poor little rascal, she'd been so sick, but now she must be feeling better since she was back at school and her mother spent the afternoon with that insignificant man.

Things would be different with a competent daddy around—very different. If their daughter were ill, he'd be certain she was completely recovered before sending her back to school. He would have to teach Holly some important lessons about parenting.

Well, that's what he was here for.

He lowered his binoculars. Lucky for him, he'd been able to park at such an angle that he caught a nice view of her kitchen. She'd been cooking in there all afternoon, going hog wild. She hadn't even noticed him standing only feet behind her in Point Loma Seafoods. He could still smell her perfume. If he wasn't mistaken, it was Issey Miyake. Pure, sexy, good. Good enough to taste.

She'd ordered enough shrimp to feed a crowd and then headed back down to Rosecrans and into Vons where she'd spent about an hour shopping. Must be a special night. He'd remained slumped down in his car, his baseball cap pulled slightly below his eyes, tipping it up occasionally to see if she was coming out. He knew he looked like the quintessential husband waiting for his wife.

He waited several minutes after she'd loaded her groceries into the car and driven away before leaving himself. He knew where she was going. Anyone who bought groceries like that went straight home.

But now it seemed as if the day's festivities were coming to an end. At least for him. He had to go to work. A good dad always paid the bills on time.

Holly had walked out of the kitchen and hadn't reappeared during the past fifteen minutes. Must be showering, getting ready for her big night with the loser. Right now, Gunter ached to get out of his car and walk around to the back of the house where he was sure her bedroom must be. The bulge in his pants insisted he do just that. But Gunter hadn't gotten this far by only listening to one part of his body.

He was a smart man, and in due time, Holly Jennings and her daughter would be his.

33

Darla pulled into the festive town of Puerto Vallarta shortly after dark. She'd made a few stops for cold drinks on the way down, and at one point she'd had to take a beach towel out to a secluded beach and take a nap. She could definitely get used to this: the sounds of the ocean, the warm sand, and the tranquility. It couldn't be that hard to find herself a good man down here and start all over. The thought of a passionate Latino man warmed her loins. But how long could it last? Without Gunter, she wondered if it was really worth it at all. She knew she should forget him. He really was trouble, and contacting him could lead her into really big trouble. But he was an addiction worse than any she'd ever had, including the ones that she'd had to a few potent prescription drugs.

She still liked to party with booze once in awhile, as she had over these last few days, and she hungered for Gunter with everything inside her.

She drove around the town until she spotted what she was looking for—an Internet café. Of course it was closed. She supposed it would have to keep until tomorrow. Maybe tonight it would be a good idea to try and find that passionate Latino, make her forget her troubles—her lover. Her brother.

34

Holly tossed and turned all night. The evening with Brendan and the girls had been great, but that dark cloud had hung over her. The girls had bounced around all night long, their energy never letting up. There was no way to relax around that. Even after tucking Chloe into bed, she couldn't relax enough for the promised massage. She and Brendan both decided it would be better to delay anything heated between them for another time.

When the sun came up before six, Holly was already packing her clothes—the decision to take a hiatus and go to Mammoth was much easier to make today than it had been yesterday. The girls had all worked hard on convincing her last night. Both Chloe and Meg were all for missing school, but Maddie would have to drive up with her dad on the weekend. She was upset as Brendan reminded her that she had a dance recital that coming Thursday, and she was performing on her own. But Maddie swallowed back her own tears when her softy old dad cheered her up with a bribe of Princess Barbie and her horse and carriage.

"You are so easy," Holly said.

"I am. I know." He winked at her. "I tell you, bribery is the secret to parenting."

"Really now? And I heard it was about boundaries and discipline. Granted, love, too."

"Don't let them experts fool you. I guarantee they either don't have children of their own, or if they do and you peeked into their perfect lives, you'd find plenty of bribes going on. She's not crying anymore, is she?"

"Isn't that called spoiling?"

He waved a hand at her and blew out a puff of air. "Hogwash. I call it well loved."

She had to agree. The girls were definitely loved, and she was impressed by his ability to parent them so well. There was nothing wrong with the occasional bribe. He made her think of own dad quite a bit. They both had a very gentle manner, and if truth be known, Holly had also been one of those well-loved children.

Thinking about Brendan and spending the weekend together invigorated her and took the edge off her worries. She even put a Sheryl Crow CD on and sang loudly to "Soak Up the Sun," stopping her packing for a minute to dance around the room.

But her unpleasant, complicated thoughts from last night remained locked away in the back of her mind: the dark and dismal ruminations about Jack alive, Jack dead, Chad, Brooke, and faceless child killers. All of it made it so much easier to pack up at the first rays of sunlight.

At six thirty the car was packed, and Holly was on her third cup of coffee. She called Brendan's house, and he answered in a sleepy voice on the third ring. "I'm going," she blurted out. "I'm taking your advice and going to the snow. On one condition."

"What's that?"

She loved his sleepy voice. It was terribly sexy. If she could only sidle into bed with him right this instant, she would. "That you and Maddie come on Friday instead of Saturday."

"I think that can be arranged."

"Good. Now when can Meg be ready?"

"I'll get her moving. When do you want to go?"

"Now," said Holly. "Everything is packed, and all I have to do is wake up Chloe and load Petie into the car."

"Wow. Okay then. Come on over. I'll wake my daughter, but you know how teenage girls are. She takes a bit to get ready. And you know that dwarf in Snow White, the one they call Grumpy? She makes him look like St. Peter in the morning. Don't expect much chatter from her on the drive until somewhere past ten. But come on, and I'll make you some breakfast while you wait."

"Lovely." Holly hung up the phone and then woke Chloe, who sleepily got dressed.

"Grab your pillow, baby. It's gonna be a long ride."

Holly got Chloe's medication, put her and Petie in the car, and ran back inside to grab the unpaid bills. They had certainly piled up lately. She'd been so absorbed in the case that everything else had fallen by the wayside. She also grabbed the files that Chad had left her and the mail she hadn't gotten out of the box the day before.

She noticed a priority letter. She put it in with the rest of the mail that she'd take a look at up in Mammoth. She knew what it was. Her sister's husband, who was a stockbroker, had made some real-estate investments on some apartments back in New York that she and all three of her sisters and their dad were going in on. These were the documents that she needed to sign and return. Nothing that couldn't wait until she got settled inside Brendan's cabin and could take a breather. Right now she wanted to get on the road.

A few minutes later, she pulled up in front of Brendan's house. She and Chloe walked hand in hand to the front door. Chloe, who was fully awake now and excited at the prospect of missing school and going to play in the snow, could hardly contain her seven-year-old energy.

The scent of bacon wafted outside the front door, and Holly's stomach growled. She'd already been up for nearly three hours and had only consumed caffeine. Some breakfast would do her good.

Brendan opened the door before they even knocked. "I thought I heard your car pull up."

Boy did he look cuter than ever with a complete mess of bedhead and an emerald green robe that matched his eyes. He topped it off with a pair of worn leather slippers. This could be love, love, love...the song by Madness from her high-school days sprung into her mind.

"Don't mind me. I know I look like something out of a bad horror flick. But if you remember right, I clean up well," he commented.

"I do remember, but actually I am kind of liking this look."

He pinched up his face and growled. "It's the real me, monster man, and it's how I look every morning."

"Hmmm. I think I like monster man." She smiled at him, ushering Chloe inside and heading for the kitchen. It was beginning to feel a lot like home around here. "Wow. You certainly didn't have to do all this. At this rate, I'll grow fat before you know it," Holly said.

Set out in front of her was a spread of bacon, French toast, sliced oranges, and cheese-and-onion omelet.

"I wasn't sure what you wanted, so I put a few things together. It was nothing," Brendan said.

"Nothing? It's absolutely wonderful." Holly picked up a plate from the kitchen island and began piling on the food.

"I also know you've got a long drive ahead of you, so I figured I'd fill you three up, and you'll be good to go for a bit."

Meg came into the kitchen, hair pulled back in a long ponytail, eyes bright, and dressed in a cute red sweat suit. "Ready when you are."

"Okay, now you're making me look bad, girl. You can't come in here all sweet and smiley-like. I told Holly the truth about you."

"How can I be a grump, Dad, when I'm going snowboarding, and I don't have to go to school? And the best part is that I don't have listen to Maddie for a few days."

"Impossible," he replied, running his hand through his messy hair. "While you three eat, I'll load up Meg's snowboard," Brendan said.

"Thanks, Dad."

They wolfed their food down. As they finished, Maddie came strolling in. "I want to go now, too," she whined.

"But you get Princess Barbie, remember?" Chloe said. "Your daddy said so, and then we can play castle and stuff with her when you come up. It'll be fun."

"It's only a few days, brat." Meg patted her sister's head. "You go do your dance recital, and then it'll be Friday before you know it."

"Okay." She let out an aggrieved sigh and finally agreed with everybody, still not looking too happy about it.

Brendan came back a few moments later, as everyone was finishing up breakfast. He gave hugs all the way around and whispered in Holly's ear, "I'll miss you."

"Me too," she said.

"Drive carefully, and call us when you get there," Brendan said.

It was nice to have someone care like that again.

They piled into the car while Maddie and Brendan waved frantically at them as they pulled out of the driveway.

It would be quite a wonderful time for the three of them, Holly thought. Exactly what she needed.

35

Where could she be? Gunter had driven by Holly's house after he'd gotten off work at seven, and her car wasn't there. Then he'd gone on ahead to the girl's school, watching and waiting as parents dropped off their children. He never saw Holly drop off hers. He saw Mr. Insignificant though, and decided to follow him. Interesting that he was a vet.

Gunter wrote down the vet's name from what was painted on his office windows. He'd do some checking on Dr. O'Neil. It could prove handy to know one's adversary. Not that he really considered the loser a worthy opponent of any kind. For there was no other man like Gunter around.

Gunter picked up his cell phone and dialed the police headquarters. There was a burning need to slither ever further under his favorite investigator's skin, and seeing how she wasn't anywhere in sight, he figured she'd have to be at work. It was driving him nutty not knowing exactly where she was. Watching her struggle with this, battle him, go against his wits. It was good. He enjoyed it immensely. An embittered desk cop answered the phone, and Gunter asked for her.

"She's not available. Can I take a message?"

"No, no message. When will she be available, though?"

"I'm not sure. She's on a leave of absence. Is this regarding a crime?"

A leave of absence? What? "It's personal. But I really do need to speak with her."

"Then I'd try her at home. She won't be back for a while."

Gunter hung up the phone, not sure how to feel. Poor Holly. Had she lost her job because of him? That would be a ridiculous shame. She was so much fun to play with. She was the mouse. He was the cat. How could they continue to play their game if she was no longer working?

He sped home. What to do? What to do? Wait a minute. Maybe this was perfect. The powers that be, were they intervening in this game of love? They must be! No one wants his wife to be a cop. It's so not feminine. And Gunter liked his women feminine. Strong, yes, but not too strong. Now, to find her and claim her.

But where was she, and how was he going to find her? He turned down his radio. Had to think. Impossible with the Red Hot Chili Peppers blaring in the background. With the radio turned down, a plan took hold and evolved. It was beautiful. Glorious in fact. How silly of him to even momentarily think that they couldn't continue their game. Of course they could, and it would be even better than before.

First, he'd have to get rid of the vet. That presented a problem, but he could handle it. He didn't like leaving anything messy behind. The vet was a key part of his plan right now. If anyone knew where his beloved was, it would be him.

He picked up the phone again, dialed Holly's home number. No answer. Damn! Fine. That was fine. She was really very good. So good. He couldn't take the chance of driving past her home again. Soon there would be no more need to stalk her anyway, because Holly Jennings would be Holly Drake.

Gunter pulled into his own drive and entered his home through the back door. "Here kitty, kitty. Come to Daddy." A slinky feline came running. Gunter picked her up, cradling her like a baby. "We have to go see the doctor."

Forty-five minutes later, he entered Dr. O'Neil's office. "I know I don't have an appointment, but my wife is out of town, and it's her kitty...I think the cat is sick, and man, if something happened to her on my time, I'd be..." He slid his finger across his throat.

The receptionist winced, peered inside the kitty's travel cage. "What's her name?"

"Holly."

"Let me see if the doctor can see you and Holly. He's finishing up in surgery. What was your name, sir, so I can get your file?"

"You know, I don't think you're our regular vet. Silly me, I couldn't remember who is. Like I said, Holly is my wife's kitty."

"Okay."

Ten more minutes and Gunter was ushered into the examining room.

"Hello, I'm Dr. O'Neil." The loser came in, stretched out his hand. Gunter took it. Strong grip, but nothing compared to the grip Gunter could put around his neck.

What did she see in him? Irish fuck. So he was probably considered good-looking by women's standards, but not like Gunter himself. Tall, dark, and handsome. He'd been told that line plenty. He had a mystique, a dark, romantic mystique. The only thing mysterious about the vet was why he hadn't shed the gay accent a long time ago. Did he think women liked that? How fucking annoying.

The vet glanced over the cat's chart. "Holly, huh?" He sort of laughed.

"She's my wife's cat. Is there something funny?" Gunter asked.

"No not at all. It's sort of amusing the cat's name is Holly. My girlfriend…" He hesitated on that word, Gunter noticed. "Her name is Holly, too."

"Good name."

"Mhhm," the vet agreed. "So what seems to be the problem?"

Gunter hoped this was going to go as he'd planned. He had to find out where Holly was, and he knew that this ass knew exactly where she was. He'd tell him if he had to wring it out of his goddamn neck. "She's my wife's kitty, and my wife would kill me if anything happened to her. My wife is out of town for the week, and I can't get Holly to eat, and she seems really lethargic. She's usually a very active cat."

"Maybe she's depressed. Have you tried wet cat food?" The vet took the cat out of its carrier and stroked it gently.

"They can get depressed, huh? I suppose they could, why not? I'm pretty down that my wife is gone, too. I really miss her. See, we were supposed to take this trip together, but I've got work to do."

"I know how that can be. So what do you do?"

Nosy ass, wasn't he? Good. Gunter would lay it on thick now. "I work up at Children's Hospital. In the emergency reception area."

"That's wonderful. I have two girls. You have any kids?"

"No. My wife hasn't been able to get pregnant. We only have the cat, and that's her baby. So you think she misses Laura like I do?"

"Possible. I'll take her temperature and see if she doesn't have something else going on." The vet stuck the thermometer up the poor cat's butt. Gunter winced. Funny how that could make him squirm. He still wasn't getting the info he needed from the doc. "I can't wait until my wife gets back from her trip next week."

"No fever. Yep, I'd say she's bummed out. You both are, sounds like it. I can relate. My girlfriend and her daughter and one of my daughters left this morning to take a bit of a break. Heading up to a cabin I own in Mammoth for the rest of the week. I'm sure by tonight, I'll be singing the blues, too, friend." The vet winked at him. "Nothing a tip of the whiskey bottle won't cure for you till your lady gets home. And as for your Holly here, try a bowl of cream. It's an old remedy, but it might snap her out of it. Otherwise, I'd let it go. Looks like she's not one to miss a meal, so expect that when she gets hungry enough she'll come charging for the food bowl. As long as she's drinking some water and going to the bathroom, she seems okay to me. I believe she'll have a change in her attitude when your wife makes it home."

"Good. Me too."

"Watch her for any diarrhea, and hopefully she'll take a bite by this weekend. If not, give us a call, and we'll have another look. My associate will be here over the weekend. I'll be out of town."

"Yeah? You going to see Holly?"

Gunter noticed the vet shift his weight from one foot to the other and cross his arms in front of him, almost defensive like. Uh-oh, he shouldn't have used her name like that. Had he fucked up? "I mean going to see your Holly?" He laughed and placed the kitty back into its container. "My Holly and I are going to head home and see what we can do about getting her to eat some cream." He smiled and hoped it worked.

"Yes, okay. Well, my receptionist will take care of you up at the front."

Gunter paid the bill and quickly headed home. He'd get on the Internet and locate the address of the cabin the vet owned. It should be easy enough. By this afternoon, Gunter would have a plane rented, fueled, and ready for the flight to Mammoth. Good thing for him that he'd gotten his pilot's license a few years ago. He knew that when he and his family took vacations together, having his license would be a benefit. He'd always loved planes. So had his daddy.

It would be only a matter of a day, and he'd have Holly out of that damn cabin and into his arms before the vet made his way up there on the weekend. He had to assume that was where he was going. Gunter thought twice about leaving this morning. Maybe he should take care of the vet first. Nah, if anything, the man appeared to be a decent father to his daughters, and that wasn't really what Gunter was after. He really did not enjoy killing people, but sometimes it went with the territory. He'd let the bastard live. For now anyway. Besides, there was a lot to do yet, before he could even leave.

He wasn't too worried about the outcome of all this. He knew exactly what it would be. Holly would be his. She would see the error of her ways and forget the vet. It was destiny. She would complete his family and make life whole again.

They would be the perfect family together.

36

"Well, I'll be Mario and Luigi's uncle," Martin Landon muttered under his breath, referring to his favorite video game. He pushed his Coke-bottle glasses back up from the tip of his nose. "Lady Godiva is sending out mail." The techie was going on his tenth hour of watching the computer address of Lady Godiva, aka Darla Monroe, to see what she might be sending out, if anything. Landon had thought it was fruitless, figured she would be more careful. But he was doing it for Holly.

Landon went to work tracing the origin of her outgoing message, and then getting inside the message. It took him almost an hour to read the post. Very interesting. It was addressed to Daddyman. Okey dokey. Boy these folks were freaks. However, they *were* calling this case "the Family Man." Landon picked up his phone to call Chad, then set it back down again. He stood, went to the door to his office, and closed it. Holly had been shafted. Landon cared about her. She was a good cop who worked hard, and for some reason Greenfield had a hard-on for her and was always giving her a difficult time, looking for any excuse to knock her around a bit. No one really understood why, but Landon figured it had to do with the fact that she was a woman—a very beautiful woman who ran circles around all the other cops.

Landon sat back down and dialed out on his cell phone. He called Holly at home and got her answering machine. He then looked up her cell phone number in his book and gave it a try. A recorded message came on saying that the phone he was trying to reach was out of range. Where could she be? Landon wanted to hang on to this information on the screen for a while longer. He really wanted to pass it on to Holly before the traitors upstairs got a hold of it.

He typed in Holly's e-mail address. Maybe she'd take a look.

Lady Godiva is trying to make contact with someone called Daddyman. He hasn't opened his mail, but I'll try and trace a location on him. I don't have an originating city yet for Lady Godiva, but I should by tonight. Give me a call. I'm holding out on the team. I thought you should have first crack at this. But once I get all the info pulled, I'll have to pass it on to Chad and the others. I won't have a choice. Best, Landon

Landon attached the message from Lady Godiva. He didn't understand it, but figured the detective would. He read it again. Interesting, indeed. But more than interesting, Landon also felt there was something very seedy and sick behind the e-mail. Goose bumps trailed across his arms. It took a lot to send goose bumps up and down any part of Landon, but this bizarre e-mail had done just that.

37

"You've got mail. You've got mail," screamed Gunter's computer in the other room, just as he arrived back home to make his preparations.

"I don't have time for this," he muttered. He walked back into his den anyway. He was curious and didn't like to leave anything behind, even if it might only be junk mail. He sat down behind his desk and typed in his screen name and password. Ah. There she was—his broad, his slut, his sister. And where had she been? Gunter opened the e-mail to read the pitiful words inside. How bad she needed him, wanted him. They should be together. When would she ever learn that they could not be together? It really wasn't a right kind of relationship. She served her purpose, and now she really should get lost.

Besides, he was so perturbed by her messy slaying of William James.

He sent her a reply.

Leave me alone. Go on with your life. We are better off without one another. Besides, I've found the perfect one, and by tomorrow I will be married. She's truly a Christmas delight, with the name to go with it.

Arrivederci mi amor, Daddyman

There, that should take care of her. Maybe she'd be so heart-broken she'd off herself. It would make his life so much simpler without such loose ends hanging around. There was still the other one out there. But something told him that his baby sister was very far away and would never make a peep about him or the family she'd grown up in. Gunter was sure of that. She'd always been the fraidycat in the family. If by chance she'd heard or read anything about the Collinses or McKays or Greenes, wherever she might be, he was sure she'd be so scared that she'd find a rock to crawl under. Nah, he didn't worry much about her.

He threw some belongings in an overnight bag, and then went to his garage. He retrieved some of the goodies that he would need to take care of the kids and convince Holly that being with him was the perfect and right thing to do.

It was already two o'clock in the afternoon. Where had the time gone? He called in to work.

"Children's Hospital."

"Emergency room, please."

A moment later, the phone was answered by his boss, Virginia Applebee.

"Hey, Ginny, I can't come in today. I'm not feeling so well."

"I'm so sorry, Gunter. Get well."

"I will. I think it's nasty one, so you may want to get someone to fill in for me over the next few days. I'll call and let you know."

He hung up before his boss could get a word in. She was a nosy bitch. He wouldn't be going back. He had no need to find any more women and children to be his family. No more need for the computers at Children's, with all of their info about who was married and who was not. It had been a spectacular way to track down potential family members. The only downfall was that two of the women belonged to dating services—Patricia and Shannon—and they happened to be the dating services Darla worked with! Darla (or Jennifer or whatever she was calling herself these days) had at least been helpful in providing information about Shannon. He'd appreciated that. But that whore figuring out his scheme had been the one glitch, and hopefully it wasn't the one glitch that could put him behind bars, away from his true family—his Holly and Chloe.

He couldn't allow that, and once he had Holly in his arms and convinced he was the one to be with, he would move them so far away that no one could find them. Love would transcend all boundaries.

38

The cabin was beautiful. It looked more like something out of Robert Redford's Sundance catalog than what Holly would've considered a typical cabin. Either Brendan was one helluva vet or he had some lucrative investments.

They'd gotten in late the night before and watched a DVD together before tumbling into bed. They'd spent all day snowboarding. Well, Holly skied and Meg snowboarded. Chloe took lessons. Holly and Meg met up for lunch and got to really talk.

Over fries and a burger, they shared quite a bit. "Meg, I'm sorry that I didn't get a chance to take you over to the station. I know we planned on it, but things got a bit out of hand on the case I was working, and I couldn't make it happen."

"I understand. Maybe some other time." Meg squeezed a load of ketchup onto her pile of fries.

"You know it. I always try to keep my promises."

"I believe you. I didn't think too many people kept promises anymore after my mom left us, but I trust you."

Holly didn't know what to say. There was quite a bit to live up to in this girl's eyes. The hurt was all across her face at the mere mention of her mother. Holly crossed her fingers that she would never let Megan down.

"You know, when she left, I thought for a long time that it was all my fault, and then I thought for an even longer time that it was all my dad's fault. But you know, what I've come to realize is that it's nobody's fault but my mom's. She chose to leave us. My mom has always been kind of selfish, and to be honest, I don't think she ever really wanted children. I think my dad did. I think she had me to make him happy and that my sister was an accident." She kind of laughed at that. "Sometimes I think she was a big accident. Just kidding. I love her, but you know sisters. They can be a real pain sometimes."

"Do I know sisters? I've got three, and I can tell you some stories. We'll have to talk over marshmallows and cocoa tonight."

"Very cool. I'm into that. You're not anything like my mom. It was after Maddie was born that things really went downhill. You would think with a new baby that she would've wanted to be with us. But she was never home with us. I mean, my dad was always trying to do nice things for her, make her happy. But nothing worked. She didn't love us."

Holly took a sip from her soda. "That must make you upset." Holly didn't know what else to say to her. She was sad for this child, for Maddie, and for Brendan. Who would ever want to leave them? She was also extremely impressed with the maturity that Meg showed at fifteen. She was certainly a far older fifteen-year-old than Holly remembered herself ever being.

"Not really. Okay, I guess kind of. But when it comes down to it, I know my mom has some real psychological problems, and if being away from us keeps her somewhat sane, then that's better for us." Meg lifted up her cheeseburger and took a bite.

"You're strong, Meg. I think you'd make an excellent cop." Holly smiled at her.

"Really?" She chewed her burger then added, "You inspire me. I want to be like you. You have no idea how glad I am that my dad met you. I haven't seen him this happy in ages."

Holly couldn't help but giggle. "It's not me."

"Yes, it is. He really, really likes you. You should hear him around the house carrying on with Holly this, and Holly that. He's worse than me with a crush."

"Truth be told, Meg, I like your dad a lot, too, and I'm really happy I met him and you. What do you say we finish up and meet Chloe after her lesson? It's time for her to take her medicine. She's only got a few days left on it, but the doctor insisted that she take all of it, otherwise the infection can come back twice as bad."

"Let's go, then."

They ate their lunches and met up with Chloe, who obediently took her medicine.

The day had been smooth and easy, as was the call to Brendan when they'd returned to the cabin from their day of fun in the snow. He was missing them.

"Ah, Holly, I want to pack up and leave now. But Maddie has been working so hard on her little dance thing, I can't do it to her."

"Of course you can't. Don't worry about us. It's good to be missed. Besides, there is a saying about the heart and loneliness."

"Phooey. I'm racing up there as soon as Maddie gets finished with the recital. I think we'll leave right after and drive all night."

"Not a good idea. You'll be too tired."

"Nope. I'll be thinking of you the whole way. Trust me, that'll keep my motors running."

"Whatever you say."

He sure was sweet. Holly put another log on the fire and stoked it. She could get used to the seclusion of the cabin. The snow outside, the barely running stream that hadn't quite frozen over yet only feet away from the front door. She put on a Norah Jones CD and thought about the night that she and Brendan spent together, until it was so abruptly ruined by the brutal attack on Lynne and Kristy. She hadn't forgotten about the bastard who'd killed them, or the promise that she had made to Kristy the day before she'd died.

She pushed those thoughts away and focused on the fire and Brendan. She was warmed more quickly by her thoughts than the fire itself. She couldn't wait to see him. Maybe once she did, all those dreams, thoughts, even the nightmares about Jack, would vanish. They had to. She wanted his memory to leave her alone. And she could not stop thinking about what Anne had said. Did he really perish in that fire? For a long time, Holly had been convinced that he was alive, walking around with amnesia or something. That could happen, couldn't it? What if it had? What if he was alive and she found that out now? What would she do, knowing that she was falling in love with another man?

Jack couldn't be alive.

No. He was gone. He was definitely gone.

She walked back into the kitchen. The girls were at the coffee table, playing a card game and watching a *Charlie's Angels* DVD. Chloe loved it. Holly had loved it as a little girl too—the TV show with the original angels. Holly had always liked pretending that she was Kelly Garrett, Jaclyn Smith's character. But the gang of women was different now, and so was their technique of shoot 'em up.

"Is that what you do, Mommy?" Chloe asked.

"What's that?" She looked up as she poured herself a glass of wine.

"Kick you-know-what?"

Megan laughed. Holly watched the movie for a minute as Lucy Liu pulled some kung fu shit on the bad dudes. "Not exactly, baby. I'm not nearly as tough."

"I doubt that," Megan said.

"Flattery will get you everywhere, my dears. Anyway, figure out what you want for dinner. I'm going to hook up my computer and check my e-mail, then I'll fix us something to eat. And, Chloe, have you taken your medicine again as I asked?"

"Oh, Mom," she whined. "I left it in the car."

"Chloe, you have to take it or the infection will come back, and it could get even worse, honey."

"I'll go get it out of the car when the movie is over," Megan said. "It's almost done."

"Thanks." Holly headed back to the bedroom and hooked up her laptop. She got online and saw that her dad had sent her another e-mail.

Sorry, honey. We've been busy here. Your mom has me looking at all sorts of vacation homes or maybe even a permanent residence. She says she loves the weather and beauty. I'm along for the ride. Whatever she wants. She's been quite an investor through the years, sneaky one she is. She's nearly tripled my 401(k) and pension without ever letting on. She's pretty pleased with herself. When I asked her what if we'd lost the money, she told me that wouldn't have happened. That's your mom for you.

Holly nodded and laughed out loud.

Anyway, honey, I'm a little concerned for you. I'm sorry about work. I think you got railroaded, and it sounds like we need to get together and talk about what's going on. This case you're working has still been nagging at me for some time, and I haven't been able to figure why. I want you to be very, very careful, okay? I'm worried about you. Keep in touch. I love you and Chloe very much. Love, Dad

She jotted him a quick note back telling him where she was and that she was fine, in case he wanted to call. She told him that she thought a house in Hawaii was a fine idea, and if that was what they decided to do, then she'd certainly have to get over her fear of flying.

She also saw that Landon had e-mailed her. She opened it up, read the note about Lady Godiva and the attachment.

Daddyman,

I need you. I always have. I've done this for us. I now know that you finding that perfect wife and family is only a farce. You never can find or have them. You've found what you need in me. Please see this and come be with me. We can disappear. We can be together and be married in a place where others don't care. Please contact me so that I can tell you where I am, and we can be forever always. I love you always.

Lady Godiva

Another e-mail had come in a few hours later from Landon. Dammit, why hadn't she opened this earlier? See what taking time away does? And you made a vow to Kristy! The next e-mail was the reply back from this Daddyman. It was crass and cruel and held the telltale truth that Daddy didn't care one iota about this Lady Godiva. The weird part was that he'd found the perfect woman with a Christmas-like name.

Shit! Holly was a Christmas name.

Please. Now paranoia had set in for sure. Joy is a Christmas name. Noel. Mary, even. Maybe December. Holly once knew a gal named December. They called her Dee Dee.

It bugged her, but she knew it was silly.

The third e-mail was again from Landon. It said:

I'm sorry, Holly. I haven't heard from you, and it's getting late— almost seven here. I'll have to let the powers that be know what I've found. I'll hold off until tomorrow morning if I can. Chad's breathing down my neck as is. Please call.

Holly looked at her watch. Dammit. That was nearly two hours ago. The wind howled outside. Probably going to be a fresh bout of snow. The lights flickered in the cabin. Chloe yelled out.

"It's okay, honey. It's just the wind," Holly yelled back to her from the bedroom. "I'll be out in a minute. Meg, why don't you two make some hot cocoa with marshmallows? I'll be right there. We'll have that talk about sisters as I promised."

"Sure thing," Meg hollered back.

Holly turned back to the computer and noticed she'd been booted off the Internet. She tried to reconnect with no luck. She picked up the phone to dial out. The lines were dead. Dammit. Her cell phone was on the charger. She'd have to wait for the battery to charge before she could get a hold of Landon, if he hadn't already left the office. Maybe she should try Chad? But what use would that be? It would only get her buddy Landon in trouble.

She quickly picked up the mail and thumbed through it, deciding to take her mind off of what she couldn't do anything about. She tore open the priority-mail letter from her sister and was shocked to see that it wasn't from her sister. Out dropped a photograph. Holly gingerly picked it up, studying it. It looked like an Olan Mills photo from the '80s. The picture was of a man, sort of handsome in a very white-trash way. He was smiling, but his eyes were like those Holly had seen one too many times—psychotic, dangerous, empty. Killer's eyes. The woman with him was a strawberry blonde, somewhat attractive. Like a young Sissy Spacek. She looked tired, worn, defeated. The smile on her face was a mere upward turn at the end of her lips. Her eyes were brown, sad, and not scared exactly… but just not really all there. They were as void as the man's, but they were not a set of killer's eyes. Then there were three children. The youngest was a very cute little girl of about three, with her mother's strawberry-blonde hair pulled into a couple of pigtails, and hazel eyes. Her eyes were lively, yet that tinge of sadness that was reflected in her mother's was also in hers. What had this family been through?

The next little girl was probably Chloe's age—somewhere between seven and eight. Very pretty. Something about her struck a chord with Holly, almost like she'd seen or recognized this girl. But how could she? The girl's hair was very long and, like the father's very blonde. Her eyes were sad, too, but there was some mischief behind them, and if Holly didn't know better, she'd have to say that in them, too, she recognized a bit of that psychotic look. Boy, this group would've probably had a doozy of a story to tell on *Jerry Springer*. Then there was the boy, maybe twelve. Handsome. That was the word for him, but his eyes were exactly like his father's, and a shiver went sailing down her back.

What the hell was this? Who had sent it?

Holly turned over the photograph and read the back. There were names above all the children. The youngest was Kimberly Drake, then Jennifer Drake, the boy was Gunter, and the parents were Mary and Frank Drake. Weird. She looked at the postmark. Brooklyn. Who could have sent this? And why? It nagged her. She scratched her head as if trying to pick at an answer.

Drake? Drake? Wait a minute. Wasn't Drake one of Darla Monroe's aliases? Fucking hell. She tried to get back on the Internet and to make another call to Landon, but had no luck connecting to either. Something was not right here. She walked out of the den and went into the front room where the files on Darla Monroe were. Her cell phone was still charging, and she hoped that it had enough juice in it to call down to San Diego.

She knew this was big and felt it definitely had something to do with the case. She had to get a hold of Chad, even if it meant either taking a back seat on this case or killing her career entirely. But if this thing went down and was solved because of this photo, she wanted some respect. No, actually what Holly wanted was the sick bastard who was behind these killings. She looked back down at the photo in her hand—at the eyes of the boy and the man. They were both very disturbed people. It was obvious, and the three females seated with them were victims of some sort. That much Holly knew and felt for sure.

"Mommy?"

"Yes, baby?" Holly glanced up.

"What are you doing? I thought you were going to have hot chocolate with us."

"I am, Chloe. I'm just finishing up some work."

"You should come watch this movie. It's pretty good," Meg chimed in. "Maybe when it's over we can watch something else."

"We'll see. It's getting pretty late, and we want to hit those slopes early. Give me twenty more minutes, okay? Oh hey, did you get Chloe's medicine from the car yet?"

Sorry," Meg replied, "I'll do it now."

Holly took Darla Monroe's file into the back room with her and started reading it over. As she got to the second page she noticed that there was no noise coming from the other room. Odd. The girls were wide awake not fifteen minutes ago, waiting for her to join them. Holly looked up at the clock. No, she hadn't lost track of time.

"Girls?" she yelled. She hadn't heard Meg go out the door to get Chloe's medicine from the car, but an eerie quiet had crept in and there was no response from either girl.

Paranoia or instinct? Holly headed for the locked nightstand on the other side of the bed. She was getting her gun.

As she turned the key in the lock, a male voice said, "Uh-uh, Holly. I wouldn't do that."

Holly turned around, key in hand, and saw a man with one hand clasped over Meg's mouth and the other with a gun pointed at her head.

"Don't hurt her. Whatever you want, we can work this out, but please don't hurt her."

"I don't want to hurt her, Holly. It's me, baby. Daddy's home."

Holly's stomach sank as she looked into the eyes of the man standing feet from her. The man poised to kill Megan. She looked deeply into those eyes and knew she was looking into the eyes of the boy in the photograph—Gunter Drake.

The Family Man.

39

Brendan had been trying to reach Holly since first light. He hadn't slept well. It was more than missing her, Meg, and Chloe. Something made him toss and turn, and he even had an odd dream about the strange man who brought his cat in the day before. The one with the cat named Holly. Something was not right, and Brendan felt it in his gut. He picked up the phone again. It rang and rang. Where were they? He thought about calling the ranger's office in Mammoth.

Aw, Holly was a cop after all. If anyone could take care of herself and those kids, it would be her. She'd probably do a better job than he could, that he'd bet on. Maybe they'd decided to head out already so they could get home early and be rested up when he and Maddie showed up before the sun dawned on Friday morning.

However, now it was evening, and there was still no word from Holly and the girls. Maybe it wouldn't hurt to call that cop she worked with. What was his name? Her partner? The one who had basically railroaded her? Chuck something? No, Chad. Yes, that was it. He didn't want to phone him, but he didn't have a better idea. Besides, even though he thought that her partner had given Holly the shaft, Brendan could tell that Chad respected her. He'd seen that when Chad had accompanied her into Brendan's offices. Maybe there was even little something more than respect there, too. If Brendan was right, he could see that this Chad cared a great deal for Holly.

He picked the phone up and dialed, hoping Chad might have some answers, or that he could at least help ease his mind. If not, Brendan had already made the decision to hop into his Land Cruiser and head north himself. A winter storm was settling in up there. He had watched the news, and maybe that's all that was unsettling—too much snow coming down and the lines were dead. But the excuse didn't make Brendan feel any better, and even though his Holly was a tough cookie, he had the strong sense that she, Chloe, and his daughter were in deep trouble.

40

Chad shut the door to Brooke's office behind him. "Looks like we're both burning the midnight oil. You want to go grab a bite, maybe a drink, and call it a night?"

"I don't know, honey. I'm working through some paperwork," Brooke said, looking up from her the papers on her desk.

"I really need to talk to you. It's about Holly and this case, and…"

Brooke leaned back in her chair and crossed her legs. "Sounds serious."

"It is."

She shuffled the papers and stuffed them inside her briefcase. "What is it?"

"I don't know if we did the right thing by her." Chad sat down across from her.

"Of course we did. She was harming herself and this case. She's a good cop. I'll give her that. But she wasn't good enough to know when to get out. For goodness' sake, she knew the Greene family."

"I know. But she is very good at what she does, and I'm her partner. I sold her out, Brooke. I did. She would never do that to me."

Brooke shifted in her chair. "If she cared about you, she would have."

"I don't know. I don't feel right about it. And I've been trying to call her, but I can't get through." Chad crossed his arms in front of him.

"Why are you calling her? You don't owe her anything. She messed up. Face it. She did. Now you and the rest of the team are trying to get through Holly's blurred lines. What in her investigation was fact, and what was based on emotion? She certainly didn't know. Leave her be. If she's the smart cookie I think she is, then she took everyone's advice and went away for a few days."

Chad stood. He was seeing Brooke in a very different light. "Why are you so crass when it comes to Holly?"

"I'm not. I'm realistic, and it's my opinion that the two of you have an unhealthy relationship. You're too close. Your boundaries are too lax. You're too inextricably wrapped up in each others' lives."

"Is that your personal or professional opinion, Dr. Madison?"

"Honestly? Both. If you want the truth, I am only human. I have emotions, you know." She looked down at her manicured hands and wrung them together.

"Are you saying that you're jealous of me and Holly?"

She didn't reply.

"That's ludicrous. Holly is my partner and my friend."

"Is it really that crazy? Are you sure that's as far as the feelings go? Sometimes it does seem like you're a little more than just friends."

"That's absurd."

"Is it?"

"I'm going to tell you something that I've never told anyone before, and I'm trusting that you'll keep it confidential."

She shrugged her shoulders. "I am a psychiatrist. It's my job to be discreet and confidential."

"I do feel a bit responsible for Holly. She's had it tough. After Jack died and she went through her pregnancy alone, I felt very protective of her. You know Jack and I worked the force together for quite some time, and there are things that Holly is not privy to regarding Jack."

"What could a wife not be privy to? What are you hiding from her?"

Chad took a deep inhale, and blew it out. "Jack was a mercenary for the CIA before he met Holly and came to work for the department."

"What kind of mercenary, Chad?"

"He took out some pretty bad dudes down in Nicaragua and helped plan several drug raids."

"Are you serious?"

"Why would I make it up?" He crossed his arms again. Was this something he should be telling her?

"And he confided this in you and not his wife?"

"He didn't want to frighten her. As a rule, the CIA does not employ the most forthright group of people. He didn't want to frighten her, but he did need to talk to someone."

"You."

"Me. We were like brothers, and Holly is like a sister. Nothing more."

"Fine. Why are you telling me this?"

"You know, I'm not sure. A couple of reasons, I suppose. In a way, I carry around some guilt knowing this. A few weeks before Jack died, he asked me to look out for her if something ever happened to him. He said that he was afraid he was being watched... and he was thinking about leaving Holly so that she wouldn't be put in any danger."

"He thought the CIA was after him for some reason?" Brooke now looked fascinated as she pushed her glasses back onto her nose.

"He had information about them that he knew they wouldn't want to see the light of day. He also thought that it could be any number of Nicaraguan or Columbian drug lords hunting him down."

"He was actually thinking of leaving her?"

"In order to protect her."

"What are you saying exactly?" Brooke asked.

"Jack was very savvy and connected. There is a possibility he did survive that explosion and disappeared." He paused. "There's also a chance that he planned the explosion himself."

"And you've kept this from her for all these years?"

Chad nodded, looking down at the floor. "What choice did I have?"

"The truth is always a good way to go."

"Be reasonable, Brooke. I swore to Jack that I would protect her at all costs. I gave him my word that I would never, no matter what the circumstances, tell her about any of this. And now you've given me your word. You cannot tell her! For heaven's sakes, she's finally dating someone who she really likes, and Jack would want that for her, whether he's alive or not. I have my doubts that he is, but let's leave the past where it belongs."

"Fine. But for the record, I think that she should know."

"Noted." Chad turned to open the door and leave.

"I thought we were going to grab a bite to eat?"

He looked back at her, but before he could say anything his phone rang. "Euwing here."

"Chad? Is this Chad? Holly Jennings's partner?"

"Yes. Who am I speaking with?"

"This is Brendan O'Neil. I'm Holly's friend. We met the other day in my office when you brought the dog in. Petie."

"Sure, hi, Brendan. How can I help you?"

"It's Holly. She's been up at my place in Mammoth for a couple of days with Chloe and my daughter Meg, and I haven't been able to reach her all day. I've got a bad feeling."

Great. A vet with instincts. Chad stifled a laugh. "Brendan, Holly is a cop. I'm sure the girls are fine. Trust me, Holly can take care of herself."

"I'm worried."

"Okay, I'll make a few phone calls, see if we can't get a cruiser over to your cabin. Give me the address. I've got to warn you, though, she'll probably be chapped with you. Holly isn't into the Prince Rescue routine."

Chad hung up. "That one has it bad. Look, let's take a rain check on that dinner."

He walked out of Brooke's office, perturbed and confused by the woman he'd thought he'd been falling in love with. Now he wasn't so sure. He'd seen a side of her this evening that he didn't care for.

He went back to his desk to make the phone call for Brendan O'Neil, when Martin Landon showed up.

"I've got something you should see," Landon said and updated him on what he'd discovered on the case.

What bothered Chad the most was the implication that the killer had found himself the perfect mate in someone who had a Christmas name. Brendan O'Neil's phone call was beginning to trouble him now. He picked up the phone to get the number to the police station in Mammoth. Like Brendan, Chad was sensing something out of the norm as well.

41

The sun was still shining hot on the Oahu coastline. Holly's dad, Ben, sipped his second mai tai of the afternoon. But he wasn't enjoying it as he'd hoped. There was a bad feeling in the pit of his stomach, and it wasn't from the fresh fish that they'd had for lunch. It was the case his daughter Holly was working. She'd e-mailed him tidbits here and there, and he didn't like the sound of it at all. Something really nasty about her case rang a bell.

Normally it went against his grain to get involved in Holly's investigations. She called and wanted advice sometimes, but he trusted her instincts. Besides, he was a retired FBI man, and he wanted to leave all of that in the past. However, today he made the decision to get involved.

He went back into his oldest daughter's kitchen. Everyone was out at the beach. He picked up the phone and dialed the number to his former office at the FBI in Los Angeles. "Tyler Savoy, please." He asked for the young man he had helped to train. Tyler was an elite profiler. If anyone could give him some answers about this case, it would be him.

"Hey, Ben, long time. What are you up to?"

"Well, kid, I'm out here sunning myself in amazing Hawaii, drinking a mai tai, and overlooking the surf."

"You old dog. Then what the hell are you doing calling me?"

"I've got a tick bugging me. You know my daughter Holly?"

"Sure, we've met. She's a crime scene specialist with San Diego."

"That's the one."

"I know they've got a nasty case right now. In fact, looks like we might be getting involved soon. Their chief gave us a ring, and we did some checking. There was a similar murder up here in Los Angeles in '92, a kid and his mom murdered. No leads, nothing. Is your daughter working that case in San Diego?"

"She was." Ben filled him in on the politics and what had happened.

"We all know the politics are a bitch. So are you doing some covert hunting for her? A bit of info gathering?"

"You could say that. What I need is for you to look up crimes in which the victim's ring finger was cut off. I'm vaguely remembering something like that about twenty-five or so years ago, before you ever came onto the scene. If my memory serves me right, and believe me it doesn't always serve me anymore, I recall something like that with a case up in the Oakland area. I was working the LA office, but that was when profiling was just getting going. Although I don't think that the bastard who was responsible for that murder was a serial killer, my boss noted his method only because it was so absurd."

"And this bad man down south is cutting off ring fingers?"

"Yep."

"Let me see what I can do. I'll get on the computers and see what old files I can dredge up. It might take some time. Something tells me your old hound dog nose is on to something."

"My gut more than my nose. The whole finger thing has been bugging me for a bit now."

"I'll call you back."

Two hours and two more mai tais later, Tyler called Ben back. "Got something for you. Does the name Drake ring a bell?"

Ben leaned back in his chair. He thought for a minute. "Drake, huh? I don't know. Should it ring a bell?"

"You had a partner named Carter, right?"

"Yeah. Jimmy Carter, like the president. We worked together for a few years until he moved back up north. We talked occasionally thereafter. Poor buzzard has Alzheimer's now."

"Too bad, because Jimmy worked this case up in Oakland. Husband beat the shit out of his wife in front of their three kids. The youngest was only four at the time. The oldest, a boy, was about twelve."

"Ah, good old dad, setting up his young ones for a lifetime of psychological problems."

"No kidding. Anyway, after he did her in, he chopped off her finger, wrapped her in some tarp, and sent her on a deep-sea fishing trip in the San Francisco Bay. The dad played the bereaved husband for some time, claiming that his wife was manic and had disappeared. Everyone fell for it hook, line, and sinker. But the little one kept telling her preschool teacher that Daddy had cut off Mama's finger."

"The mouth of babes. Their honesty is so refreshing. So how long did it take before things started happening?"

"After about a month of the little one carrying on and then showing up at school with some nasty bruises across her back and legs, the teacher grew suspect and gave the police a call. A week after that, the mother's mangled body washed up on shore."

"How do they know that the finger was cut off and not eaten by the fishies?"

"Straight cut across. Fish gnaw."

"Right."

"Dad got away. Somehow he caught wind that the police were on to him, and he's never been seen since. Hopefully he's lying in his own grave, but he could be on some island enjoying life. Who knows? The kids were all separated and sent to foster homes. There was suspicion that the boy was also abusing his sisters."

"The apple doesn't fall far."

"No, it doesn't. Check this out: the kid spent five years in juvie after cutting the finger off of one of his foster siblings. Of course, those records are sealed, but we have our ways."

"Are you thinking what I am?"

"That maybe this kid, who would now be a man, is the dude down south doing the terrible deeds."

"I'm thinking it could be. I'm also thinking that I better give Holly a call. I'm worried, though. It's eight your time, and I've been ringing her at the cabin she's at in Mammoth for the last couple of hours."

"Probably out for dinner, Pops."

"Hey, watch who you're calling Pops, kid."

"I'm not exactly a kid anymore. I'm graying at the sides. Listen, why don't I take this info to Holly myself. Claire and I need a few days away. Our two-year-old is driving us crazy running the roost. We'll take a flight up in the morning. I'll head over to Holly's place, fill her in on what we think we know. If she wants to take it a step further, I might call in my guys and kick the asses of the SDPD coppers who pulled her from the job."

"She might like that."

"Are we good to go, then?"

"Yep."

"Good. I'll give you a call when I land and fill you in before and after I see your daughter."

"Thanks, Tyler. I appreciate it."

"No problem, old timer."

"I'm gonna kick the crap out of you when I see you if you don't knock off this old-timer shit with me."

"Go drink a mai tai for me."

Ben laughed and hung up the phone. Although he knew Tyler was a very good agent and that he'd be true to his word about going to see Holly, Ben still couldn't help thinking time was of the essence.

42

Holly was trying to remain calm. She knew the importance of doing so for the girls' sakes.

Gunter made Holly tie up the girls on the bed. He kept the gun going back and forth, pointing it between Chloe and Meg.

"I'm sorry girls, but Mommy and I need to talk, and we can't be interrupted. Good job, Mommy. Now, no funny business." Gunter inspected the knots while keeping the gun on the girls. "I'm a nice guy, you'll see."

Holly watched as Chloe's eyes filled with tears. She shook her head no and made their little wave at her with her index finger. She knew it wasn't much consolation, but hopefully it made her daughter feel a hint safer. Meg looked wide-eyed and completely frightened.

"Alrighty then, Mommy, you did a good knot."

Hopefully Meg had been a Girl Scout, because Holly devised a knot that a Girl Scout might be able to get out of. Hopefully. This nut job hadn't been a Boy Scout, that was for damn sure.

"Mommy and I are going in the other room to have a talk, and then we'll come back and tuck everyone in."

He gave Holly a shove out the door. Once around the corner, he smacked her hard on her butt. "Nice," he said.

She cringed.

"Okay, babe. Well, I'm hungry and want some dinner. You think you could get things going for me?"

"Do you think you could perhaps keep the gun out of my face?" she asked, trying hard to sound pleasant.

"Yes, I do see your point. Okay, I can do that, but here's the deal. If you do anything funny, anything at all, my little handy dandy phone here…" He pulled a cell phone from his pocket. "I'm a gifted man, and I read a lot. A real lot. It is amazing what you can discover on the Internet. Not only can you learn the smartest way to stalk people and find out things about them that not even their mothers or best friends know, but you can also learn how to build a bomb. Kaboom! So what I did, just to ensure that our little engagement and future happen smoothly, is I placed an explosive device in the crawl space under the cabin, and if anyone does anything to mess with our relationship, then I will flip open my phone, press one number on the keypad, and we will all be sent skyward in a matter of seconds."

"Why would you want to kill yourself?" Holly wasn't buying it. Most psychopaths were so ego-oriented that suicide was not a method they chose. Unless they thought someone else might try and take them out first.

"Because, sweetie, what would life be without you? You are perfect. I've been watching, waiting, seeing you work your case, trying so hard to find me. You knew that eventually you would, and now you have. It was destiny."

She took out some bacon and started frying it up for him. She didn't want to believe him about the bomb, and if it was just her here in the cabin, she'd take her chances. But she had Meg and Chloe here, and she would not risk their safety on a hunch.

She would play along. She would follow his lead in this sick game. "Would you like something to drink?"

"Now you truly are a woman who understands a man, aren't you?"

"I do." She forced a shy smile.

"Ooh, I love the sound of those words. I do, I do, I do. And you will, too! Oh, yes, you will. I'm not a big drinker, but I do like wine."

"I've got a bottle chilled in the fridge."

"Nice. A Chardonnay?"

"Yes."

She took the bottle out and wondered what the odds were of being able to get him drunk enough that she could get the phone away from him. If she could do that, she could also get the gun out of his pants. It was slim to none that he would get plastered, even if he drank the bottle.

She poured him the glass.

"Thanks, honey. Do you remember the first time we met?"

Holly stared long and hard at him. "Why don't you tell the story again? You do it so much better than me."

"Children's Hospital. You brought Chloe there in the middle of the night with a fever. I checked her chart later after you left, and poor thing—a bladder infection."

Holly remembered him now. Not only were his eyes the same as the boy's in the picture she'd received earlier, but also the same as the man in the receiving area at Children's Hospital. The one who'd followed her out that night as she put Chloe into the car. That was how he found his victims. It had nothing to do with dating services. That was simply coincidental. But there was still something here regarding William James and Darla Monroe. Then it clicked—Darla Monroe was Jennifer Drake. The man before her sipping wine was Gunter Drake.

Darla was also Lady Godiva, and he was Daddyman.

Oh, God. They were involved in some twisted incestuous thing.

She couldn't let on that she knew anything about any of it. She would have to play this game as long as possible in order to keep herself and the girls alive.

Her brain was swimming as she pieced together Gunter's story. And William James was their patsy.

"You know, Chloe is still not well. In fact, she has another infection and hasn't taken her medicine. I really should take her to the bathroom."

"She's fine," he replied coldly and sipped his wine.

Holly finished fixing him a BLT sandwich with chips and orange slices. She took her time, letting him drink the wine, refilling his glass.

"Trying to get me in the mood, huh, babe? You don't have to work too hard, I'm already there." He grabbed his crotch.

Her only hope was to get him out of the house and away from the girls, then pray either Meg could undo the restraints and get them away, or that someone came looking for them. The phone lines had been dead all evening. She now knew that they'd been cut rather than downed from a storm. "Listen, I've been thinking."

"That's another thing I like about you, honey, you're smart. So tell me, what's going on upstairs in that pretty little head of yours?"

"We never really had a proper ceremony. Maybe we should."

"Well, damned if I wasn't thinking that myself."

"I am an old-fashioned girl, and I'd like to be married before we, you know, consummate anything."

"I don't know about that." He set his wine down and shook his head. "I'm a horny guy. I've got needs, Mommy. And looking at you drives me wild." He slid his tongue across his lips.

Holly lowered her voice. "But the girls."

He finished off his second glass of wine. Holly went to pour him another. He held his hand up. "That's enough for me."

Damn.

"I see your point. But maybe a little preview would hold me over."

"What do you mean?"

"I don't know. Why don't you come here?" He pulled out the cell phone and showed it to her, then put it back in his pocket.

She had no choice. She went over to him. He slid his hands under her shirt, then under her bra, groping her breasts. He shoved his tongue in her mouth. Her entire body went ice cold.

"Mhhm. I wonder how you taste, huh?" He reached his hand lower, into her pants. His fingers sinking into her skin as he moved between her legs, violating her. She wanted to scream. She thought about kneeing him hard in the groin, then maybe luck would be on her side and she could at least get the gun and kill him in time. Her mind flashed back to the mutilated bodies of Patricia Collins, Shannon McKay, and her friend Lynne. He brought his fingers up to his nose, smelled them, licked them. She thought she would definitely be sick.

"You know, I think I would like a glass of wine," she said, her voice shaking. Anything to kill more time. She needed to keep her head on, stay straight, but after what had just happened, some liquid courage might help to get them out of this.

"Yes. The wine might help you loosen up, honey. You seem on edge."

She walked back around the kitchen counter and took the bottle of wine, pouring herself a glass and forcing back the bile that had risen moments earlier. "Look, you know I'm good on my word, and I've let you have your preview of things to come. But please, will you allow this to happen out of here. There are children, and you work around children and understand them. It might take some time for them to appreciate our relationship."

He looked like he was pondering this. "Okay. But, hear this, baby, tomorrow morning you and I take off, get married, and then I'm gonna fuck you like there's no tomorrow. You'll be sore for days." He grabbed himself again.

He was so foul and so repulsive. Holly hated this man with every fiber, every nerve ending, every part of her. She tried to control her shaking. Before he ever laid another hand on her, she would go down fighting. "I hear you."

"Looks like we've got a few hours to kill. It's only eleven."

She couldn't believe he'd already been in the house for almost two hours. "I should really go check on the girls."

"Okay, babe, but no crazy ideas, or boom! Kaboom, sayonara, see you later, alligator. Hasta la vista, baby."

"No crazy ideas," she assured him.

Holly went back into the room where the girls were. They were both still tied together on the bed. Holly could see that Chloe had fallen asleep, tear stains across her face. Meg was watching her. She took the tape off of Meg. "Shhh. He's here still, and he has a bomb. I'm going to try and get him out of the house before the morning. The knot I made can be worked with. I want you to work the knot loose and go for help. Wait ten minutes after we're gone, okay?"

Meg nodded. Chloe moved. "I'm going to take the tape off of her, too. Neither one of you can talk or cry out, or he'll make me put it back on." She slowly removed the tape from Chloe who opened her eyes in horror. "No, no baby. It's going to be all right, okay? Meg is going to take care of you through the night, and by morning everything will be okay. I promise. Mommy will get rid of the bad guy just like Charlie's Angels. But do everything Meg tells you."

Chloe nodded.

"Okay. Listen for the door to close. I have faith in you. It's going to be just fine." She kissed both of them on top of their heads, held back her own tears, and went into the other room.

"The munchkins are sound asleep."

"Good."

"You know, instead of waiting until tomorrow, there has to be a justice of the peace open somewhere. We are pretty close to the Nevada border."

He studied her.

"Let's get married tonight. The girls are asleep, they won't know the difference. Then you can get what you want much sooner than daybreak."

"I like that idea. And just in case you're not telling me the truth about them being asleep, that's okay, because if they somehow get loose and open the door, if anyone opens the door, then the cell will ring." Gunter grinned. "This place will blow sky high! Good protection, huh?"

Holly gasped. Now what? He walked over, took her by the hand.

"No worries, darling. As long as they're good little girls and stay inside while Mommy and I are gone, there won't be any problems. I've already set everything in place, and the only way for the bomb to be disarmed is if I do it myself. I'll grab us a couple of jackets in the hall closet. No one would do anything stupid, right?" He held up the cell phone. "I'd hate to have to blow my new family out of this world, especially since this is a new start for all of us."

Holly nodded. "No one is going to do anything stupid. Why don't you go ahead and grab those jackets."

Gunter walked out of the room. It took all her mental strength not to bum rush the door and get the girls out of there. But even if there wasn't the threat of a bomb, Holly knew she couldn't get the girls untied, out the back room, and through the front door before he came back into the room with the gun. She didn't even have time to tell Meg about the bomb. He came back with the jackets.

"I know you want to go and tell the lovelies our secret. Don't worry. I did it for you. Kind of scared them. I thought you said that they were asleep. I don't think anyone will be leaving this house until we get back."

He held the gun to Holly's back as she stepped out into the cold night, then he dialed something into the cell. He'd reset the bomb.

For perhaps the first time ever, Holly was at a loss.

They raced down the highway in a rental car, and then onto a back road, through some very tall, snow-capped evergreens. The road opened into a clearing. Straight ahead sat a small plane.

No!

"I told you I'm multitalented. I'm a pilot, too. We should be in Reno in no time."

"But the weather," Holly said.

"Fuck the weather, baby. What's a bit of snow? We're in love! Going to the chapel!" He started whistling the tune.

He was sick. Irrevocably sick. She had to get away from him, out of his clutches and back to the girls. But the only way to ensure their safety was to get that phone. He opened the door for her. She got in. She thought about making a run for it but knew she couldn't.

He got into the cockpit and cranked the engine. "Good plane, you know."

She hoped so. She closed her eyes as he turned and faced the plane down the dirt runway, sleek with snow. He was totally insane. The plane skidded from side to side and he laughed like this was an everyday event. She felt it pick up speed, but knew that it couldn't be fast enough to take off, not with the snow and sleet around them.

"Open your eyes, baby. Here we go."

Holly didn't know if it was a morbid sense of fascination that made her follow his instructions, or if she simply wanted to see as death came reaching for her. As she opened her eyes, the plane barely cleared a group of trees. She was going to vomit. "What the fuck are you trying to do? Get us killed?"

"Living on the edge, baby. Living on the edge. And now that we're here in the night sky and all..." The plane fluttered and bounced around. Holly's hands hit the roof, trying to stabilize herself. "Don't be scared. I'm very good at this."

"Right. So you want to tell me about Lady Godiva?"

"What's there to tell, baby? Every man needs a dalliance. I knew she'd be the one, though. I just knew she'd blow it. If there ever was a reason for the police to catch on, it would be because of something stupid she did. Dumb bitch."

Holly tried hard to calm her stomach. Her thoughts kept wandering back to the girls, Brendan, her parents. "So since we will be joined in holy matrimony, maybe you should tell me about your other families. I do have a right to know, don't I?"

He sighed. "Oh, I suppose so. Look, I am a patient man, I really am, but when I get angry, things can get ugly."

That's an understatement, you sick fuck!

"I met the women and the kids through Children's. It was easy. Everyone who comes through the door has to fill out paperwork. I looked over the paperwork, liked what I saw, and bam. Now Lynne and Kristy, that was different."

Holly's stomach tightened at the mention of her old friend.

"I saw them inside a Starbucks. I was probably too hasty. They were not perfect by any standards. Royal pain in the ass, those two were. The hard part for me was when they brought Kristy into the hospital still alive. I had to do something about that, you know. I couldn't ever move on with her alive. Put a little something in the IV to help her pass on."

Holly wanted to reach across the plane and throttle him. A rage rose up through her body and into her face. She never wanted to see anyone dead as much she did him.

"But what a coincidence when, come to find out, my Lady Godiva knew Shannon. They were into some interesting games. When things didn't turn out well for Shannon and me, my Lady figured it out after reading the paper and such. She thought she would help me, make it look like that disgusting pervert James was the one to do poor Shannon in. Didn't work. She really is pitiful. Didn't quite get it right that one. Totally inept, but she gets points for loyalty. I will give her that much. She'd do anything for me. And can she give one fantastic blow job. I hope you can, too. In fact, I'm counting on it." He turned and faced her. "I love getting head."

Scratch his eyes out, now. Just do it, Holly.

"Shannon was decent. Patricia didn't even want to try and play ball. Lynne, now there was a fine hooker. Man could she suck…"

That was it. Holly didn't think. She reacted. All the rage and fear welled up in her. "Really? Well, I'm the best at it. Want to see?"

"Hell, yes. That's my girl."

Holly unzipped his trousers and bent to put her mouth on his penis. She thought of all the people she loved and knew she had to do this if she was going to have any chance of making it out alive and saving her daughter and Meg.

"Oh, yeah, baby."

She slid her mouth and tongue over the shaft of his penis, forcing herself not to stop until this vile man was soundly caught up in the pleasure she was giving him. And then she bit down, bit down as hard as she could. He screamed out in raging pain. The plane took a fast, quick dive as he yanked her head from his lap. He punched her, slamming her head against the window, just as the plane was thrown into a tailspin.

Oh, dear Jesus, please save my daughter. Please save my child, dear God, please save her.

Gunter struggled through dire pain to get control over the plane. It seemed impossible, and Holly could see the ground coming up fast. Gunter was able to get the nose back up, just before they started scraping trees. It was the trees, along with a fresh powder of snow, that softened the blow as the small plane hit and broke apart.

For Holly everything went black.

Holly was out for mere minutes, she figured, because she could still hear the sound of the plane's engine running. She opened her eyes. Pain was shooting through every part of her, inside and out. She had no idea how badly she could be hurt, but she knew that she was. She tried hard to stand. She looked around for Gunter, but didn't see him. She was finally able to get up and brace herself against what was left of the plane.

Gunter came screaming around the other side of the plane like a madman. He drew back his hand and backhanded Holly, knocking her to the ground. She tried to bring her hands up to her stinging face, but he pinned them down next to her as he turned her over and sat on top of her.

"Now why did you have to go and do something as stupid as that? Crashing the plane was not a real smart move, and doing what you did to the family jewels was very, very bad. But trust me, they survived. And now, love, you will pay. I ought to send your little girl and your buddy's kid to the moon."

Holly shook her head. She could feel and taste blood trickling out of the side of her mouth. The wet snow had seeped inside her pants and down her backside. She started to shake, more from fear than the cold. He apparently was running on complete adrenaline.

"No. I'm sorry. I wasn't trying to crash the plane. I was only trying to get the gun away from you. That's all. I'm sorry." It hurt to speak every word. "Do you really think I would crash the plane on purpose with my little girl back at the cabin? C'mon. And I didn't hurt you on purpose. The plane made a jarring move. That's how it happened. I'm sorry." Her ankle was killing her, and she knew it was either badly twisted or possibly broken.

"You know what? You're like all the rest of them. Nothing but a lying bitch. You should've never done any of that. Because now I'm really fucking pissed off. You never wanted to be with me. You were just fucking with me." He spat in her face. She struggled to free herself. But against his strength, it was impossible.

The propeller on the plane was still going at half speed, and the noise of it grinding against the crumpled-up metal was loud and ear wrenching, but watching that propeller go round and round while he continued to berate her gave Holly an idea. It was a slim chance that it might work, but she had to give it a try.

"You don't want to do this. Maybe we can work it out. Let's try. Please?" Holly begged.

"Nah, I'm done trying to work it out with you and waiting around for you. You're another typical woman—all talk and no play. Well, honey, it's time to pay the piper," he said as he yanked open her shirt.

The cold wind hit her and she gasped for air. With him keeping her arms pinned under his elbows, he had a difficult time unfastening her belt, but he did with far more ease than she could have hoped for, and she'd gotten him no closer to the propeller.

"Okay, okay. But I'm cold, can't we get inside the plane?" Holly tried to struggle under his weight again and moved him a bit closer to the propeller.

He slid on a patch of ice and she was able to get an arm out from under him. She held her palm flat and shoved it out as hard and fast as possible, nailing him right on his chin. He fell back and hit his head on the rim of the propeller.

"Fuck!" he screamed.

Instead of having the intended effect, his pain only angered him further. He quickly unbuckled his pants, dropping the gun in the process. Quickly, Holly tried hard to scramble up to get it. He made it there first. Then her hand was on it. He kicked the gun out from underneath and stepped down hard on her hand. She screamed out in pain. She was feeling pretty damned defeated as he jumped on top of her again, pinning her legs under his body.

"You want to be feisty? Fine. Have it your way. We can play real rough." He yanked off her bra, and pulled her jeans down below her ass. "If that's how you like it, that's how you'll get it."

This was it. She could survive this. She could live through this kind of hell, hunt this motherfucker down sometime in the future and destroy him. Sure, the future. There probably wasn't going to be a future after this. Before now, she'd been totally pissed off at this psychotic prick, and now all she felt was fear and desperation and the strong desire to say good-bye to Chloe. To let that beautiful child know how much her mother loved her. For the first time ever, she said a silent prayer to Jack. *Jack if you're up there, can you help me out of this? Please. I need God's help right now. I need your help.*

She was completely helpless, but the arm connected to her broken hand was free, and as she lifted her head slightly, she saw a gleaming sharp piece of metal that had broken off of the airplane. With strength she never knew she had, strength that had to have come from somewhere or someone else, she grabbed the object. As Gunter was trying to arouse his bruised penis and stick it inside of her, she summoned every ounce of strength she could and pulled the sharp piece back to her side.

Against all hope, she struck the monster who was about to rape and murder her, digging the sharp metal into his torso.

Gunter screamed out. She wiggled out from underneath him and scooted back toward the wreckage. She'd stabbed him on his right side, and he spurted blood all over the white snow. He tried to reach out to grab her. More blood splayed out from his mouth. "I'll fucking kill you for that."

She stood and limped over to where he'd kicked the gun, and picked it up. She turned around and pointed it at him. "No, you won't, you son of a bitch. Because I'm going to kill you."

She pulled the trigger.

The shot rang out through the frozen, desolate woods. It hit Gunter in the forehead, and he immediately fell back. She dropped the gun to her side, standing there in shock. As fresh snow began to fall and hit her near-naked body, the reality of where she was hit her. She picked up her shirt and put it on. Most of the buttons had been torn off. She found her jacket inside the wreckage and pulled it on, zipping it up and pulling the hood tightly around her head. It didn't help much. And now with Gunter dead, and the immediate fear he'd proposed gone, the pain of her twisted ankle and broken hand pulsated.

She climbed inside the plane and leaned back against the seat, letting out a long sigh. She picked up the radio, and for the second time that night asked Jack, God, whoever was listening, to lend a hand and get her home.

43

Chad hadn't had any luck with the Mammoth PD. The report they'd sent back down to him was that the lights were off in the cabin, and nothing seemed out of the norm. They didn't want to disturb anyone and would go by in the morning. Totally incompetent. By morning's light, Chad was on a flight out of San Diego and into the Mammoth area. By the time he reached the cabin, there was a man who he didn't recognize walking up the front steps.

"Excuse me?" Chad hollered stepping out of his rental car.

"Yes?"

Chad flipped open his badge. "I'm a police officer with the San Diego Police Department."

The man opened his wallet and took out a similar badge, only with a bit more pull behind it. "Nice to meet you, Detective Euwing. I'm Tyler Savoy with the FBI. Looks like we might be here for the same reason."

Chad didn't know what to say. Tyler knocked on the door. The sound of a child crying rang out from the other side. It was Chloe. Chad moved, ready to bust in the door.

"Hold on. We don't know what's going on in there." Tyler pulled out a 9 mm Glock.

Chad didn't have his weapon. He didn't think he would need it, and he hadn't wanted to go through the hassle with it at the airport. He simply wanted to come up here, check on Holly, fill her in, and apologize to her.

"No, no!" An older child's voice sounded out.

"We've got to go in," Chad said.

They both heard tapping coming from a window at the side of the house. They walked around to see two very frightened, tearful girls. One was Chloe. Chad wasn't sure who the other was. Through the glass, the oldest one was gesturing wildly. Chad got it: There was a bomb. The goddamn house was rigged to blow.

Within an hour, the FBI had flown in a variety of special agents and a bomb squad. As they gathered, Brendan pulled up in his Jeep with another little girl.

"What's going on?" he asked, unable to disguise the alarm in his voice. "I had to drive up through the night. I was too worried to sit still. What in Mother Mary's name is going on?"

He looked around at the barrage of vehicles, and Chad could see on his face that the man understood the situation was grave. In a low voice, he relayed as much as he knew.

"What? You mean to tell me that my child is in there, and some lunatic has set a bomb? Where is Holly?"

"We don't know yet."

"What? You don't know? She's not in there?"

"From what we can decipher from your daughter, no."

"She wouldn't have left them," Brendan said emphatically. "I know her. She wouldn't have left unless she had to."

"We're in. I've got it," the bomb squad leader yelled. "Quite a contraption he built."

Brendan bolted to the door and barged in, wrapping his arms around both girls. Their happiness didn't last long, as the girls explained what had happened, and that they didn't know where Holly was.

Brendan's heart sank. Holly had just come into his life, and he wasn't about to lose her now.

44

Gunter's cell phone rang. Holly was shivering and couldn't feel her fingers, but she could hear the phone. She saw it lying on what was left of the front seat. She tried hard to reach for it, but a night in the elements had made it impossible. The phone seemed outrageously far away. She knew it was hopeless.

But the phone rang again and again and again, and Holly knew they were looking for her. She willed herself to find the energy and strength that she needed. If she wanted to live, she had to get to that phone. *I want to live. I'm going to live, goddamn it!* She yelled out in pain as she forced her body to move. But she got the phone. Oh God. Did she answer it? Gunter had said that it was a detonator to the bomb he'd claimed was under the cabin. He said that he'd have to dial a number to set it off. Holly knew enough from her training that without that code, if there really was a bomb that it would not detonate. She answered the phone.

"Holly! Holly!" It was Chad.

She barely breathed out "yes" before she passed out. She knew that was all that she needed to say. They could find her now.

The signal to the phone held long enough, and the troopers searching for her by air and land located her three hours after she'd answered the call.

Eighteen hours after Gunter Drake had first entered the cabin, Holly was airlifted to the closest trauma center and hospitalized. Two days later, she was released with a broken hand, a twisted ankle, and some frostbite. But she was alive, and so were Meg and Chloe.

Chad and Tyler Savoy came to visit her.

"You are one helluva lady," Tyler Savoy said, after Chad officially introduced them.

"I only wanted to save the kids. I took a chance, and it paid off."

She was seated on the sofa inside the cabin, sipping a cup of hot tea and being catered to by Brendan. The girls were still shaken, but every cop around had brought Chloe all sorts of Barbies and candy, and plenty of goodies for Meg as well. The girls were being thoroughly spoiled, and they deserved it. Maddie was kind of out of the loop, but Chloe did a good job sharing all of her treats with her friend.

"If you guys hadn't traced down Gunter Drake's phone number and found me…I might have died out there. You're the real heroes."

"I beg to differ, Holly," Chad said.

"Me, too. Because of your courage and what you figured out about this case on your own, and also because I've got a feeling about you and your gut after knowing your father, I'd like to extend an invitation for you to come and join us," Tyler said.

"The FBI?" she said.

"Yep. You can start training at Quantico this summer after you heal up all the way."

He grabbed a pen off the table next to her and signed her cast. Chad looked back and forth between the two of them.

"Wow. That's quite an offer."

"I think you might have what it takes to be a good profiler."

"Really? You're not only saying that because you're my dad's friend?"

"Nope. Besides, your father can be a real you-know-what, and if you come to work for me, I've got a feeling he'll be bugging me from here to the moon. That should tell you how much I believe in your capabilities."

"He's been calling you too, huh?"

"Three times a day trying to get an update on you and what happened. I don't know how many times I've relayed the story."

"That makes the two of us," Holly said. "At least I convinced him to stay put on the beach drinking his mai tais. For now anyway."

They all laughed.

Chad cleared his throat.

"Think about that offer, Holly," Tyler said. "I know that you're tired, so rest up and then make a decision. I've got a wife waiting for me a few miles up the road, and I promised her a bit of my time, so I'll get going."

"Go, go. Thanks again."

"You can thank me by joining my team. Call me when you get home, and we can go over the details."

After Tyler left, Chad sat down on the couch next to her, scooting her leg over a bit to make room. He took her hand. "Will you ever forgive me, partner?" he asked.

"Don't give it a second thought."

"You gonna take his offer?"

She shook her head slowly. "No. It's flattering, and I can't say that you and I might need to work some stuff out. I'm a little hurt by all that went down. I'm a big girl though and I just said that you don't need to give it a second thought. So, I think you're stuck with me."

He gave her a hug.

Neither one of them said anything for a few moments.

"So I think we figured out how the messed-up DNA got inside Shannon McKay's body," Chad said, breaking the tense silence.

"Darla Monroe, or Jennifer Drake, put it inside her before she was dead."

"I figured it out, too. James and Monroe went to play with Shannon earlier in the evening. Monroe knew of Gunter's plan, even egged him on a bit, always wanting to make her brother happy and do what he wanted and needed. Monroe had sex with James, and then she collected his semen, which is totally disgusting but it worked. Monroe then stuck James' semen inside Shannon, probably with a baster. It had Monroe's menses on it, not Shannon's. No one was the wiser. Monroe knew her brother would kill the poor woman, and so she planned it in hopes of setting up James and then being able to convince Gunter to be with her."

"Wow, you are good. I hadn't figured out the psychology of it all."

"Your girlfriend should have."

"That fire has died down."

Holly decided not to ask. She honestly didn't want to know. Besides, if she knew her partner like she thought she did, he'd work it out with the tall blonde.

"Um, Holly."

"Yes."

"There's something I need to say to you."

"What?" She could tell this was serious. He didn't speak for a minute then took in a long breath.

"I wanted to say that I love you, you know, I mean that you mean a lot to me, to us—the team, and I'm happy you're sticking with the team. We really do need you."

She thanked him, but deep inside her she knew there was something else he needed to tell her. What it was, she wasn't sure, and because it seemed so heavy, she didn't think she really wanted to know anyway. She'd had enough heaviness to last her a lifetime. Chad would have to carry whatever it was on his own.

45

News of the case was all over the media. CNN had called, and the local channels were ringing the phone off the hook. Greenfield had sent over roses and a letter of apology inviting her back on the team. Everything was happening so fast that Holly was happy to be lying next to Brendan, tucked away in a cabin miles from the one in Mammoth. They were now in Lake Tahoe, where the reporters couldn't find them—all expenses comped by the police department. The FBI had provided the private plane to take them to the undisclosed location. As a precaution, and in order to maintain some privacy, there were security guards stationed in close proximity.

The girls were asleep, all of them in a pile in the front room before the fireplace while *Legally Blonde 2* flashed on the television. Meg and Chloe both seemed to find comfort in constant sound around them after what they'd been through. The girls were still coming to terms with the violence they'd encountered in their innocent lives. Brendan went into the front room and tucked in the girls.

Now a precious silence enveloped Brendan and Holly. Holly had wondered only a few days before, as she lay face down in the icy snow about to be raped by a monster, if she would ever know such soothing feelings again.

"Been through a lot, kid," Brendan said.

"I'll be fine. It's the girls I'm worried about."

"I think they'll be fine, too. We all have each other. We'll get through it together."

She liked the word together and knew he meant it. "I suppose we will."

"Looks like the police force has pulled out all stops to get you back," he said.

She laughed. "Yeah, well. They should be kissing my butt."

Brendan kissed her on the top of her head. "Suppose that is the only place not hurting you," he said.

"Maybe a few other places," she said, a discreet smile on her face.

"Yeah? Like maybe here?" He kissed her nose. She nodded. "And here?" Her cheek, her eyelids, and then her lips.

Their game went on for quite some time as a fire grew between them. Holly found herself wanting him more than she'd ever wanted any man. The guilt of that desire almost made her stop as Jack's face appeared in her mind. *Go away, would you?*

"What's the matter?" Brendan asked.

"Nothing. Kiss me again."

He did. Pulling away, he looked at her in a way that warmed Holly to the inner core. He was so tender and sweet. She was in love, and there was no denying it. She took the initiative, surprising the both of them, and climbed on top of Brendan, making love to him fiercely, ignoring all her aches and pains, reveling in the pleasure of the moment as she rocked them both to ecstasy.

When it was over, they both inhaled deeply, neither one of them saying a word, not ever wanting to lose the moment.

46

Holly poured herself a second glass of Syrah, tasting the full-bodied grape flavor. She was tasting, smelling, hearing, touching anything and everything as if it were the first time. If the past couple of days had taught her something, it was that life was too short, and it was to be enjoyed. She was elated to be back in the comfort of her own house. With Christmas just a few days away, the reporters had gone on to do holiday-related stories. Hers had been told, and now was time for cheer, which suited Holly just fine.

She turned up the stereo and hummed along to the music of Ella Fitzgerald. It felt so good to be alive. It felt passionate. That was what Holly was feeling—passionate about the wine, the music, and even the onion she was busy chopping, preparing a romantic dinner for just herself and Brendan.

She glanced up at the clock. Brendan should be arriving in a half hour. It didn't give her much time. The girls were all over at his house. She couldn't help but look forward to where the night would likely end up. The thought of being in his arms was an exciting prospect.

Chopping, humming, swaying, and sipping, Holly was lost in her dreams when Petie suddenly started barking wildly from the other room.

"Petie," she rang out. "Hush! What is it?"

Brendan must be early. She peered through the peephole on her front door. Maureen? All Holly could see was the back of a head with bushy red hair. Maybe she got her night confused. She opened the door and started to say her colleague's name when the woman turned around, gun pointed straight at her.

It was not Maureen.

Holly took a step back. It was Darla Monroe.

"Aren't you going to invite me in?" the one-time blonde said.

"I'd rather not," Holly replied.

"Well, honey, looks like you don't have much of a choice." Darla shoved Holly out of the way. "Nice place you got here. Why don't you be a good girl and close the drapes for me? We don't need any pesky neighbors seeing that we're having a party over here, do we?"

Holly nodded and went to work closing the drapes, her little dog still going berserk.

"Shut that fucking rat thing up before I blow its brains out!"

"Petie, hush! Come here." Petie ran to Holly with his tail tucked between his legs. She scooped him up.

"I don't know if you want to do that. You might want to lock him away considering I am going to blow your fucking brains out. Unless you want to take the dog with you."

Okay, keep her talking. Keep her talking. Brendan will be here soon. "Follow me. I'll put him in here," Holly said and walked down the hall to her office, where she locked Petie in the room.

"Into the bathroom." Darla pointed the gun at her.

Holly didn't like the sound of this.

"Turn around."

Holly did and faced the bathtub of her small Nantucket-style bathroom.

Darla reached into her suede coat pocket and pulled out a pair of handcuffs. "These come in real handy. Multipurpose deal. Great for sex games and for dealing with bitches like you. Gunter always liked handcuffs. We had a lot of fun with them through the years." She snapped them shut over Holly's wrists.

"You don't have to do this."

"I don't? Yes, I do. Now get in, and sit down."

Holly stepped into the bathtub. If she could just kick her...But Darla had her positioned so that it was nearly impossible. Her hope was that she would play along and Brendan would arrive soon. But Brendan didn't have a gun either. He might wind up getting hurt or killed himself. Holly had to think quick. Darla proceeded to tie her ankles together into a very tight knot. Holly didn't realize that the woman was so strong. She then placed a strip of masking tape over her mouth.

"Now you get to listen to me."

This ought to be good.

"You murdered my one and only love. Oh, sure, many would say that what we had together was sick, but it wasn't. It wasn't at all. Gunter loved me. He did. And I loved him." Darla reached over Holly's head and turned the spigot on. "Ooh, nice freezing water. The kind you killed my Gunter in. You destroyed any chance of us ever being together, and now you're going to pay with your life." With that Darla brought her arm back and swung hard, hitting Holly on the side of her head with her gun.

Holly's head bobbled and she fell to the side of the tub. Everything was hazy, but she wasn't completely knocked out. Not yet.

Hang on, just hang on. She had to fake unconsciousness for a chance at staying alive. But what then? She was exhausted, shackled, and near blacking out. Bile rose in the back of her throat. This was not good. The water was getting higher. As she started sinking into the water, she thought she heard Darla say, "Who the hell are you?" But it was so distant that she wasn't sure anyone was saying anything. It was like being in between dreaming and waking up, fuzzy and confusing, and Holly felt she was going deeper into the dream state.

"Leave me alone!" Darla screamed. "You're always ruining everything! I knew you'd come back! I just knew it! How did you find me?"

"Turn it off, Jennifer. Turn the water off and let her go. Don't ruin your life. They're gone now. You don't have to pretend anymore. You're not like them. You're good. Please, Jennifer. Daddy and Gunter are gone. You can get over this. Turn the water off."

A woman's voice. Who was it? Who was Darla Monroe talking to? Jennifer? Darla Monroe was Jennifer Drake. Who was the other woman? Was Holly dreaming? Was she dead? Where was Brendan?

"You never understood. You never will," Darla yelled. "You weren't one of us. You hated us because we loved each other, and the only one who ever loved you was that bitch mother of ours."

"She was the only good one. And you're right, she did love me, and I loved her very much. But you don't have to be like them. You don't have to be like Daddy and Gunter. Please put the gun down, turn the water off, and leave. Go! You don't want to kill her. Think of all the horrible things they did to you. That wasn't love, Jennifer. It wasn't. It was cruel and hurtful. Gunter did not love you and neither did Daddy. They couldn't love anyone. Please, please don't do this."

Crying. Darla Monroe, or whoever she was, was crying.

Then the other woman was screaming, "No, Jennifer! No, don't do it!" A loud bang.

Crying of a different kind. Water covering Holly's face. Was she dead? Was this what it was like to be dead? Had Darla Monroe shot her, and who in the hell was the other woman?

Someone lifting her. Water not running anymore. Her face out of the water.

"What the hell?" She heard Brendan yelling.

"Call an ambulance, please! Call an ambulance. I didn't do this. I really didn't," the other woman said.

Seconds, minutes, hours later, Holly wasn't sure, she was being lifted onto a gurney and prodded with needles.

"Looks like she got hit pretty hard."

"I'm okay," Holly muttered.

"Holly?" It was Brendan.

"What happened?" She opened her eyes. Brendan stood over her, a concerned look in his eyes.

"You got thunked on the head by a lunatic, that's what happened to you."

"No. I know that. Who was the other woman in the room?" As Holly asked, a woman of about thirty approached them and looked down at Holly on the gurney.

"I'm Kimberly Drake. I'm sorry about this."

"Kimberly Drake? You're..." Holly said.

"Yes, I'm Gunter Drake's sister, and the woman who did this to you was our sister, Jennifer Drake."

"Darla Monroe."

Kimberly nodded as tears came to her eyes. "Yes."

"What happened?" Holly asked again.

"She shot herself," Brendan replied.

Holly knew by the look in Kimberly Drake's eyes that her sister was dead. "I'm...sorry."

"It's okay. Maybe now I can let it all go and leave everything behind. I'm the one who sent you the photograph of my family. I was set to leave for France when I did that, but something pulled me back. Against all that I ever wanted to do, I came out here. By the time I arrived and had the courage to track you down, the fiasco with my brother had already taken place. But I knew deep down it wasn't over. Nothing with Gunter was ever over. I had hoped I could find my sister and track her down before she came here. I looked everywhere. Then I decided to come and speak to you tonight and warn you that revenge is huge in my family. That you were in danger. I got lucky when I saw my sister's car out front. At least I hoped it might be her car. The plates said 'Godiva', and everyone in my family always called her Lady Godiva because of her long blonde hair. It made her feel special. I didn't think…I just walked into your house, knowing she was inside and that something bad was going to happen."

Holly smiled and took her hand. "I understand."

"Okay folks, we need to get her to the hospital and checked out," the EMT said.

"Will she be okay?" Kimberly asked.

"She should be."

"My girl is tough," Brendan said. "She can take a lump on the head." He stroked back Holly's hair. His look didn't match his words.

"I'm fine. I'll be okay. You're right, I'm plenty tough."

"Would you like me to go to the hospital?" Kimberly asked.

"No, please. Don't worry about me. Thank you for saving my life. The best thing you could do for me is to go and catch that plane to France."

Kimberly Drake leaned over her and said, "Thank you for saving my life, too. If you get a postcard from a Karen Whitley, just know that's me." She smiled.

And that was the last Holly saw of Kimberly Drake.

47

It was all behind them now. Gunter Drake was dead. Jennifer Drake, aka Darla Monroe, was also dead. Kimberly Drake had moved to the French Riviera to put her childhood and the horrid memories behind her once and for all. Holly took in a deep breath as she reflected on the past few days, during which she'd escaped death more than once.

She had one more item to take care of before she could really move forward. She picked up the phone and placed the call.

When she hung up, she kissed Chloe on the cheek. Meg was on the sofa watching TV. Brendan and Maddie would be by in a couple of hours. He'd taken her to the latest Disney movie.

"Meg, can you watch Chloe for an hour? I have to take care of something."

"Sure."

So she had at least an hour to put this to rest.

Holly made her way up to Birdrock. She walked up the front porch and knocked on the door.

Anne Nickels answered. "I thought you'd be back eventually," she said and swung the door open. "Come on in. Tea is already brewing. Chamomile, right?"

Holly nodded and followed her inside the house, where she sat down on the chenille sofa. "I want to apologize for the way I acted the last time I was here. Seems that many of your predictions or feelings about my case were correct. We did catch him."

Anne nodded. "You don't need to apologize. Sometimes the things I say are not what people want to hear, but I have a responsibility to my clients to relay what I intuit, even if I don't understand it myself."

"I'm here because obviously so much of what you said was accurate, and now I need to finish up on a personal note."

"Jack?"

"Yes." It amazed Holly that she knew his name and knew exactly what it was that she'd come to discuss.

"When we spoke before, I felt this sense about him, that he hadn't died, that somehow he was alive. I saw the fire, but usually when someone passes on, I see a grave or some other type of object that is reflective of a passing. I did not get that with him. I saw a handsome, vital man, still very much alive."

"Okay." Was this what Holly wanted to hear? She wasn't sure, but she had to know. "Is that what you still see?"

Anne set down her teacup and closed her eyes momentarily. "Actually, no. Interesting." She paused and crossed her legs. "I now understand why I saw things the way I did on your first visit. The reason I saw Jack so alive was because you had kept him that way, Holly. You were not willing to let go, and because of that he was so prevalent in spirit within your heart and mind. That's what I was reading," she said gently. "You've let go, and that is all Jack ever wanted. Now he can go on into the light and be where he's supposed to be. You see, if we hold the dead so strongly with us, they cannot truly pass on. So it's good for both of you."

Holly didn't know what to believe.

"Also, Jack is aware of the new man in your life." Anne smiled.

"Huh?"

"He likes him. He says go for it and live your life. He says that you and Chloe have an angel watching over you, but that you should let this new man be your angel here on Earth."

Holly teared up. The sense of fear that she had felt for so long was replaced with relief.

She stood and gave Anne a hug. "Thank you."

"Anytime."

Holly closed the door behind her, got in her car, and headed home to her Earth angel and their girls.

Acknowledgments

I'd like to acknowledge my readers who make this job the best one in the world! I want to thank a good cop and friend, Scott Willeford, who always is willing to give me valuable information and to fact-check. And I want to thank my family, who allows me a lot of time and space to write.

About the Author

A.K. Alexander is an internationally best-selling author. She resides in San Diego, California, with her family and many animals. When not writing thrillers under the name A.K. Alexander, she is writing mystery and young-adult fiction under the name Michele Scott. You can find more information about the author and her work at http://www.michelescott.com.